CRACKER

ONE DAY A LEMMING WILL FLY

ONE DAY A LEMMING WILL FLY

Liz Holliday

ST. MARTIN'S PRESS ≈ NEW YORK

Library of Congress Cataloging-in-Publication Data

Holliday, Liz.
    Cracker : one day a lemming will fly / Liz Holliday.
      p. cm.
    Adaptation by Liz Holliday of a screenplay by Jimmy McGovern.
    ISBN 0-312-18072-1
    I. McGovern, Jimmy. Cracker. II. Title.
    PR6058.044654C73   1998
    823'.914—dc21   97-37426
                                                     CIP

First published in Great Britain by Virgin Publishing Ltd

First U.S. Edition: January 1998

10 9 8 7 6 5 4 3 2 1

This book is dedicated to my mother, and to the memory of my father – who probably wouldn't have approved.

With thanks to the staff and students of the Clarion SF Writers' Workshop 1989, and to Chris Amies, Tina Anghelatos, Molly Brown, Mary Gentle, Chris Horseman, Ben Jeapes, Roz Kaveney, Andy Lane, Barbara Morris, Jim Mortimore, Julia Quine, Gus Smith, Alex Stewart, Charles Stross and Kim Whitmore; and to Karen – wherever she may be.

FIRST ICE

Tears on the classroom floor.
I start to grieve.
He opens the classroom door,
Tells me to leave.
First Ice isn't nice.

CRACKER

ONE DAY A LEMMING
WILL FLY

ONE

The boy ran through the woods, feet sliding on the soft wet earth, arms flailing, face made ugly by fear. His breath came in ragged little gasps, making his throat burn and his chest ache. He put a hand out to steady himself against a tree but he didn't dare pause or slow.

The other was behind him, coming up fast. The boy had no time for thought, no time to watch where he was going or to choose a path. No time to offer up a prayer or even a hope. The wind whipped tears from his eyes.

Behind him, a branch cracked, as if a foot had come down heavily upon it.

Fitz was happy again. Happy like Gene Kelly was happy, in *Singing in the Rain*, only without the rain. He almost danced down the street, because Judith was by his side and they were talking, just talking normally, like any married couple.

Happyish, anyway. He wasn't fool enough to believe it could last.

They threaded their way through the heavy traffic outside the cinema. They'd been to see a film.

What a simple little thing to do, Fitz thought. Once, it would have meant nothing much, just a way to pass a Sunday afternoon. But that was before Judith had left him and the world ended and he'd had to find a way to make it new again.

'Bogart at the end of *Casablanca*,' she said. Even on a Sunday, she was impeccably dressed and made up. The sun, struggling to shine through the low cloud, still managed to find a few highlights in her chestnut hair.

'Nah,' Fitz said. 'He doesn't die.' It wasn't a fair objection, really. When they'd started this discussion about great sacrifices in the movies, he hadn't specified life or death situations. Judith didn't seem bothered, though.

Her perfume drifted up to him, even through the exhaust fumes from the traffic. Yves St Laurent. That taste she'd acquired when he bought her a bottle after a particularly heavy blackjack session. A hint? he wondered. She'd said she didn't want to share in his winnings. So was she saying she'd changed her mind about it? But Judith wasn't devious enough for that. She'd have come straight out and said it.

That's it, Fitz told himself. Don't you dare get your hopes up. Stay cynical. Cynical is safe, cynical doesn't get hurt. Bloody hell. When had he started to be scared of taking a risk? Very well then. He'd believe she was wearing the perfume because she was trying to tell him she still loved him. There was no greater gamble. His heart was in the kitty, and he'd nothing to up the ante with. It was time to fold or show.

He looked down at her. She was a small woman. Hell with that. She was a big woman, maybe the biggest he'd ever known. Big hearted, emotionally strong. Tough as old boots, he sometimes thought. Only his own hugeness – physical, mental – made her seem small. He'd hurt her with it, with his need to push the limits, to dance on the edge of the abyss, to stare down into it and face the night. She was his light, and he'd driven her away. But she had come back. Was coming back, he corrected himself.

She'd said this was boring, this need of his to find a pure motive in an impure world. Well, she didn't seem to find it boring now. Perhaps she never had. Of course she hadn't – he knew it with that unerring instinct that told him what drove people.

Not boring. Unbearable, perhaps. He'd have changed himself if he could. Made himself small for her. But he

2

couldn't, and he wouldn't promise what he couldn't deliver.

'*Angels With Dirty Faces*,' he said. Now there was a man promising the earth, and delivering it.

'No,' she said.

'Oh come on,' he said. 'Pat O'Brien asks him to scream,' Fitz dropped into a corny American accent, 'and he says, "Don't do this to me, Father. Don't take away the only thing I have left – " '

'He screams because he's frightened,' Judith said. She made a derisive sound, and tossed her head. Her long earrings danced and flashed in the dull light. She grinned.

Ah, he loved it, Fitz thought. Arguing for argument's sake about something really important. And he loved Judith for being able to take part in it with him, for standing up to him.

But this conversation was more than that. If he was honest with himself – and he believed he was, always – he had to admit that. She knew what *Angels With Dirty Faces* meant to him. She'd watched it with him twice, maybe even three times. She'd never said this before.

'No no no,' he said quickly. 'No. He wants them to think he's frightened. Right?' It was important she agreed with him. Why? he wondered. The argument itself was the thing. Ah, that was it. It would prove that she could have her own opinions but still end up on his side. That she could go away and yet come back to him. That he would win her, in the end.

But he was avoiding the subject. Why had she chosen this time – out of all the times they had talked about the film – to do this? Maybe she had only just thought of it. That was a possibility, but it didn't seem likely. Fitz knew when he was clutching at straws.

' – So that they don't follow his example and end up on death row,' he finished, with a barely perceptible pause in the conversation.

'He's a Catholic,' she said, as if it explained everything. She seemed to be enjoying herself. Before the separation, she had always seemed to like these conversations.

'So what?' Fitz said. Religion. Wish fulfilment. Something for the small people who were scared of the world. Scared to dance on the edge and stare down the night.

'He's about to die,' she said, then something else that was lost in the roar of the traffic. 'Heaven and hell. It could be true.' She gestured, talking as much with her hands as her mouth. She did care, even if she'd once said she thought this search of his was boring. That still rankled, but he forced himself not to think of it, to think of the present, and of their future. Their future together.

'OK,' she went on. 'It's a million to one – ' she shot him a sharp glance. He knew what she was thinking. Odds like that, he'd have gambled. But then, Fitz would gamble on the chance of snow in the Sahara. That was the problem. Most of it, anyway.

And then he knew. Revenge. She was taking away something he cared about. This film. The closest he'd ever got to finding a truly pure motive.

But Judith was going on. 'So he does it to save his own skin, because it's his only chance left.' She stuck her hands in the pockets of her smart blue jacket. She'd bought it herself out of her own salary.

His only chance left. Just as Fitz only had one chance left to make his marriage work.

'Impure motive,' she finished, making the most of the words as if to say, argue with that if you can. She looked up at him.

'God,' he sighed, feeling obscurely satisfied that she'd won the debate, that she was good enough to do that. Masochist, he thought. 'My all-time favourite movie, and you've ruined it for me.'

Judith smiled.

Jane Penhaligon nibbled the edge of her pizza. Her boyfriend, Peter, sat across the table from her. It wasn't the most

4

romantic place to eat, just somewhere they came when neither of them felt like cooking; it had been a long time since they'd been anywhere else.

Peter picked at the remains of his tagliatelle. 'You sure you don't want a dessert?' he asked.

'No time,' Penhaligon said. 'Not if I'm going to change before I go on duty – '

'Heard it all before,' Peter said. It was true. These days she always seemed to be rubbing his nose in how important her job was to her. But at least this time he was smiling. 'So,' he went on, 'you won't mind if I help you out?' His hand darted out and grabbed an olive off her pizza.

'Be my guest,' she said.

'Seriously, Janie – you ought to ease off.' He grinned at her hopefully; that little-boy grin had been the first thing about him she'd noticed. The trouble was, little boys weren't much use when what you wanted was a grown man. 'I mean take tonight . . . why don't you call in sick – '

'Don't, Peter.'

' – we go home, and I'll run you a bubble bath – '

For one second, she was tempted. 'Don't – '

' – and then we can get cosy in front of the fire?'

He was always doing this to her, trying to make her feel guilty that her priorities hadn't changed when he'd moved into her flat. *That* hadn't even been her idea. It wasn't her fault that he was happy to drift along selling furniture, never quite making it to departmental manager. He'd known the way things were when he'd moved in. 'Because I take my job a damn sight more seriously than some people I can name, that's why!' she said.

He nodded. 'Yes, well some of us work so we can have a good time. We have lives, not just careers – '

'Then go and find a good-time girl, Peter,' Penhaligon said.

'Yeah,' he said. It was amazing how much of a guilt-trip he could fit in that one word, Penhaligon thought. He picked

5

up one of the little sachets of brown sugar and started to fiddle with it. 'Look, I've been thinking. I reckon you work too hard.' He tore the corner off the packet and dribbled the sugar across the table.

'Very artistic,' Penhaligon said. 'So tell me something I didn't already know?'

'I reckon we ought to take a holiday – '

'You know, that's not a bad idea.' It would get her away from Fitz for one thing, she thought. Maybe without him distracting her all the time – and Bilborough and Beck getting at her in a thousand and one little ways – she'd be able to put a bit more into her relationship with Peter. He didn't really deserve the flak she gave him. Not all of it, anyway. 'Where do you want to go?'

'I thought maybe Greece – some island-hopping, maybe?'

'That's a bit touristy, isn't it? What about Venice? A bit of culture – '

'I was more thinking of sun, sand. Sex.'

'You always do.' They both laughed. He was good-looking, Penhaligon thought, in a fine-boned kind of way. When she'd first met him, he'd seemed like a real catch. It wasn't his fault she'd met Fitz. 'What about Portugal?' she said.

'Just as long as it's hot,' he said, grinning slyly.

'I expect that can be arranged,' Penhaligon said. 'I have to go.' She picked up her bag and slung her jacket over her arm.

Before she had pushed her way clear of the table, he said, 'Hang on. Are we still on for *Made in America* tomorrow night?'

'What, me miss Whoopi Goldberg?' Penhaligon said. 'No chance.'

'Great,' Peter said. 'I'll pick up the tickets tomorrow, then.'

It didn't take much to make Peter happy, Penhaligon

reflected as she left him to pay the bill. It was just as well, really, considering what he got.

'There you go,' Andy said. He sat down next to Melanie and put her Bacardi and Coke on the table in front of her. She smiled at him, and said something he couldn't hear because of the music from the juke box. She was very pretty, and she had a nice figure. A real good-time girl. Had a good job in Boots, selling make-up. Andy was lucky to have her, and she made sure he knew it. He put his arm round her, and was glad when she snuggled up close to him.

Nine o'clock on a slow Sunday night. The King's Head was half empty. Andy had arranged to meet Melanie and some other friends, but that was before his brother, Tim, had failed to come home. Silly little bastard, Andy thought. I'll wipe that stupid smile right off his face for upsetting Mum like this.

'You right, then?' Andy's friend Mike appeared in front of him. 'I hear you had a hot time at the Blue Moon after we left, hey Melanie?'

'Leave it alone,' Andy said. One of these days, Melanie was going to find out that he'd told Mike – all right, Mike and some of the other lads – that they were sleeping together. Then the shit would fly, that was for sure. Specially since she'd said no, repeatedly.

Mike's girlfriend Alison arrived and draped her arm over him. She whispered something in his ear. Mike blushed and pushed her away. 'Get off, Ali,' he said. She giggled. 'Get you another one, Andy,' he said, gesturing at Andy's pint.

'Not for me – ' Andy said. He'd only come out to tell them what had happened. He really didn't want to leave Mum on her own for much longer.

'Tim's gone missing, Mike,' Melanie said. Andy looked at her gratefully. He hadn't known how to say it.

'What, that little wanker? Run off with a nun, has he?' Mike said. Andy stared at him, thinking, shut up. Just shut your fucking face. 'Hang on,' Mike said after a moment. 'You really mean it, don't you?'

'Yeah,' Andy said. 'It's probably nothing, but my mum's been in a real state all day. Keeps saying she's going to call the police.' He picked up his pint and stared at it without drinking.

Andy finished his drink. Melanie was giggling with Alison over something, but when he said, 'Let's go,' she seemed willing enough.

He walked her home. He grabbed a long, wet kiss in the alley at the top of the road, but when he tried to slide his hand up her blouse, she slapped it away. She giggled though, so that was OK. She was pretty, he thought. He could imagine her on the cover of some magazine or other. Kate Moss wasn't a patch on his Melanie. The moonlight turned the tarnished blonde of her hair to silver, almost the colour of Tim's hair –

'Shit,' he said.

'What?' she asked. She was repairing her lipstick, which had smudged when they kissed. A cloud slid across the moon, so that the alley turned suddenly dark. 'Damn,' she said.

'I forgot about Mum,' Andy said. 'Look, I have to go. I'll ring you, OK?'

She might have nodded in the dark. He couldn't really tell. They went back to the road, and he headed to the bus stop. Halfway there, he looked back. Melanie was just turning the corner, cutting back the way they'd come. She's going back to the pub, he thought. Good-time girl. He'd lose her if he ever forgot it, he was sure.

By the time he got home, it was beginning to spit with rain. He went into the kitchen and made himself a cup of coffee. The whole place was spotless – floor, doors, windows, the lot. It meant Mum had spent the day cleaning. She did that when she was upset. He didn't remember the place ever being this clean before Dad had left.

'Mum,' he yelled. No reply. He went into the hallway and yelled again up the stairs. 'Mum, has Tim come back yet?' No reply, but now he could hear the radio playing in her bedroom.

He went upstairs quietly, and paused outside her room, then knocked quietly on the door.

'Come in, love,' she said.

Andy opened the door. His mother was sitting on the edge of the bed. She had dumped a dressing-table drawer out onto the bedspread, and was sorting through the mix of odd earrings, half-finished lipsticks and old photos. A picture of Andy's father stared up out of one of them.

Never here when you need him, Andy thought.

'Tim not back yet?' he asked.

His mother shook her head.

'You ought to phone,' Andy said.

She dug through a tangle of old necklaces for a moment, then held up a broken string of pearls. 'Do you think it'd be worth getting these restrung?' she asked.

'Phone him,' Andy said. He felt himself scowl at her. He didn't want to. It wasn't her fault Melanie was pissed off.

His mother started to untangle two chains that had got knotted up with some sewing thread. She didn't answer. Just talk to him, he thought. If she'd only talk to Dad, maybe things would be OK again. Wasn't going to happen though, he was pretty sure of that. He walked out.

He went into the front room and threw himself into his favourite chair, picking up the remote for the TV as he went. He pushed a button at random. The TV crackled and came to life. Jonathan Ross leered out of the screen at him. He'd kill Tim when the little bastard got home. Zap with the remote. Some foreign film. Subtitles. Little wanker had it coming to him. Zap. Clint Eastwood hotrodding a car in some American city. He stuck with that until the love interest came on, all blonde hair and white teeth. Made him think of Melanie. At the pub. With Mike. Zap. Bob

9

Monkhouse. Godhelpme, he thought, OK, so it's Sunday night and we went out last night, but she likes to be out every night. She'd told him so, repeatedly. He knew if he didn't give her what she wanted, she'd find someone who would, quick enough. I'll kill that little sod when he shows up here, he thought.

He sipped his coffee. It had gone cold. He hadn't even noticed the time passing. His mum came into the room. She didn't speak to him, didn't even look at him, just went straight to the phone.

He heard her punch a number.

'Steve?' his mother said.

Andy smiled. OK, so maybe it had taken some crazy stunt by the little poof to get them talking. That didn't mean it was a bad thing.

'It's Julie.' She sounded tense. That was hardly surprising. She hardly ever spoke to the old man, except to talk about Tim. 'Are you in bed?' Now she sounded startled. It's nothing to worry about, Andy told himself. Why shouldn't he be in bed, except . . . 'Tim is there, isn't he?' There was a pause. Andy felt his heart thudding in his chest. I didn't mean it, he thought. Just be there, you silly little git. 'Has he left?' his mother said. 'He said he was going to yours yesterday.' She was panicking now. Andy twisted round in his seat. I didn't mean it, he thought again. 'He never got there,' she said to him; and then into the phone, 'I'll phone you back.'

'He'll be all right,' Andy said. He has to be all right. I never meant any of it, he thought. Just be all right, kid. Just be all right.

His mother made another call. The connection seemed to take forever.

'Police,' she said.

Judith watched Fitz swill whisky round in the back of his throat. He swallowed. The conversation – argument? she

10

didn't know what he'd call it – had rankled him. She knew that. She'd been scoring points, and they both knew it. It was stupid. His whole bloody obsession with other people's motivation was stupid, come to that; but that didn't mean she had any business teasing him about it. That's all it had been, really. Teasing. Yet somehow, he'd made so much more of it than that.

She'd loved him for it once. Being around someone who just didn't give a damn about what other people thought had exhilarated her. But that was long ago. It had been part of the reason why she left him.

'I tell you, if Cagney's in Hell, he's watching English films,' Fitz said. He dropped into that fake American accent he did so well. 'You dirty rat. *Room with a View* for the hundredth time.' She started across the room towards him. 'Where's Eddie G? Where's Bogart?'

He stared at his glass for a minute, then took another gulp. He wasn't a man who sipped. Not her Fitz. When she'd married him, that had been another of the things she'd liked about him: the way he'd take life by the scruff of its neck and give it a good shake. She could smell the whisky on him, feel the heat of his huge body.

He turned to her. She stared up at him. He wasn't a good-looking man. Not by conventional standards. But that just proved how foolish conventional standards were. She ached for him suddenly. Her mouth went dry with desire. She put her hand on his shoulder, felt the solidity of him, the sheer bulk of him that no-one else could ever match.

'Sleep in our bed tonight, Fitz,' she said. She moved her hand across his arm, across his chest. She would have kissed him, but she didn't quite dare. Even to herself her voice sounded slow, languorous. He sighed; it was a sound halfway between anger and despair, she thought.

'Please,' she said. She wondered if he could hear the pleading in her voice. She knew she could. And she didn't care.

• • •

11

They lay in the bed together, not speaking, not touching, certainly not sleeping. Fitz wasn't fool enough to think that Judith was asleep when he'd finally had enough. He slid out of the bed and dressed in the darkness. He told himself that if she cried, he'd stop, go back to bed, wait out the night until the morning came. But she didn't cry, and he didn't have to find out whether he was lying to himself or not.

Fitz walked into the casino like he was coming home. He loved the noise of it, the voices calling out, the clatter of chips falling on baize, most especially the tension of fortunes being won and lost. The place reeked of sweat and cheap perfume gone sour. And fear. Oh yes, thought Fitz. Fear. Why else gamble if you aren't afraid? And what point gambling if you don't stand to lose?

This place, or a hundred others like it – they were all the same to Fitz, and infinitely better than lying sleepless next to Judith, with her careful lack of reproach. By the time he'd left the house, he knew every slight imperfection in the ceiling. Damn painters. You just couldn't get the staff nowadays . . .

He was no longer happy: the afternoon at the cinema seemed like lifetimes ago. But he could feel his blood starting to sing in his veins, feel the rush of adrenalin, and that would have to do. The game was on. It was time to play or pay.

One of the dealers called out, 'Evens spades, six to four hearts, five to one clubs and diamonds.' Fitz turned. The woman's hair was as brassy as her voice, and only the low lighting saved her make-up from looking garish. He considered for a moment. He wouldn't bet much. He owed Judith at least that much . . .

'Place your bets . . .'

Last chance. Fitz ambled over. The other punters round the table were betting fivers or tenners. Pocket change, really. Well, he wasn't going to do so much more. Just fifty or so . . .

'Six hundred on hearts,' he heard himself say. Damn, but he hadn't meant to make it so much. Maybe Judith was right. Maybe he was out of control. But there it was: the edge and how to dance on it with the adrenalin surging in his veins.

He watched the cards, refused to be distracted by the dealer's jangling bracelets and flashing rings, or the tawdry promise of her cleavage. Her cheap perfume cut through the cigar smoke. How could she compare when there was Judith at home, begging him to share her bed?

Flack, flack, flack went the cards as the dealer laid them on the table. The rings on her fingers glinted. Watch the cards, not her hands. At that he almost missed it.

'Diamonds wins,' the dealer said. The woman next to Fitz turned to her partner gleefully.

The dealer was good, he had to give her that.

'No,' he said. Everything went quiet. Pay or play. He'd damn well better be right about this.

His fingers flicked through the hearts as he counted them up. Eight of them. Then the diamonds. He pulled the ace of hearts out from where she'd snugged it down between the two and five of diamonds, and held it up. The tension stretched almost to breaking point.

'Nine,' he said quietly. 'Hearts win.'

A sigh of disappointment went up from the people round the table who had won on diamonds.

'I'm sorry,' the dealer said. She was flustered. So she damn well should be.

'Yeah.' He almost laughed. 'If it's any consolation, you very nearly got away with it.'

She had a lot of sense, that dealer. She knew danger when she saw it, even when it came wrapped in one of Fitz's gentlest smiles.

'It was a mistake – ' she sounded desperate. Fitz wondered if it was because she was afraid of him, or of someone else. Tough titty.

13

'Yeah.' Smile. 'You owe me a grand.'

A bit later he walked down the sodium-bright streets with a couple more whiskies burning in his belly and most of the cash tucked safely in his back pocket. He'd buy Judith, what? – maybe some sweet little black number, or maybe that green chiffony thing she'd liked so much, or – no, dammit. She'd said she didn't want any part of his winnings. So, what then? Maybe he'd use it to pay off part of the overdraft. She'd like that, Judith would. Sensible Judith. He wondered what her wonderful Graham would say about that. That Fitz was trying, no doubt. Yeah. Very trying. Well, there was always the three o'clock at Aintree. He'd heard that Bottom Line had legs –

Something slammed into his face. He went down hard, got his hands up to protect himself, but not before he took another punch, this time in his belly. He rolled but didn't even try to get up. Blood stung his eyes and he could hardly breathe for it clogging his nose. Hands patted him down. He tasted copper and salty snot, felt quick, professional hands moving over his body. Nothing he could do about it. They had the wallet and were gone before he'd even figured out what they were doing.

'Christ,' he muttered into the darkness. 'Christ.'

TWO

The woman ran through the woods. Moonlight silvered the tree branches as she crashed through them. It might have been pretty, if she'd had time to stop and look.

But she hadn't. He was after her. She thought she could hear him breathing, hear the long rasp of his breath as he sucked air so he could run faster and catch her. Or maybe she was making the sound herself. It hardly mattered.

He was closer though. She put on a burst of speed. Behind her, she heard him stumble. She stepped off the path.

She watched through the branches. He got up, then walked slowly on, looking from side to side as he went.

She stepped out and grabbed him, pushing him back before he could protest. She slapped him lightly on the chest, then grabbed the edge of his leather jacket and pushed him back against the tree.

'I won,' she said, before he could do a thing. She reached up and kissed him fiercely. His mouth tasted of tobacco and toothpaste. But her senses were too full of him for her to think of anything at all. His arms went round her, and she was pulling and he was pushing and somehow they ended up on the damp leaves, with her hands clawing at his back and tangling in his hair, and one of his on her breast and the other fumbling up under her skirt and both of them fierce and urgent and they hadn't even stopped kissing to come up for air yet, and she wanted it to take a long, long time, but she wanted it to be now, now, now.

She rolled underneath him, because whatever anyone said

15

she liked it that way, and opened her eyes wanting to see his face urgent with desire for her, but his head was moving downwards, his lips seeking her nipple and so she looked up and saw the thing hanging there in the tree and she screamed and screamed, her mouth opening wider than she'd thought it ever could to let out that noise, and by the time she'd stopped screaming she was almost back at the car.

But he was with her, so that was all right. They clung together for a moment, silent, screamed out, all desire vanished into the terror. It was only then that she'd been able to make sense of it: the body, hanging there in the trees, the feet turning slightly in the cold air.

They drove.

It was never going to be any different. Judith lay in bed, listening to Fitz come in. She glanced at him through the open door as he went to the bathroom. He'd been beaten up. She wondered if he expected her to care.

But she did care, and she even knew the exact moment she'd been forced to admit it to herself once and for all.

It had been the moment, the July of last year, when she'd finally got the police to admit that he'd gone to talk that boy – what was his name? Sean, that was it – out of blowing himself sky high, and that blind girl with him. Fitz the hero, walking straight into that house with the petrol scattered all around and the gas full on. The only wonder was that he hadn't taken a cigarette in with him.

By the time they'd told her, it was too late for her to go and wait outside for him. Not that she could have done anything, anyway. She'd had to stay back at the station, wearing holes in the damn carpet tiles with all her pacing.

The last thing he'd said to her before he left was that he wanted to rape her. That he wanted to put his mark on her, prove she was his, not Graham's. She'd slept with the man once, out of despair and loneliness, and – she had to admit it – the need to provoke Fitz to an emotional,

16

unrationalised response.

Well, she'd done that all right. He hadn't meant the rape threat. Not literally. She knew when he was trying to shock. But for that to have been the last thing he ever said to her would have been more than she could have lived with. Then he'd walked in, cracking Clark Kent jokes and pretending nothing had happened. Only she'd seen his hands shake as he lit his cigarette, and that night they'd gone home together. Home. They'd made love with a passion she had been scared they had lost. The next morning he'd rationalised it, of course: 'It's mother nature trying to beat death: see death, have a fuck, make more babies. Same thing I told Tina,' and he'd looked at her and walked away, towards the French doors; but before he'd gone into the garden he'd turned back and said, 'She didn't believe that was all there was to it, either.'

Damn him. He always did know the easiest way to hurt her. She almost despised herself for staying with him after that. But she knew that, although with him she might not have everything she wanted, without him she had nothing that she needed.

She might as well not have bothered, she thought now, feeling the cold space in the bed next to her. It had been downhill all the way from there. He hadn't quite forgiven her, oh no. At least he hadn't pretended. After that first night, he'd gone back to sleeping in the spare room – had, in fact, tried to act as if it hadn't happened, until she'd accused him of dishonesty.

Then this. It wasn't the first time they'd slept together since then. The other times had been just like this. Lying next to him, not touching, not speaking, staring into the darkness, until finally he left. She wondered where he went, what he did. She supposed he went gambling. Certainly he drank – she could smell it on his breath.

It would have been so much easier if only she hadn't cared.

● ● ●

17

The truly shocking thing was how seriously the police took Tim's disappearance. They were very young, but full of professional sympathy. They sat in Julie's front room, listening carefully, taking notes about everything she said.

'He didn't take a coat,' Julie said, not meeting their eyes. What kind of mother must they think she was, letting him go out like that? 'He had no money.'

There's a trick to not crying. She'd learned it when Stephen had left her. You take big slow breaths, and you concentrate on the next thing you have to say.

The next thing you have to say: something, anything to make them realise they had to do something. 'His dad's less than a mile away.' No response. 'He hasn't been seen since last night.'

Take another breath, and another. Sometimes all you can do is keep breathing.

Just his bloody luck on a Sunday night, Jimmy Beck thought. Freezing cold, in the woods, with the rain pissing down, looking for some little brat with feathers where his brains ought to have been. He wanted to be back at the station, maybe, with a good cup of tea and a gander at the *News of the World*. Failing that, a cafe somewhere, pretending to follow up some lead or other. Anything but standing here with the rain dribbling down the back of his neck, and the mud seeping in over the tops of his shoes. Not that finding the kid wasn't important. Course it was, and if anyone could find him, he would.

He flashed his torch around. Trees, trees, more bloody trees. The boss had sent as many men as he could, but there wasn't a hope in hell of finding the kid. Not in this muck.

He yelled the kid's name. So did a lot of other people. There was no reply.

It looked like the search through the woods would be a waste of time, David Bilborough thought, as he sorted through the photos of the missing boy.

He'd been down there earlier, as they'd struggled through the mud with the rain pissing down and the sky so overcast they couldn't see a bloody thing, and not enough people to do the job properly anyway. It was still going on, of course, and would do till they got a result or someone – maybe him, maybe someone higher up – decided there was no point going on.

But for now, here he was, sitting with Mrs Lang with no idea what he should say. She sat very upright on the floral sofa, with her hands folded in her lap. Her eyes were hard with grief. She was very still. In her place, he'd have been beating his head against the wall.

It didn't help that Penhaligon was watching him. She was sitting on the edge of the sofa, trying not to look too ladylike, taking notes. She was just waiting for him to say something stupid, he was sure. She was a good officer, but the most judgemental person he'd ever come across. Except Fitz, of course.

He put another photo on the pile. The lad, Timothy, stared up out of it. He had been a lovely-looking lad, Bilborough thought. A bit girlish, maybe. Pretty, with hair the colour of corn and wide blue eyes. Had been. Bilborough was fairly sure of that.

He wasn't going to tell Mrs Lang that though. Christ no. Leave it till they had something to go on. He was going to do it himself this time, too. Sod Penhaligon. He'd show her he could be as sensitive as any woman.

'You didn't think of ringing to see that he'd arrived?' he asked. These people. God, if Catriona was OK – if the baby was OK – he'd never let it out of his sight. He'd seen too many of these cases, sat with too many frantic parents.

'He often goes round to his dad's,' Mrs Lang said. She sounded irritated. Guilt, he thought, or maybe just the worry. He was beginning to sound like Fitz. The thought didn't amuse him.

19

'Can you remember what he was wearing?'

'Trainers. Black denims. Long-sleeved tee-shirt,' she answered. Her hands were long and pale. She started to pluck at one of them with the fingers of the other. It was the only sign she made that she was upset.

Trainers, Bilborough thought. Denims. Great. That would take in ninety per cent of the kids in Manchester. He paused, trying to think of a question that would provoke a more detailed response.

The doorbell shrilled through the silence. He saw Penhaligon flinch. She was expecting the worst, just as Bilborough himself was. He nodded to her and she went to answer it. He leaned forward in his seat, hoping to encourage her to keep talking. The husband might be difficult. They were sometimes.

Mrs Lang twisted her wedding ring round and round. 'That was the last thing I said to him, actually. I said: "You're not going out in that. And put your coat on." ' She smiled slightly, the kind of smile you might make because otherwise you would cry.

The door banged open, and a chunky middle-aged man walked in, shaking the rain off his jacket. Penhaligon followed him.

'Police?' he asked. Bilborough liked the directness of that.

'Yeah,' Penhaligon said from behind him, before Bilborough could answer. He stood up.

'Any news?' the man asked.

When no-one said anything, Mrs Lang sighed raggedly and said, 'This is my husband.' Bilborough noted that she didn't sound delighted about it.

'I don't live here,' Mr Lang said. 'We're separated.' He sounded about as happy as his wife.

It was quite amazing, Bilborough decided, how much tension one additional person could generate in a room.

'I'm DCI Bilborough,' he said, to try and ease it as much as anything. 'This is DS Penhaligon.'

'DCI?' Mr Lang asked. Bilborough nodded. He knew very well that he looked far too young for his rank. He wondered if Mr Lang were about to make something of it; it wouldn't have been the first time, nor the first time he'd got stick from someone because they were upset; but Mr Lang just repeated, 'DCI.' His mouth started to work, and then he said, 'Oh Jesus, they think he's dead.'

He stifled a sob, but he couldn't stop his shoulders shaking. Mrs Lang looked at him without speaking. Bilborough couldn't tell what she was thinking.

Penhaligon moved forward and put her arm round Mr Lang. She looked at Bilborough over his shoulder. 'You want to make a cup of tea, sir?' she asked.

Sir. Bloody hell. Nevertheless, he went off to explore the kitchen.

Andy stood at his bedroom window, staring out into the rain-filled darkness. He had his light off, and the sky was overcast, so the only illumination came from the houses across the garden.

Tim was out there somewhere. Attention-seeking little git, Andy thought.

Someone knocked on the door. 'Come in,' Andy shouted.

He turned round. His father was standing in the doorway.

'What do you want?' Andy said.

'The police are here – '

'Yeah. I know.' Couldn't fail to bloody know, could he?

'They think it's serious – '

Oh yeah, Andy thought. Tell me another one. Little poof's probably holed up with some bloke as pretty as he is.

'What do you want me to do about it?' he asked. Even as he said the words, he regretted them. It wasn't that he didn't care. It was just that he couldn't believe anything was seriously wrong. And anyway, it would just turn into another opportunity for Dad to have a go at him.

'They're searching – the woods, you know – '

21

'I'll get my jacket,' Andy said.

'No need – '

'He's my brother, for Christ's sake. You're always telling me he's my brother – '

'The police said to stay here.' For one terrible moment Andy thought he might cry. He'd never seen his father cry. 'I think . . . I think they're afraid of what we might find.'

Jesus, Andy thought. They think he's dead. They think they'll find his body in some ditch somewhere. He couldn't say anything. He took a step forward. He wanted to hold his father. To touch him. Something.

He couldn't do it.

'I'm going to get some of the neighbours to help. George Lindsay and the rest of them. Stay with your mum.'

Andy nodded. His father turned and left.

A little later, he went downstairs. His mother was sitting in the front room in her favourite place on the sofa. It was amazing how calm she seemed. The red-headed woman copper was with her, and another one, a bloke with a moustache.

He ought to go in and sit with her. He ought to say something. He'd promised Dad. But he couldn't. He just couldn't.

He turned and went back upstairs.

It was still raining when Bilborough got back to the woods, a thin driving rain that bit straight through his clothes and stung his eyes. He wrapped his hands round a mug of coffee. Benefits of rank.

Light from half a hundred torches flashed in the darkness, turning the trees into silhouettes and the raindrops into jewels.

It might have been pretty in other circumstances. To hell with that, though. All the darkness and the rain meant was that you could hardly see three feet in front of you. They'd been searching for hours and he really didn't think they'd find anything. Maybe it would be better to wait till morning. It wasn't very long till dawn now, and they'd do better in daylight, surely. He could go home then, be with Catriona when she needed him. If the baby came while he was here . . . but he couldn't help remembering Mrs Lang's huge dark eyes staring at him, and her husband's awful silent sobbing. He scuffed at a sodden tussock of grass with his foot. There was a dead body somewhere out there. He felt it in his gut. The kid might have been abducted, he supposed; but his instincts said not.

There was a sudden shout from somewhere. He looked round. One of the constables was waving. He was surprisingly close to where the cars had been parked. Bilborough ran over, him and just about everyone else there. The constable had found something. He held it up on the end of a long stick. Bilborough peered at it. It could have been anything – a piece of clothing, a clump of grass, even a solid lump of mud. But it wasn't. It was a trainer.

THREE

Jane Penhaligon stared round at the Langs' neat suburban living room and sipped her tea. The other Detective
Sergeant on her team, Jimmy Beck, came back into the
room. He raised his eyebrows at her, though he must have
known there'd been no news in the few minutes he'd been
upstairs. She shook her head very slightly, hoping the Langs
wouldn't notice.

Usually, Beck was all swagger, but after this long waiting
in the funeral-parlour atmosphere of the Langs' front room,
even he was subdued. He sat down in one of the armchairs
and stared at the blank TV screen. After a second, he stroked
his moustache as if psyching himself up to say something.

If he asks if he can turn it on, I'll kill him, Penhaligon
thought. She glared at him. Just as well only ITV was still
broadcasting this late at night – he almost certainly would
have asked, if there had been any sport on.

Mrs Lang sat nearby on the couch. She hardly seemed to
have moved in hours. Her husband was another matter.
He hadn't gone anywhere near Mrs Lang, but since he'd
returned an hour ago he'd managed to pace all round the
room just the same. Now he hovered in the background,
staring first at his wife, then at the floor, then at his wife
again. Penhaligon wondered whose idea it had been to split
up. She'd have taken bets it hadn't been his.

She sipped again at the tea. It was almost cold. She felt as
though she'd drunk more tea in the last twelve hours than in
the rest of her life put together. It's something people do in a

24

crisis, she thought. You can waste an awful lot of time with tea. First asking everyone if they'd like some, then making it – that was good for quite a while, especially in a strange kitchen – and, finally, drinking it. It saved some of those awkward silences. Like now, with Mrs Lang sitting watching her with those huge Bambi eyes of hers. Penhaligon wondered what the other woman was thinking, whether she thought Penhaligon had answers she wasn't telling. God. Most of the tea was gone. It was a bit too soon to make another pot.

The phone rang. Penhaligon jerked round, but Beck had already gone out into the hall to answer it before she could move. She heard him murmuring something. Mrs Lang just sat and stared, with only her restless hands betraying her anxiety. Beck came back in. Mrs Lang followed his every move with her eyes.

'Mrs Lang,' he said. 'What size shoe did Timothy take?' he asked.

God, Penhaligon thought. That was just typical –

'Did he take?' Mrs Lang murmured, almost to herself, as if she were trying to extract the meaning from it.

Beck glanced at Penhaligon. He looked embarrassed, which, she thought, he had every right to be.

'Sorry,' he said. 'Does he take.'

'Seven,' Mrs Lang said, without raising her voice; she looked as if something inside her had died.

Beck nodded and left the room. Penhaligon heard him pick up the phone again. She followed him.

'Seven,' he said into the mouthpiece as she came out into the hall. He saw her looking at him and moved the handset away from his face. 'Slip o' the tongue,' he said to her. His Irish accent had become thicker, as it always did when he got upset.

Penhaligon just stared at him. She couldn't think of anything to say that would be adequate in the face of such insensitivity.

'Thanks for being so understanding,' he said after a minute.

Tough, Penhaligon thought. She made a show of examining the floral pattern on the hall carpet, and said nothing.

Beck listened down the phone for a moment longer. He muttered something inaudible, then, louder, 'Right. Right.'

He looked up, and folded the aerial of the cordless phone away. 'They found a seven,' he said, sounding more shaken than Penhaligon had expected.

Penhaligon leaned against the wall. Damn, she thought. Here we go. 'I'll tell them,' she said. One of these days, she would stop doing this. She would let the men handle the messy parts of the job, the parts that involved destroying innocent people's lives. But not today. Not when that would mean letting Beck go in there and trample all over their feelings with his size nines.

She only wished that were funny.

Andy couldn't stand it any more. The woman copper had said they'd found a trainer and it was as if all the air had been sucked out of the room.

He'd had to leave. He couldn't stand seeing the hurt in Mum's eyes, the reproach in Dad's. As if it was his fault. As if he'd done that to Tim. Stupid little bastard, always getting it wrong.

Andy had meant to go for a walk, maybe go and see Melanie; but it was pissing down with rain, and there was a little knot of people gathered by the gate: he recognised one or two of the neighbours, a couple of Tim's teachers, a journalist from the local paper who'd been hanging around all day, waiting for someone to come out. Shit. If they were lucky, they might even make the *Sun*, he thought. But he didn't feel like talking, and in the end he'd just stood in the porch next to the copper who was on duty there. At least this one had a uniform on. Meant you knew where you stood.

26

A cop car drew up. The wet road glistened in its head-
lights. He'd just about forgotten that they would be bringing
the trainer round for his mum and dad to identify. Tim's
trainer. He knew it would be his brother's; knew it in his gut,
the way he knew a few other things about him that his
parents would rather not think about.

It was no use. He had to go. He strode quickly towards
the gate. Mr Lindsay, one of the neighbours, stepped towards
him. He grabbed Andy by the shoulders. 'It means nothing,
Andy,' he said, urgently. Andy shrugged him off and kept
walking. 'Nothing at all,' the man said behind him. Andy
began to run down the road, into the dawn.

This time, Bilborough thought, he'd do the talking. He
knew what Penhaligon thought – that every time he opened
his mouth he said something stupid or hurtful or both – but
this time it would be different. He put the trainer, in its clear
plastic bag, down carefully on the dining table. The plastic
crackled loudly.

Mrs Lang got up and crossed the room without being
asked. Her husband followed close behind. She stopped
when she was halfway there. Her hands were still for once,
folded in front of her. She stared at the shoe impassively for
what seemed a very long time, though it couldn't have been
as much as a minute. She turned and nodded to Bilborough.

Her husband pulled her close into him. Christ, Bilborough thought. What do you say? What do you *say*? At
least they had each other. But then Mrs Lang shook her
husband off impatiently. She went and stood by the sofa,
where she'd spent so much time in the last couple of days,
while Mr Lang watched her helplessly, and, Bilborough
thought, hopelessly.

She ran her hand through her dark hair, pushing it back
from the pale oval of her face. Bilborough saw Penhaligon
watching her, watching him. Say something, he thought
at her. But she didn't say anything. The silence became

27

unbearable. Damn Penhaligon anyway.

'There could be a perfectly innocent explanation, Mrs Lang,' he said. His voice sounded too loud.

Wrong. The woman's face crumpled. She brought her hand up to cover her mouth, and she began to cry, as she had not cried at any time since this began. Not to Bilborough's knowledge, anyway. Bilborough couldn't see Mr Lang's face, but he didn't need to. The man's shoulders were heaving with the effort of suppressing his sobs.

Bilborough jerked his head towards the living-room door. Penhaligon went out. He followed her. She was pissed off with him. He could tell by the set of her shoulders. He should have left the talking to her, Bilborough thought. She was so much better at that kind of thing.

'Get Fitz,' he said quietly.

Penhaligon turned towards him. He realised she wasn't so much fed up with him, as depressed with the whole situation. It was hardly surprising. She'd sat with the Langs longer than any of them, hours, waiting for the search parties to find something.

'We don't know he's dead yet,' she hissed back at him, giving him one of those disapproving looks of hers. 'Sir.'

'He's been gone two days, he's no coat, he didn't take any money and we found his shoe,' Bilborough said. He extended the aerial of the mobile phone. 'Do you really think he's alive?'

The rain battered at Andy as he ran. It means nothing, George Lindsay had said. Andy didn't believe him. He's dead, he thought as he ran. The pounding of his feet echoed the pounding of the thoughts in his head. Tim's dead. My brother's dead.

He slowed to a walk, eventually. He wasn't surprised to find that he had ended up near the woods. The sun was just coming up, a dull grey light filtering through a leaden sky that promised nothing good for the day to come. The path

28

that led into the trees had been churned up by cars and people on foot. He followed it for a bit, with his feet sinking further into the mud at every step. He knew these woods – he'd played in them as a kid, and later he'd hung around in them drinking illicit cans of lager and smoking ciggies when he'd skived off school. But now, in the pale dawn light, with the mist curling round the bases of the trees and the smell of wet mulch clinging to the back of his throat, it was easy to believe he'd fallen into some strange wildwood.

Soft, he thought. I'm going soft in the head, like Tim.

He hadn't gone much further when he began to hear voices calling his brother's name. He came to a halt just before the path joined the road that entered the woods from the other direction. Several cars were parked there, with a few people standing around drinking coffee from Thermoses.

Andy hesitated. He was furious with them for taking even a moment's rest. He knew he ought to go and offer to help. But he was sure of what they would find: Tim, dead in a ditch, with his eyes staring into nothingness, and his skin cold as ice.

He couldn't do it; but he wasn't able to face going home yet, either. He decided to go to Melanie's place instead. He glanced at his watch. Six-thirty. He had plenty of time to get there before she left for work.

Andy hammered at Melanie's door. He was tired and cold, and soaked through to the skin, though the rain had stopped a while earlier.

'Hang on,' her mother shouted. There was a clatter of keys turning in locks. The door opened a crack. Mrs Johnson peered out of it, then opened the door properly. She was dressed for work, and already fully made up.

She said, 'Andy, love, you look – ' She paused. ' – this is about that brother of yours, isn't it?' Andy couldn't speak. He just looked at her miserably. 'Come on in.'

29

Andy followed her into the kitchen. It was warm and full of the smell of toast and bacon. Mrs Johnson pulled a chair out for him, put the kettle on and then called Melanie, all without demanding to know what was going on. He had always liked the way she didn't nag him. He'd told Melanie as much, but she'd said, 'Well, she isn't like that with me.'

Melanie came down just as Mrs Johnson finished making the tea. She was wearing a towelling dressing-gown, and though it didn't reveal much, Andy couldn't stop himself from staring.

'It's Tim, isn't it?' she asked.

Andy nodded. She seemed very cool. Andy thought maybe he was embarrassing her, so he looked at the floor between his feet. 'They found his trainer,' he said. 'They haven't said, but I reckon he's dead.'

'Oh no, love,' Mrs Johnson said. 'Surely not – '

Andy wanted to say, *Don't be stupid. If he's dead, he's dead. There's no point hoping for anything.* But he could hardly say that, so he just shrugged. He wished Mrs Johnson wasn't there, so he could hold Melanie. He needed to hold something. He realised that he was close to tears. I won't cry, he thought. I just won't.

'It'll be OK, Andy,' Melanie said. 'You wait and see.'

'That's a promise, is it?'

'Wait and see.' She took his hand. He looked up at her. There was something odd in her expression, but he couldn't understand it. 'I have to go and get ready for work,' she said.

'I'm afraid I have to go as well,' Mrs Johnson said. 'But you ought to be getting home, Andy. You don't want your mum and dad worrying about you, too.'

'I suppose so,' Andy said, though he wanted to ask if he couldn't just wait there until the two of them got back from work.

'Wait for me,' Melanie said. 'I'll walk as far as the park gates with you.' She still sounded strange. Maybe it was just that her mother was there, he decided.

A little later they walked along the road together. He took her hand, glad of the contact; after a moment or two she slid free of him and put her hands in her pockets.

'What's the matter?' he asked.

'Nothing.'

'Oh, come on,' Andy said. 'You should have seen your face in the kitchen – '

'I don't want to talk about it. Not now – ' Her face held that same strange look, but he recognised it now. It was as if she were angry and didn't want to admit it.

'What?' he demanded. It was hard not to shout, because suddenly all the anger that had built up during the night was burning in him.

Melanie pursed her lips. 'Go home, Andy. Find out what happened to Tim. We'll talk later.' She started to walk away.

Andy followed her. 'No,' he said. She kept walking. 'Tell me what I'm supposed to have done.' He grabbed her arm and pulled her back, forcing her round to face him.

'Take your hands off me,' she said.

'Tell me,' he demanded, but he let her go.

She glared at him. 'Ask Mike,' she said finally, and walked away.

He stared at her as she left him, until she turned the corner and there was nothing left for him to do but go home.

FOUR

Penhaligon waited in the car outside Fitz's house. It was finally morning. There had been times during the previous night when she'd thought dawn would never come. She wound the window down a bit, hoping Fitz wouldn't want to smoke in the car. There were limits.

She'd taken half an hour to rush home, have a shower and change. Peter had asked her to come to bed – he could be quite persuasive, at times. She'd resisted the temptation, and the shower had woken her up a bit, but she still felt like death only slightly warmed over.

And now here she was, doing what she was told like a good girl, getting Fitz so he could bully and cajole the Langs into giving up whatever information they were concealing. If they were concealing anything, which Penhaligon doubted; Bilborough would see it differently, of course; Beck certainly would, but then he set a lot of store by his detective powers. Jumped-up little wanker, she thought.

She sounded the horn. No point getting impatient. Fitz would just go that bit slower and take the opportunity to explain to her in great detail the childhood trauma that had made her hate waiting around.

The front door opened. Penhaligon leaned across to open the car door. The Manchester Constabulary didn't run to central locking. She glanced up and realised that the person coming out of the house was Judith, not Fitz. She tried to look away, to watch the marmalade cat that was sunning itself on

32

the pavement, but she couldn't. This was Judith, wonderful, wonderful *bloody* Judith. Fitz's wife. Penhaligon found that she was watching in the rear-view mirror as the other woman walked down the road. Class act, Penhaligon thought, and felt her mind skitter away from: and a difficult act to follow. Despite the financial problems she knew Fitz's gambling must bring in its wake, she couldn't believe Judith really knew what it was to go short. She certainly knew how to choose clothes. And how to wear them. Penhaligon suddenly found she was acutely aware that her blouse, though fresh on that morning, was slightly rumpled.

Bloody Judith, she thought again.

She had always imagined Judith as dowdy and plain. There had been that horrible moment when Penhaligon had seen Judith for the first time, when she had turned up with Graham, in the same restaurant as her and Fitz. Penhaligon had had to admit to herself then that she had a fight on her hands, but then she'd thought it was one she could win. Now she wasn't so sure.

If she were honest with herself, Penhaligon had to admit she had thought she would be one of very few women who found Fitz attractive. After all, he was hardly the standard issue male pin-up. Then again, apparently she and Judith had both been attracted by the same things: Fitz's intelligence, the edge of danger about him that actually hid a teddybear centre, his manic energy. And physically – well, physically she wanted very much to get physical with him.

Judith disappeared out of sight. Penhaligon thought, I may have lost the battle, but the war's hardly begun. She smiled lazily, beginning to get into a fantasy where she and Fitz went away together, and Judith lived happily ever after with her counsellor chappy, and then – she realised she had been hearing someone tap on the side window of the car for a while.

'Open up,' said a voice with an exaggerated American

accent. 'This is the police.'

Penhaligon turned. Fitz knocked on the door again. Then he realised it was already open, and got in. He'd been in a fight. There was a fresh scab above his left eyebrow, a graze high on his cheek, and a long scratch across his chin.

'What happened?' Penhaligon asked.

'Tripped over the kerb and smashed into a lamp-post,' Fitz said. He was very quiet, Penhaligon thought, as if the phony accent he'd used just then had only been for show.

'That what you told Judith?'

'Judith had better sense than to ask,' Fitz said.

Fitz was in a better mood by the time they got near the Langs' house. He produced a bag of sweets, took one out and unwrapped it. Without even asking her if she wanted one, he reached over and popped it in her mouth. His fingers brushed her lips as she took it from him; the frisson of excitement that shivered through her was out of all proportion to the event itself. He was watching her. She liked that. Whatever it was that Judith had, Penhaligon knew he wanted her.

Penhaligon quite often thought men, including Fitz – especially Fitz – were pretty adolescent. Look who's talking, she thought: you with a crush a mile wide on a married man. She grinned. I bet he doesn't know why, even though he thinks he does, she thought. Her grin widened.

'It speaks volumes about a person, Panhandle,' Fitz said. 'The way they suck a sherbet lemon.'

Oh yeah? He was going into dissection mode. He'd done it to her once before, when he hardly knew her: the Hennessey case; he'd been very ruthless and very accurate, and he'd done it in public. She'd hated him for a while, but she'd forgiven him for it eventually. She'd forgiven him for a lot of things, most of them involving Judith.

'Me, I'm a cruncher,' Fitz said. 'Like to pop 'em in – crunch – exposing the sherbet. Instant gratification.'

34

This, Penhaligon thought, is a set-up. Good fun, but a set-up nevertheless.

'Judith is a roller,' Fitz went on. She'd been bound to come into the conversation somewhere, Penhaligon thought. 'She likes to roll them around in her mouth for ages,' Fitz went on, then paused. 'Noisily,' he finished, as if it were a judgement; but that would come later: with Fitz, it always did.

Class act Judith, making slurping sounds with sherbet lemons? Penhaligon could hardly imagine it.

'You see,' Fitz continued, leaning slightly towards Penhaligon, as if telling her something in confidence. 'As a child she got more pleasure out of making the other kids jealous than she did out of the sweetie itself.'

Penhaligon laughed. He was funny. That was a large part of the attraction, of course.

He looked at her slyly. Careful, she warned herself. He's setting you up; but that was all right. This was all just a bit of fun.

'I think you're probably a sucker,' he said slowly, though Penhaligon thought he'd probably been leading the conversation in this direction all along. 'I think you probably like to make it last. Am I right?'

Penhaligon laughed. All right Fitz, she thought. Let's see what you make of this. She took her eyes off the road for an instant to glance at him. 'Yeah,' she said, making her voice deliberately slow and low. What else could I make last, Fitz? she thought at him. What else might I like to suck? Wouldn't you just like to find out? He glanced at her out of narrowed eyes. He'd got the message all right. Good.

'I bet you could suck that sherbet lemon wafer thin before you got so much as a hint of sherbet,' Fitz went on. He sounded almost admiring.

'Yeah,' she said again, wondering if he were thinking the same thing she was. No doubt she'd find out when he told her triumphantly that it indicated a secret sexual predilection. Not fellatio – too obvious. S&M, maybe, or –

'Thus indicating a massive guilt complex,' Fitz said.

Penhaligon scowled at him. He'd won again. Sucker, she thought at herself.

The copper on duty outside the Langs' house looked bored as hell, Fitz thought as they drove up. Good job too. They probably weren't paying him enough to have a good time.

The door opened even before Panhandle had finished parking. Bilborough rushed out. He looked as crumpled as ever. Anyone would think he'd been wandering through the woods all night.

'Stay in the car, Jane,' he shouted as Fitz got out.

Jane, Fitz thought. Now there was a thing. He'd hardly ever heard Bilborough – or anyone else, come to think of it – use Panhandle's first name. In fact, he'd have laid odds that Panhandle didn't think of herself as Jane, at least while she was at work. So why would Bilborough suddenly call her it? Wanted her to do some shitty bit of scut work, maybe? Nah. He'd just tell her. He was too insecure ever to *ask* someone to do something. Hardly surprising, with him being just out of nappies and all. But what would have made him call her by her first name, then? It feminised her, that's what. Made a woman out of her. A vagrant thought led him to wonder about the prospect of making a woman out of Panhandle. *Bad Fitz. Down boy.*

Back to the matter at hand. Bilborough – ah yes, Bilborough's wife was pregnant. That would be it, then. She'd gone into labour, thus reminding Bilborough of the essential femininity of all women, and simultaneously making him feel protective toward them; but he couldn't protect Panhandle – it was against the rules, both formal and informal, of the job; hence his use of her personal, non-professional name, which allowed him to think of her in civilian terms.

'I want to know why they're separated,' Bilborough said, in a low voice, not quite a whisper but intended only for Fitz's ears. 'I want to know why they didn't report it for twenty-four hours. The brother's hiding something too.'

Sure, sure thought Fitz. Let's get on with the important stuff, shall we –

Bilborough stuck his head in the passenger side of the car. 'My wife's in labour,' he said.

QED, thank you, I rest my case, Fitz thought.

'It looks like the kid's dead,' Bilborough went on, 'but don't tell them that.'

Fitz nodded. This was going to be nasty. He'd rather have dealt with a dozen convicted criminals than one grieving parent. He sighed, and went into the house.

The house was furnished in good, solid upper working-class style, Fitz thought. Carpet and curtains from Lewis's, furniture from that nice shop by the market, knick-knacks from some rip-off tourist shop on the Costa del Sol, or, in a really bad year, Blackpool. At least it was honest tat, he thought; not like the kind of designer crap certain jumped-up middle-class *Guardian*-reading bleeding-heart counsellors would fill their homes with. He sat down, wondering where that little diatribe had come from. He'd been rather successful at putting Graham out of his mind, recently.

To hell with it. Better to concentrate on the job. He looked at the Langs. Nice, old-fashioned nuclear family, as approved of by the Tory party, but now riven by separation in the modern manner, and about to be torn apart by becoming quite another kind of statistic: Mrs Lang, late thirties, probably oh, let's see – a primary-school helper, something like that; next to her on the sofa, Andy: nineteen-ish, maybe brighter than his school record would show, by the looks of him, but there was a hint of aggression there, like a trapped animal; he'd warrant watching, Andy would; and Mr Lang, older than his wife and not weathering the separation at all well; a manual worker, Fitz thought, but good at his job – maybe a foreman.

'Did you choose Tim's trainers?' Fitz asked quietly. He

didn't want to push them till he had to.

'He chose them,' Mrs Lang said. She sounded tired and a little bit defensive.

'Does he have any friends?' Fitz had to ask.

'Of course he's got friends.' Mrs Lang again, but this time her defences were all the way up. It was a common enough reaction to grief: guilt, anger, all mixed in till you couldn't tell one from the other. She was going to need help to deal with it, but that would have to wait until later.

Meanwhile, he had to get the others talking. 'Would you wear these?' he asked Andy.

'Wouldn't be seen dead in them,' the lad said in a voice full of contempt.

It would be worth coming on a bit stronger, Fitz decided. Bait the bear, see what happened if it lashed out: 'Because your mates would give you stick?'

'Yeah,' and then, almost without a pause, 'Tim hasn't got any mates.'

'Greg Stevens,' Mrs Lang put in, too quickly. She turned to look at Andy.

'Greg Stevens is a mental retard,' Andy said, and the contempt was back in his voice, full force.

Mrs Lang turned away. She stared straight ahead, as if hoping that would hide the hurt that was plain on her face.

Ah, thought Fitz. Now we're getting somewhere. Our poor little Tim's a pink monkey, that's what he is. It was an old experiment. You took a monkey and painted it pink. When you put it in a cage with others of the same breed, they tore it to pieces. Happened every time, even when the monkey concerned had previously been known to the group. It was killed because it was different. Tim might not have been killed because he was different from the other kids – though then again, he might, there was always the outside odds of that – but they'd certainly made his life misery. And Andy? Andy was scared that if he stayed around his brother too much, he'd start turning into a pink monkey too; Fitz would have laid odds that Andy was nothing if not a pack animal.

'Did you have a row with Tim, recently?' He aimed the question at no-one in particular. They'd deny it, of course; but it would be interesting to see who answered.

'Not recently, no,' Mr Lang said. He leaned forward in his seat; he held his hands out in front of him, and he rubbed them together as if he were washing them. It was a defensive posture, one aimed at holding Fitz off. His wedding ring was a thick gold band, noticeable without being ostentatious. His marriage meant a lot to him, Fitz thought: test of manhood, adulthood rite, all that; and he hadn't given up on it, either – hadn't taken the ring off, for one thing; for another, his attention never really left his wife; even when he wasn't looking directly at her, you could somehow sense she was at the centre of his world.

Fitz took a long drag on his cigarette and settled back a bit into his chair. It was too small of course, but Fitz was used to living in a world made for smaller people. And this time, though he might be uncomfortable, he'd made his point. He was on their territory, talking about a subject that hurt them deeply; but he was in control. He decided to cut a little deeper: time to get the scalpel out.

'Why didn't you call when he didn't arrive?' he asked, never letting the sympathetic look leave his face.

'I wasn't expecting him,' Mr Lang said. His hands stopped moving. 'Look, we feel bad enough. Don't be making it worse.'

It was fair comment. 'Sorry,' Fitz said. He sighed deeply to cover a sudden, unfamiliar moment of embarrassment. Back to the brother. 'Did you have a row with Tim recently?'

'Look, he hasn't run away,' Andy said quietly. 'He's got no coat, he's got no money and he left his books. Poetry.' Then the contempt came back into his voice. 'Load of crap.' His voice went quieter again, as if the thought of poetry had triggered an automatic response, which was now over. 'If he

39

was running away he'd have took them with him. So he wasn't running away, right?'

Fitz dragged on the cigarette again. Andy was sharp, all right, sharp as knives, and probably right in this instance, if Tim really had been into poetry. He hadn't answered the question either. Bilborough was right. He was hiding something, though Fitz couldn't tell what. He decided to let the question drop for now. There would be time later, if Tim really were dead.

He exhaled, watched the smoke rise for a second. 'Would you mind if I had a look round his room?' he asked. Andy looked at his mother as if he were willing her to refuse Fitz permission, but she nodded silently.

Andy realised that the fat guy was in his room as he went upstairs. He could hear him shuffling around, and imagined the guy standing there, looking at his stuff like it was something you'd find in a dustbin.

He'd said he wanted to look in Tim's room. Andy hadn't liked it, but Mum had said it was OK, so that was that. But now he was prying into Andy's stuff, and that was something else.

Well, Andy would just tell him where he could go. He couldn't look around without permission. There were laws, after all.

But by the time Andy got to the doorway, he'd thought about it a bit more. The man was built like a brick shithouse, and by the look of those scars on his face, he wasn't someone who minded wellying in. All in all, it was probably best to hold off, at least for a while. After all, he didn't want to upset Mum.

He lounged against the doorframe. He was right. The guy pushed a pair of Andy's underpants out of his way with the tip of his shoe. If it hadn't been for Mum, Andy would have told him where to go; but she really had been upset enough already, so all he said was, 'This is my room.'

40

'Yeah, reminds me of my son.' Oh, here we go, Andy thought. Will it be, 'You kids are all the same', or, 'I know where you're coming from'? Either way, Andy had heard it all before. Fitz said, 'Aah, the unmistakable whiff of smelly feet.'

He was trying to get Andy on his side. Made a little joke, see, we're all in this together. Well, they weren't, and he hadn't known Tim; hadn't known what it was like, having to put up with a brother like that. Why couldn't the stupid little faggot have been like everyone else?

But the big guy was carrying on with his little speech. 'You know at Christmas he doesn't hang his stocking up, he just stands it up.'

Ha bloody ha. Wonder how many times you've told that one this week? Andy thought. 'Finished?' he said.

'Yeah,' the man said. He sounded vaguely disappointed. Andy wondered what he'd been expecting to find.

'This one here,' Bilborough said, pointing at a modern semi that was just like all the others in the crescent. Penhaligon screeched the car to a halt in the drive, but Bilborough was out of the door before it had come to a complete stop.

Catriona Bilborough came out into the yard while Bilborough was still some way from the house. Penhaligon had seen her a couple of times before, but she had forgotten how pretty the other woman was. The pregnancy looked well on her, too, Penhaligon thought: she almost glowed.

Bilborough rushed up to her and started to take her in his arms, but she held him off. 'False alarm,' she said.

Bilborough pushed her away and started back to the car. 'Jesus,' he said. He looked as disgusted as he sounded. Behind him, Catriona's expression was halfway between genuine distress – and she did have a point, after all, Penhaligon thought – and a kind of manipulative, baby doll upset. Maybe he encouraged it, Penhaligon thought; he was very protective. Actually, she decided, they probably made a right pair.

'Thank you,' Catriona said. She turned and went back towards the house before Bilborough could react. Penhaligon found herself warming to the other woman after all.

Bilborough turned quickly. 'Sorry,' he said. 'I'm sorry.' He caught up with her, and touched her on the shoulder. 'Hey . . . Hey, I'm sorry,' he said again. She turned, and he put his arms round her, awkwardly at first because of her lump. She hesitated for a moment.

Penhaligon felt an overwhelming rush of jealousy. No, not jealousy. She didn't want Bilborough. God forbid. Envy, maybe. She heard, or imagined she heard, Bilborough's voice whispering, 'I'm sorry, I'm sorry,' over and over again to Catriona.

She wanted something like that. But not that. Not that safe, or that simple. She wanted to be loved and needed, to have someone who would – who would do what? Who would put her first every time, and never do anything to hurt her – someone who, in other words, would never need to apologise? No. Too bland, too easy. She already had Peter, after all. She needed . . . someone who would do outrageous things sometimes, but apologise when he got it wrong. That was more like it. And who would let her get it wrong, and still be there afterwards? But not just anyone, dammit.

She wanted Fitz. And that was all she wanted.

Fitz. The fat guy's name was Fitz. He'd told Andy as they'd gone from his room to Tim's. He stood looking round the room, eyeing up the wallpaper, the girlie lamp with the pale blue lampshade Tim had chosen for himself.

'You keep your mother out of your room,' he asked. Stupid question. Andy nodded. 'But Tim lets her in here.'

'Yeah.' Big bloody deal. His room was more of a mess than it would have been if he'd let his mum in it. At least it was his own mess. This room – well, this room was just girlie. Andy couldn't think of another word for it. Tim had liked Mum coming up here. He'd liked choosing stuff for it. Not proper things – records, posters – but the curtains, that kind of thing. So Mum said, anyway. Tim never said very much at all. Not to Andy.

Fitz was still looking around. He'd found Tim's bookshelf. Bloody poetry. Fitz pulled a book out. He made a sort of snorting noise. Taking the piss, Andy thought at first, and had to stop himself getting angry. Then he realised that Fitz admired Tim because of that book.

'Wilfred Owen,' Fitz said.

A memory of a GCSE class stirred in Andy's memory. Something about gas masks and poppies. Waste of time it had been, whatever it was.

'When I was his age, I was into Biggles.' Andy wondered who Biggles was, but he couldn't be bothered to ask. Fitz flipped through the book. 'Who's his English teacher?'

'Cassidy, that's his name,' said Andy. He wanted to add, he's a useless little twerp, just as pathetic as all of them up at the school; but he didn't. Fitz would find out sooner or later.

The man pummelling the punchbag had quite a nice body, Penhaligon thought. It wasn't the way she had expected to meet an English teacher. Marking essays, reading stories, she thought that would have been more his speed. Yet here they were in Sydney Road School's gym, waiting for him to finish his workout.

He was in his early thirties, probably; he was in reasonable shape – he obviously worked out, but only a bit, because he wasn't that well muscled – but his hair was thinning on top. He smelled of the sweat that glued his singlet to his chest.

The sound of his gloved fists banging into the bag echoed round the school gym. Whap and whap and whap whap whap. Penhaligon waited quietly, acutely conscious of Fitz's

43

bulk next to her. He was twice the size of this Mr Cassidy; twice the size, and Penhaligon thought, twice the man; but then, as she was forced to admit, in her more besotted moments she thought Fitz was twice any man on the planet.

Cassidy gave the bag a final especially vicious punch. He stopped and stood still for a moment, head down, gloves down, breathing hard. After just a moment or two he turned towards them. He had a babyish, almost unfinished-looking face. Sad eyes, like Richard Kimble in *The Fugitive*. Not Harrison Ford, David Jansen, in the TV series. She'd have to tell Fitz she'd thought of that. He was always telling her you couldn't understand the world if you didn't understand popular culture.

Cassidy was still breathing hard. Between pants he said, 'You think he's dead?'

'In confidence?' Penhaligon asked. Stupid question. What was he going to say – *I'm going to start by telling the staff, go on to the kids, then move on and see what I can get out of the Sun, or failing that, the local rags?*

'Yeah,' he said. Penhaligon wondered suddenly if he knew he had sad eyes. He'd probably hate her for thinking it.

'We fear the worst.' She was good at this, she thought; that was why Bilborough always dumped it on her – it was having Fitz nearby. It stopped her concentrating.

Cassidy steadied the bag, then whacked into it with all his strength, again and again. The last blow made the bag bounce on its rope. Fair enough. You'd have to be hard – harder than Cassidy looked – not to get attached to the kids you taught. It was bound to be rough on him – but then he stopped and grinned. He pulled the punchbag to him and held it there.

'Saves me doing it to the kids,' he said, as if Penhaligon had just told him the time of day. She knew that Fitz would be watching this, analysing it; but even she could sense there was something off-centre about the man's response. 'The art of teaching today,' Cassidy went on, as if nothing

44

was wrong, 'just keeping your hands off the little bastards.'
He threw in the last word as if trying to prove he could use
it.

Fitz was uncommonly quiet. Penhaligon felt as though
she could hear his brain working in the background, hear
him putting this response through the mill. She wondered
what answer he'd come up with.

Almost as if he'd realised there was something wrong,
Cassidy said, 'How's his mother handling it?' The smile had
vanished. A drop of sweat broke free of his hair and trickled
down his forehead.

'She fears the worst,' Penhaligon said.

Fitz finally spoke. 'Do you know Tim well?' His voice
was kindly, not the aggressive Fitz that sometimes drove
Penhaligon to distraction.

'Hardly know him at all,' Cassidy said. He turned back to
the punchbag and put his arm round it. He was obviously
upset. He banged the bag gently with his gloved fist. It was a
peculiarly male form of making tea, Penhaligon thought:
something to concentrate on, to distract the attention from
the pain of what you'd just heard. Cassidy continued, 'Bit of
a loner. Bit effeminate. Gets picked on.'

He stood away from the bag and began to lay into it
again.

'Do you live alone?' Fitz asked. It was a typical Fitz
question, straight out of left field, with no apparent connection to anything that had gone before.

Cassidy stopped boxing. 'At the moment,' he said. He
stepped towards them, grinning. 'I'm thinking about getting
married.' He seemed genuinely pleased about it. Maybe,
Penhaligon thought, he'd had a rough time with women; he
might have been on the point of giving up hope when this
new relationship came along. You'd want to brag about
that.

'To someone on the staff?' Penhaligon had never really
understood how Fitz decided what questions to ask. She

45

suspected he didn't either; but she had a good idea of the kind of answers she'd get if she asked him about it, so she didn't bother. She supposed in the end all that mattered was that he was right. It didn't surprise her any more.

Cassidy was surprised though. And pissed off. 'Yeah,' he said shortly, and turned back to the punchbag. Whap, whap, whap whap whap whap.

Penhaligon supposed it was better than a kid getting it.

FIVE

Andy had managed to push the argument with Melanie out of his mind while the coppers were in the house, but as soon as they left he remembered it all.

'Ask Mike,' she'd said. All right then. He bloody well would, and he'd do it right now, whether or not Mike was at work. He told his mother he was going down to the garage and left before she could argue about it.

Andy found Mike in the workshop. He was working under a yellow VW Beetle, with just his legs sticking out. Andy glanced round. The only other people anywhere near were a couple of the mechanics, and they were hanging around in the yard. They wouldn't be a problem.

The trouble was, Andy had a fair idea what Mike was going to tell him, and he didn't like it one bit.

He kicked Mike's boot to let him know he was there. After a couple of seconds, Mike rolled himself out from under the car. He scrambled to his feet and kicked the trolley he'd been lying on aside. The smell of oil clung to him. He wiped his hands down his overalls, leaving thick black smudges on them.

'Can't come for a drink yet,' he said. He jerked his thumb at the car. 'She's got problems with her exhaust and it's a bit of – ' He stopped and took a closer look at Andy. 'You look like shit,' he said. 'Tim not come home yet?'

Andy shook his head.

'He'll turn up. He's probably doing a tour of all the men's bogs in Moss Side – '

47

'Will you shut up?' Andy said. He'd had enough. He knew why he was here and so did Mike, and no amount of tiptoeing round it would change things. Besides, he really didn't want to think about Tim. 'What did you say to Mel?'

'I don't know what you mean, mate,' Mike said; but Andy knew he was lying, partly because he wouldn't have called him 'mate' otherwise, and partly because he'd gone pink under his layer of grime.

'Bloody well do,' he said. 'You told her I said we'd slept together, didn't you?'

'Oh *that*,' Mike said, as if it were the least important thing in the world. 'Yeah, it came up in the conversation the other night.' He took a step sideways.

I'll kill him, Andy thought. I'll fucking kill him. He stepped forward.

'Look, I've got to get on,' Mike said. 'We can talk about this tonight if you want – '

'*Now*, Mike,' Andy said. He reached forward and grabbed a handful of Mike's coveralls.

'I don't know if I can do it,' Julie Lang said. She stared at the two police officers, Penhaligon and Bilborough, as if to dare them to tell her otherwise, but all the time she rubbed her hand across the arm of the sofa. Steve stood behind her, leaning on it. He covered her hand with his, so that she had to keep it still or snatch it away from him. She didn't want to do that. Before this had all started, she'd barely been able to see him without a row starting. Now, he was the single point of solidity in her life.

That was important, now when it felt as if her home had been invaded by strangers, what with all these police in the place. She didn't care if it were only two of them this time. It seemed like an army.

They wanted her to go on television, to tell the whole world that she'd failed as a mother. Oh, they hadn't put it like that, but that was what it would mean. That living at

48

home was so awful Tim had run away; or that she had failed to keep him safe from harm.

She could feel the tears welling up inside again, and she didn't want to cry in front of strangers.

'It might make all the difference,' Sergeant Penhaligon said. She put her cup of tea down carefully on the coaster.

'Maybe we should,' Steve said. He sat down next to Julie. She shut her eyes. It was good to have him back, almost like the old days, before the boys had been born and they'd started arguing the whole time. 'It would be worth it if it would get him back. If there was even a cha–'

'Don't say it,' Julie said. Having Steve home was one thing. Having him telling her what to do was another. 'After all the times you yelled your head off at him.' She moved her hand away. She was suddenly very conscious of Penhaligon and Bilborough watching them. 'All right,' she said, suddenly weary of it. At that moment, she would have done anything to get rid of them. 'If you really think it'll help.'

'Thank you,' Bilborough said. 'Where's Andy, Mrs Lang?'

'He's gone to see his friend Mike, but – '

'It would be best if all three of you were in it,' Penhaligon said.

'Get him. I'll sort out the camera crew,' Bilborough said. 'Then get on to Jimmy Beck and ask him to set up a phone room – oh, and we'll need Fitz. Got that?'

Penhaligon nodded.

It'll be worth it, Julie thought. It'll bring my boy home to me. She reached out and took Steve's hand again.

Penhaligon found the garage easily enough. There were a couple of mechanics in the yard outside it, deep in discussion about an old van. She went over to them. They ignored her.

'Excuse me,' she said.

49

The older one of the pair glanced up. 'Can I help you?'

'Can't see a problem with her bodywork – ' said the younger, and grinned.

Right, Penhaligon thought. She pulled out her ID card. 'Police,' she said. She let them sweat for a second or two – she could almost hear the older one checking through the garage's certification in his head. Then she went on, 'I'm looking for Andy Lang. Believe he's visiting one of your staff – a Mike Black?'

'In there,' said the older one.

The workshop door was ajar. Penhaligon went inside. It was cool and dim, and it smelled of oil and hot metal. She heard Andy yelling before she saw him.

' – just keep your trap shut – ' he yelled.

'I'm sorry. I said – ' someone – Mike, Penhaligon supposed – replied.

She picked her way round a pile of machine parts. Andy was by one of the cars, squaring off against another lad of about his own age. They hadn't seen her.

'I know your game – ' Andy said.

'I've got Ali, for Pete's sake,' Mike replied.

'One's not enough, that it?' Andy pushed Mike, so he had to take a step back. 'Mates. We're supposed to be mates.' His face was flushed, and distorted by rage.

'Andy?' Penhaligon said.

He turned. 'Christ. What do – ' He stopped. The anger left his face. ' – Tim? Have they found him?'

'I'm afraid not,' Penhaligon said. 'Your parents have agreed to make a television broadcast.'

Andy nodded. 'Good.'

'I never thought – ' Mike said.

Andy turned on him. 'That's your trouble. You never bloody think, you moron,' he said, but all the anger had gone out of his voice.

'They'd like you to be in it,' Penhaligon said.

'If it'll help.' Andy stuck his hands in his pockets and

50

headed towards the door. Mike watched him go, but didn't speak.

Now what was all that about? Penhaligon wondered. Bilborough thought Andy was hiding something. Maybe it didn't have anything to do with Tim's disappearance after all.

Amanda Perry picked up her mug of coffee and went into the front room. The carriage clock on the mantelpiece said five to twelve. She sat down on the sofa and crossed her legs up under her. Just in time for *Take the High Road*, she thought, or was it *The Young Doctors*? One of them, anyway. They were all the same. Sometimes she thought she ought to get a job. She'd been a hairdresser before she'd married Barry, and enjoyed it, too. But Barry was older, and he had money. He didn't want his wife working. Amanda liked the money all right, but she was sick of what Barry wanted and didn't want.

She turned on the TV with the remote. She was a bit early. The news was still on. Something about South Africa, violence in the townships. It was too far away to seem important.

Lord, but she was done in. It was hardly surprising. She hadn't slept at all the night before. Not much, anyway. Partly, it was Barry lying next to her, snoring his head off. Pig. But there was what she'd seen in the woods. Every time she closed her eyes she saw it, the legs dangling, turning slightly as the body swung. The jeans pulled down round the knees. She kept telling herself she'd imagined it. But she hadn't. She could still remember the feel of her heart thundering as she'd run, the burning in her chest as she screamed. Imagined it. Yeah.

Only, then a woman's face appeared on the TV screen. Begging someone called Tim to come home; begging whoever was holding him to let him go. The body, Amanda thought. The body in the woods had been this woman's little

51

boy. She felt sick, abruptly; sick to her stomach and cold with terror. She couldn't stop herself thinking of the body swinging slowly in the cold moonlight.

The camera pulled back. A man and a lad were sitting next to the woman. Her husband and eldest son, Amanda guessed. *His* father and brother.

He's dead, she thought at the family on the screen. He's dead, he's dead, he's dead. But the woman didn't know. She just went on pleading with Tim to come home, begging whoever was holding him to let him go.

'Please,' the woman said. That was her final word. 'Please.' After that she broke down. She covered her face with her hand.

Amanda felt herself begin to cry. She reached for the phone and dialled 999.

Beck took the call. He was sitting in the incident room opposite Bilborough. A TV set nearby was still playing the broadcast when the call came through. It wasn't direct, it had come through the emergency services. Chances were it would turn out to be a false lead. A case like this, they could expect any number of bad calls, most of them genuine but mistaken, a few of them malicious.

Beck had already taken three calls since the broadcast started, and he wasn't the only one on the phones. None of the others looked at all promising, but that didn't matter. The procedure was the same for all of them: each one was taped, and there was someone standing by to trace the call the minute it looked like a live one.

Like this one, maybe. He knew it as soon as the woman started speaking, knew it in his gut the way he always did when he was on to something. The boss was on the other line, doing the trace.

'It's really important that you tell me,' Beck said, trying to keep the woman talking. It was easier these days, with the new digital phone lines, but it didn't hurt to be careful.

'You'd never find this place unless you knew it,' the woman answered. Keep talking, Beck thought. That's my girl. Just a minute longer. He took a hit from his cigarette. 'You have to squeeze through a hedge – '

The boss made a *keep going* sign at Beck. The television broadcast finished. Beck reached over and turned the set off.

'Could you show me?' he asked, thinking, no chance.

'No,' the woman said, 'I'm married. The man I was with is married.'.

'That's it,' Bilborough said. He put his handset down and stood up. 'She's ringing from home.'

He turned and left at a run. Beck took the next call.

Amanda heard the car draw up outside the house. Her stomach clenched. She knew who it had to be.

The doorbell rang. I'm not here, she thought. I'm not here. I'm out shopping. But the doorbell rang again. The third time it went, she got up and answered it.

Two of them. A man, a woman. Amanda licked her lips, ready to deny all knowledge.

'Police,' the man said. He held up an identity card. It could have been from the gas board for all Amanda knew. It could have been fake.

She got ready to say as much. 'Yes,' she said. 'Yes.'

Somehow, they had her in the car before she could object. In the car, at the woods, walking through the half-light beneath the leaves, all before she could really think about what she was doing. She led them on, the two police officers and the crowd of searchers.

It was only when she got to the gap in the hedge that she really understood that she would have to see it again. It. The body.

She paused before she went through. She would have gone back to the car, but there were too many of them. 'I can't,' she said to the man. Bilborough. DCI Bilborough. He stared at her without the slightest trace of sympathy. She turned to the red-headed woman, the sergeant. 'I can't,' she said again. The woman stared back without sympathy.

There was nothing for it but to go on. She pushed into the gap. Twigs scratched at her face and caught at her dangly earrings. She tasted acid, and knew that if she wasn't careful, she'd be sick.

Just a little further. It would be over soon. They'd thank her. Let her go home. She kept looking straight ahead. Carefully now. Don't look up.

'Here,' she said. The tree was directly ahead of her. They'd started to make love just about where she was standing now. But that was all right. She didn't have to think about it. Didn't have to look up and see it.

Someone shone a torch up into the tree. Amanda couldn't help it. She glanced up. The body was there. A boy. Thirteen, they said. The torchlight picked out the dead white of his flesh, the pure gold of his hair. His legs turned as his body swung. The terrible thing was that it was exactly as she'd remembered it.

Amanda realised that she was the one making the terrible crying sound.

SIX

This is it, Bilborough thought as he led the way through the Langs' front gate. There were one or two people standing by it, despite the pouring rain. He thought he recognised one as a neighbour. Another was obviously a journalist. She had a cassette recorder over her shoulder, and she stepped forward with an expression that said she wouldn't take no for an answer.

'Later,' he said, before she could ask him anything.

'But – '

'When we've got anything definite we'll let you know. Till then it's no comment, understand?' He pushed past the woman.

Penhaligon was close behind him. This is it, this time I do the business myself, he thought. He felt his throat constrict at the very thought of it, but that was just tough.

He rang the doorbell. He was beginning to hate that door; he had to remind himself that the Langs were victims just as much as their son. He just couldn't bear watching their grief, their uncertainty. At least he would be able to take part of that away from them.

'I'll do it,' Bilborough said. It was almost worth the anxiety just to see the look of surprise on Penhaligon's face.

'Are you sure?' Penhaligon asked.

Bilborough wasn't, but he wasn't going to let her find that out. 'Yep.' He fiddled with his tie.

Someone came to the door. It was impossible to tell who through the panes of thick, dimpled glass. Whoever it was peered through the clearer central panel. Andy, Bilborough decided. There was a Woman Police Constable on duty by the door, but the family probably didn't trust her to keep visitors at bay. That journalist, for instance, looked like a tough number.

The door opened. Andy stood there, his face closed, wary. He knows, Bilborough thought. He's guessed already. He felt relieved, let off the hook; but there were still the parents to come.

Bilborough went in without speaking, straight past Andy.

'You found him?' the lad asked.

'Shall we go in there?' Bilborough said, gesturing towards the front room. Well, you weren't going to talk to him on the doorstep, were you?

He followed Andy through the hall, acutely aware of Penhaligon's eyes watching him as she followed. Waiting for him to screw up. We'll see, he thought. He had it all planned. He'd say: I'm terribly sorry, Mr Lang, Mrs Lang, but we . . . we what? Oh, God, he was going to screw up. He knew it.

He went into the living room. Mrs Lang twisted round in her familiar place on the sofa to watch him. Her eyes were huge, desperate. She knows, he thought. Oh Christ, she knows. He went and stood by the television, then waited for Penhaligon to sit down. Anything to put off the moment, he thought, despising himself for it.

They were all watching him. Mrs Lang, blank-eyed with grief, Andy and Mr Lang, Penhaligon waiting for him to say the wrong thing. He could hear the sound of their breathing. That was ridiculous, but he was sure it was true. Say something, he thought at himself. Say anything. But he couldn't speak. He felt as though someone had a hand at his throat, squeezing the words back down inside him. He could hardly breathe. Say something, he thought again. But what? *Sorry, your son is dead? Sorry, we found him hanging in the woods, and oh by the way, it looks like he was raped? Sorry, I'm just here to destroy your lives? Sorry, sorry, sorry.*

Penhaligon was watching him. She wasn't going to let

him forget this. Her eyes flickered from him to the Langs and back again. He licked his lips.

'I'm afraid it's very bad news,' Penhaligon said. Her voice was surprisingly loud and determined.

Thank God, Bilborough thought. It was done. Damn Penhaligon.

'He's dead?' Mrs Lang said, in a matter-of-fact kind of way.

'I'm so sorry,' Penhaligon said. Her voice was soft now, and her face registered more than professional concern. She'd been through this with – how many families? A dozen, maybe? – yet she still managed to sound genuinely upset. Maybe that was it, Bilborough thought. Maybe she could tell them because she got too involved with them, like the text books said you shouldn't. Well, by the time she made DCI – if she ever did – maybe she'd have toughened up. Maybe then she'd know what it felt like to stand there with the words choking you and no way of getting them out.

Mrs Lang sat quietly on the sofa, as if she were trying to understand what she had been told. Andy had got it though. He was going to cry soon; he covered his face with one hand. His grief seemed genuine enough, though Bilborough was still certain he was hiding something. Girl-friend trouble, Penhaligon said. Bilborough didn't buy that.

Mr Lang bit his lip. His eyes were shut. He was going to need Fitz more than the others, Bilborough thought. He understood what the man was going through: he couldn't bear his pain, but he didn't dare let himself cry. Mr Lang started to say something, but Mrs Lang spoke first.

'How?' she said.

You don't want to know, Bilborough thought; trust me. But they always did. It was as if being told the details made the death more real to them; as if having to listen to all the dreadful things that their loved ones had gone through made the grief easier to handle, because they couldn't deny it. Bilborough didn't understand it – that was what he had Fitz for, after all – he just knew it was always the same. They'd want to see the body, too. He'd have to persuade them to wait till after it had been to Path and been cleaned up. Penhaligon would. She'd taken over dealing with the family, so she could do that, too.

But even she wasn't finding this easy. 'He was found hanging,' she said at last.

Andy broke first. He and his mother turned to each other. He put his arms round her and began to sob. She held him, but she still turned to face Bilborough. Well, he thought, to face Penhaligon, actually.

'He didn't kill himself,' she said. 'My son – '

'It's early days yet – ' Penhaligon put in, her voice almost a whisper.

' – did not kill himself.'

She was probably right, Bilborough thought. They'd need the Pathology report to be certain, though. He wondered why she needed to think it had been murder.

She clung to Andy, and the two of them sat there on the sofa, crying and shaking and trying uselessly to comfort each other. Mr Lang watched them. He didn't try to go to them, just stood there helplessly with no-one to comfort him and without permission even to try and help his wife and son. Bilborough wondered, not for the first time, why they had split up.

'My son did not commit suicide,' Mrs Lang repeated.

'It's very early days yet.' Even Penhaligon seemed help-less in front of that much grief. She glanced up at Bil-borough. He stared back, embarrassed. All right, he thought at her. All right, I couldn't do it. So what?

As they left, he heard Mrs Lang repeat again, 'My son did not commit suicide.'

Outside, it had stopped raining, though the sky was still full of leaden clouds, and the wind bit through Bilborough's parka. There were more people gathered round the gate than

58

there had been before. Kids, some of them; mothers with babies; a few men. Some of the kids looked about Tim's age. Bilborough wondered if they were the ones that had picked on Tim, or if they were the ones that had ignored him, looked the other way when he was bullied; he didn't have any friends, Fitz said.

Bilborough waited till he was well past the duty WPC before he spoke.

'I'm sorry,' he said. He went past a few of the people at the gate. They were listening. It was all he needed. Never mind. Soon be in the car. With Penhaligon doing her martyr act. That was going to be fun.

'It's all right,' Penhaligon said, as if by rote.

'It's not all right.' Bloody martyr.

'It is. It's all right.' Penhaligon went round to the driver's side of the car.

Christ, they were beginning to sound like a bloody pantomime. 'It's not all right. It's not all bloody right.' He paused by the passenger door and stared over the roof of the car at her. 'Will you stop patronising me, right?'

Penhaligon glanced quickly at the crowd, then back to Bilborough. 'All right,' she said. Her face was alight with anger. 'I thought you were gobshite in there.' She paused. 'Sir.'

Julie cried for a long time once the police had gone. Afterwards, she couldn't have said how long it had been, but it felt like all eternity. Every time she came close to stopping, she would remember his smile, that shy way of grinning he had when he knew he'd said something bright; or she'd remember a painting he'd brought home from nursery school, all green and purple splodges, but, he had assured her solemnly, a cow. Or she'd think of later on, when he'd come home quiet and sullen because the other kids had picked on him, called him names, beaten him up. She'd tried to tell him once or twice that in a year or two it wouldn't matter, that he'd have girls hammering down the door: 'Girls with more sense', she'd said, 'than to want some hulking great rugby player. There are plenty of them about, believe me, son.' And he'd smiled at her, and said, 'If you say so.' At the time she'd thought he just didn't believe her. Now – well, now maybe she had to think Steve might have had a point.

Only now it was too late to try and understand. It was too late for anything but crying. Only there came a moment when she couldn't even do that, as if she had used up all the tears in the world.

She sat crushing a tissue in her hand. How could it be that she had stopped crying so soon?

'I'll go,' Steve said, suddenly. 'Just say, and I'll go.'

Julie looked at him. There were just the two of them in the room. Andy had gone upstairs almost before the door had closed behind Bilborough.

So there was no reason not to argue, not to say whatever needed saying, if only she could work out what it was. She'd loved Steve once. It had disappeared, somewhere between when she'd had Andy and Tim getting old enough to decide what he wanted to do for himself. The rows had mostly been about the way he treated Tim, how he tried to get the boy to go to football matches, and made him join first the Cubs and then the Scouts – though Andy never had – and made him help out in the garage.

He hadn't driven Tim away from him with all that non-sense. But Julie had seen the despair in her son's eyes when he couldn't live up to his father's expectations; and that despair had driven Julie away. But that was then and this was now, and things were going to be different.

'Don't go,' she said. 'Stay with me. Stay tonight.'

OK, so I finally said it, Penhaligon thought. I probably shouldn't have said it. They were almost at the station. Bilborough hadn't said a word to her since they got in the car. He just sat glowering in the passenger seat, glancing at his watch every now and then.

If he hadn't wanted to know, he shouldn't have asked. Penhaligon turned the corner into Anson Road. There were a few people standing around outside the station. She thought about going inside, eating her sandwiches in the canteen, drinking the godawful machine coffee. It didn't appeal.

'I've got a few things to do,' she said as she brought the car to a halt. 'If that's all right?'

'Make it quick, OK?' Bilborough didn't wait for her reply. He tried to go straight inside, but one of the bystanders stopped him. It took Penhaligon a moment to place her. She was the journalist who had been outside the Langs' house earlier. Bilborough was still talking to her as Penhaligon drove off.

Three travel agents later, she was sitting in a cafe with a cappuccino and a tuna sandwich. She spread the brochures out in front of her. Out of deference to Peter, she'd picked up some that dealt with Greece and Spain, as well as Italy and Portugal.

It was going to cost a lot more than she'd bargained for. Still it would be worth it. Maybe if they could just relax together for a while they'd be able to stop bickering over every little thing. She knew Peter thought she was more interested in her career than she was in him – he'd said so often enough. If it were only that, they might have been all right. But it wasn't. It was Fitz.

Be honest, she told herself. You're really hoping that if you get away from *him* you might start feeling more for Peter again.

She stared at the page in front of her until her eyes blurred. Portugal. The Hotel des Palmas looked nice. She started to turn the corner of the page down. Then she stopped and found the brochure for Kos. The Hotel Agora. It was far too expensive. She marked the page anyway.

• • •

She was a tarty looking bit, this Mrs Perry. That was Beck's opinion, anyway – she was too old for all the heavy eye make-up and pink lipstick she wore. Must have been past thirty-five. Dark roots showed through her orange hair. The clothes looked expensive, mind you. Not your market stall crap. He'd wondered where she got them, whether there might be some leverage there; but her husband was well off – manufacturing, mind you, nothing shady, more's the pity – so that was out. She wasn't his type, Beck decided, but he could see the attraction. Oh yes.

Now she sat there in Interview Room Two, refusing to answer questions like she had some choice in the matter. She'd break in the end, of course. He'd see to it. Maybe he should tell her that. Tell her to save herself some grief.

He glanced at the Woman Police Constable seated in the corner. She stared back impassively. Great job she had, he thought. Professional gooseberry.

'Withholding his name is a criminal offence,' he said. She stared up at him through the mane of her hair. Her mouth was a thin, determined line of pink. 'What's. His. Name?' Beck asked for the tenth, the fiftieth time, slowly and carefully. He was getting bored with this. Pig sick of it, truth to tell.

Maybe he was getting to her. Her mouth worked. She looked out of the window, then down at the table. 'He's got a wife and three kids,' she said. Yeah, yeah. He'd heard it all a dozen times.

He circled round behind her. He'd seen that in a movie somewhere – now what was it? Didn't matter. An interrogation scene, it had been. Speak from where they can't see you. Put them off their guard. Well, it had been in the police training too; but thinking about the movie made him feel better, like he'd succeed where none of the others would – not the boss, not Penhaligon, certainly not Fitz.

'What's his name?'

She said nothing. Maybe her shoulders, clad in that

expensive green jacket, slumped slightly. He let the moment drag out, let her get really uncomfortable.

'Did you have sex?' He glanced at the WPC. Well, he had to ask, didn't he? It might be important. He stepped up close to her, but still out of her line of sight. Beck spoke gently. 'Mrs Perry, we've got Forensics at the scene, and if they find anything they'll want to know whether your boyfriend left it or anyone else.' Her shoulders slumped a little further. Beck let his voice soften a bit more. 'Do you understand how important that is?'

'Yes.'

Well, that was something. Time to get pushy again. 'Did you have sex?'

'No.' That was something. A straight answer, anyway.

Beck paced over to the window. It was large, but frosted and divided into smaller panes. The light pearled through it. He wondered how long they'd been in the interview room. It didn't matter. He'd go on all night if he had to. Patience was a great virtue in a detective.

'So what's his name?' he asked again, sounding more casual this time.

Mrs Perry twisted round in her seat. Her voice was full of contempt. So was her face. 'I'm not going to tell you his name,' she said.

OK, OK, Beck thought. Let's take it easy here. He went round to the front of the table and sat down. They'd just have to start again from the beginning. Sooner or later she'd cough –

Too late. The door crashed open so hard it bounced against the wall. The boss slammed in. He was steaming. Seemed to be, anyway. It was part of the game. Good cop, bad cop, the old movie cliché come to life. It would work, too.

'Here she is,' Bilborough said. 'Little bleeding Red Riding Hood.' He walked straight up to Mrs Perry's chair.

'Boss,' Beck started. 'I'm handling it – ' That was part of the script.

63

Bilborough jabbed his finger in her face. 'I'm going round to your old man right now.' Jab with the finger. 'And I'm going to tell him what you've – '

'I'm handling it,' Beck said.

Bilborough didn't so much as pause. ' – been up to.' Jab. 'OK?' Again the finger jabbed at her. He leaned across the table so she couldn't avoid looking at him. 'And then I'll find out who this fancy – ' His voice was getting louder. He was losing it. This wasn't part of the script.

'He's got three kids, boss,' Beck said. That was. Beck was Mr Nice Guy who would stop Nasty Mr Bilborough screwing up Mrs Perry's life; but Bilborough didn't seem to hear.

' – man is, and tell his missus everything.' Jab with the finger. 'Every bloody thing.' His face was right up close to Mrs Perry's now. His voice was quieter, more dangerous. Beck knew then that the anger was for real. The woman stared at Bilborough. She couldn't have got a word in even if she'd wanted to tell them everything.

'Boss,' Beck said.

Something seemed to dawn on Bilborough. He turned to Beck. 'Three kids? His kids are alive, aren't they? We're talking about the death of a child – ' Spit flew from his mouth and disappeared into the light.

Mrs Perry ran her hand through her hair. She was upset. So bloody what. There was the boss about to lose it over this kid dead in the woods and –

That was it. Didn't need Fitz to work it out. Catriona pregnant and the boss worried sick to death about her. This business with the kid couldn't help but work on him. He'd be thinking that in ten or twelve years' time it could be his child out there with a noose round its neck.

'She'll tell me, OK?' Beck said. Any minute now Bilborough was going to blow.

'A bloody child. And you've got the cheek to fart around, wasting our time.' He was shouting now. His face was distorted, almost unrecognisable with anger.

64

He slammed his hand down on the table. 'I want her banged up, right?' he said. He straightened up. Beck did too, hoping he'd be able to get Bilborough out of the room. They started walking towards the door. 'Bang her up, right now. Throw away the key, got it?' He was shouting at Beck now, shouting at the whole damned world. 'Wasting our time. Withholding evidence. Right?'

Beck watched for a second as Bilborough went into the corridor, where Penhaligon was waiting. Bilborough seemed to make a visible effort to calm down. The anger fell away from his face, and his shoulders relaxed.

He nodded silently at Beck.

Beck went back into the room. Mrs Perry was almost in tears. Even before he sat down, she said, 'Francis Bates, 81 Greenside Park.'

Beck went back to the corridor. He just caught the end of Bilborough's conversation with Penhaligon.

' – Path?' Bilborough whispered.

'He'll be about an hour. He's at a fancy dress party.'

'Francis Bates – ' Beck said.

'I heard,' Bilborough said in an undertone. 'Go round and pick him up, the pair of you. Then get Fitz. I want him here.'

Fitz, Fitz, bloody Fitz. They'd managed well enough without him just now hadn't they?

Penhaligon started off down the corridor, her sensible shoes clacking as she went. Bilborough started to follow her.

Beck called him back. He turned, with a surprised look on his face.

'Boss,' Beck said. He had to look up, just slightly, to stare Bilborough in the eyes. 'No offence, right?' Bilborough nodded. He looked wary. 'It's getting so we can't shit around here without Fitz.'

Bilborough glared at him and followed Penhaligon.

SEVEN

In better days, Fitz had loved to work in the kitchen with Judith. It was partly the room: bright and airy, painted yellow to reflect the summer sun or, as now, to brighten the dull grey light of winter. Partly, of course, it was simply that he loved being around her; loved to watch the sun strike copper highlights in her hair, loved to watch that perfect body move, loved to see her smile and hear her laugh.

But that was the easy answer, Fitz thought, as he chopped cucumber for the salad. He liked the kitchen because it was the heart of domesticity, as Judith was his heart and their marriage the heart of his life.

Which was why he hated it now, of course. He didn't feel married any more. No, that wasn't it. He felt married, but as if Judith was sheering away from him. Soon, he thought, he'd go to look at their wedding photos and find that they had been torn raggedly down their centres. Judith here. Fitz here. And never the twain shall meet. He sighed.

It was Graham's fault, of course. Bloody therapist. Fitz whacked the knife through the cucumber. He only wished the bloody man hadn't had the wit to take Judith off his client list before he slept with her. Then Fitz would have made the shit fly. He whacked the knife down. Oh yes. Whack. I'll make it fly and you can bet it'll stick. Sleep with a client, will you? Whack. Sleep with my *wife*? Whack, whack, whack.

Fitz had been all for getting the man disbarred. Then Judith had pointed out that she'd stopped seeing him as a

66

client long before she'd slept with him. Doesn't matter, Fitz had said. I'll do him anyway. There are ethics involved, you know. Only, then he'd thought about Judith's face smeared over the gutter press, and he'd known he couldn't do it.

If Judith hadn't slept with him, Fitz wouldn't be so blazing angry all the time. Maybe he'd even be able to control his drinking, his gambling. Well, probably not. But anyway, Judith had said it had been as much her fault as Graham's. That the man hadn't raped her. Oh no, of course he hadn't. He'd raped Fitz, that's who he'd raped.

It wasn't cucumber Fitz wanted to be chopping. It was Graham's dick.

Fitz whacked wildly at the cucumber. The knife sliced down, through the deep green skin, into the yielding centre and clean through into the soft birch chopping board.

Grandpa Freud had the right of it after all, Fitz thought. Graham's dick under his knife. That was the least of it. There was something even more primitive: here he was, in the kitchen, the heart of his home, struggling to take back his woman – his woman, Christ, listen to him, you'd think he was living in the Dark Ages – by preparing food for her. Yet the food was, in some odd sense, a symbol of Graham. His enemy. What was it those primitive cave painters in Lascaux had believed? Eat your enemy, take on his strength. Sympathetic magic. Right, well, he'd eat the bloody cucumber – take part in whatever tame little domestic rituals Judith required of him – and he would get her back.

He stared down at the pile of cucumber. The pieces were odd sizes, rough chunks rather than the neat cubes he'd intended to make. There was far too much of it. How much cucumber could one family eat, anyway? He picked up a piece and ate it. It was crisp but bland; he'd always thought cucumber a bit of a waste of time, really.

Now, where was he? Sympathetic magic. Oh yes. Justifying his unjustifiable urge to hurt Judith by pretending to be a primitive. He ate another piece of cucumber. It really wasn't as bad as all that. The wine Judith had marinated the lamb in was close by. He picked the bottle up. It was half empty. Aha, he thought. And, Doctor Fitzgerald, when did you change from being a person who sees a half-full bottle to being one who sees the bottle half empty? And in reply: Oh, I've always been that way. It's just recently I've known I'm right. Before I only thought I was.

The wine glowed ruby in the light from the window. He poured a couple of fingers of it into a mug and drank it in a single swallow, only then stopping to look at the label. Bull's Blood – cheap Spanish plonk. Dear God, he thought. Are we really that broke? Still, it was the perfect accompaniment to what had been, in effect, Graham's dick.

Except it was far larger, I expect, he thought; and then, Bad Fitz. Mustn't be petty.

Judith was off somewhere, on some errand or other. He'd never thought the day would come when the mood in a room would lighten because she'd left. It happened all the time now.

It would be good to get the salad done by the time she came back. Show willing, all that.

Damn, he thought. I knew I shouldn't have eaten that cucumber. I'm starting to sound like Graham now.

Tomatoes, done; peppers, done; celery. He pulled the bunch towards him and hacked off the feathery green tops.

She was coming back. He could hear her heels clicking softly on the hall carpet. Oh joy, he thought, and wished he weren't being ironic.

She was holding a letter, and her face had that hard, determined look it had had so often recently: the mouth slightly pursed, the chin tipped up. She slapped the letter down on the counter next to him. 'From the bank,' she said, in the tones of a school marm confronting an unruly pupil with a blotched exercise book. She walked straight past him.

Fitz picked the letter up and turned to face her. She was

standing by the kitchen table, haloed by the light from the kitchen window. She was slicing a carrot.

You want phallic symbolism? Fitz thought. We got phallic symbolism. He glanced at the letter. He didn't need to read it to know what it said – overdraft up, credit card payments not made, cheques bounced. Same as ever.

She'd want to talk about it, of course. Lately, he thought her attempts to discuss this kind of thing had been more an attempt to punish him – *punish him! After what she'd done!* – than to sort things out. She wanted to extract a promise from him that things would be different. That he would gamble less, drink less, God only knew what else – eat polyunsaturated margarine and jog five miles a day like that jumped-up *Guardian*-reading super-trendy little pipsqueak?

It wasn't even worth trying to talk about it. He walked over to the table, holding the letter.

'God,' he said, sounding appalled, then paused for effect. 'His grammar is atrocious.'

He'd hoped for a laugh. A smile at least. Something to tell him his revenge theory of Judith was wrong.

She scowled. 'Your economics is worse.' Not a glint of humour.

'I know people who owe more than this.' You want a challenge? You got one, Fitz thought.

'Robert Maxwell, maybe,' Judith said.

Ha bloody ha. Fitz folded the letter and put it down amid the clutter on the table. As he turned back to the work-surface he said, 'Well, I think we've got bigger problems than that, haven't we?'

'Such as?' Jesus, she just wasn't going to let it drop.

Oh Judith, Fitz thought. Where did I lose you? Once, he'd thought they were Bogart and Bacall, Gable and Leigh, Taylor and Burton, living out lives that were somehow larger than life, charged with importance and immune from the mundane details of existence. Now they were more like

69

the Odd Couple. Worse. They were like an episode of *Neighbours*. They'd have to be careful they didn't start talking in Australian accents.

As for the rest of it, it wasn't worth talking about. Not now. Why ruin a good meal, when they both knew they weren't going to find any easy answers? She'd ask him to give up gambling. Why? Because of the money, she'd say. He'd explain that he needed that edge, that adrenalin surge. She'd insist. He'd explain for the thousandth time that he wouldn't make promises he couldn't keep. It was pointless. Chunk went the knife through the celery. Point – *chunk!* – less.

'Do you know you use up more calories eating celery than the stuff actually provides?' he said by way of changing the subject.

'Such as our marriage,' Judith said, answering her own question. Fitz concentrated on the celery. Chopping off a finger would certainly provide a distraction, but it seemed a bit drastic. 'I want to solve those problems, Fitz.' God, but she had a beautiful voice. 'You don't.' On the other hand, losing a finger was probably a small price if it would put her off the scent. 'You like crises. Gives you an excuse to drink and gamble.' He heard her slosh something into a bowl. Salad dressing, he decided. Good old Judith. The world could be coming apart around them, but if Judith had her way there'd still be crème fraîche and sun-dried tomatoes and home-made vinaigrette with the salad. 'You take away the crisis and you take away the excuse.'

Now that was just stupid. She'd obviously been listening to him too much. He'd always known his constant analysis of the people around him would have a bad effect. Either that, or – more likely – Graham had been getting to her. 'Bullshit,' he said. He thought, let's just get on and eat the meal. Let's at least pretend to be a happy family.

She wasn't having any of it. 'Bullshit as in, "I can't think of an answer right now, so I'll just pretend it's all beneath me"?'

Oh for pity's sake. Fitz gave up on trying to rescue the afternoon and went to tell Mark and Katie that supper would soon be ready. Maybe by the time he got back, she'd be prepared to drop the subject.

They were in the living room, sprawled all over the sofa. They were watching some soap opera or other. Fitz didn't recognise it, but he did recognise the glazed look on their faces when he said, 'Ten minutes.'

He waved his hand in front of the TV screen. It didn't seem to bother them at all. Christ, didn't they know they had their very own soap opera going on in the kitchen? 'Ten minutes,' he said again, and supposed he was lucky when they grunted a response at him.

He went back into the kitchen and returned to his salad-making without speaking to Judith. Watercress. Where was –

'I'm going to have to lay it on the line,' Judith said.

What? She was going to what? 'You don't have the right to lay anything on the line,' Fitz said. He suddenly realised how far down he'd been tamping his anger. Now it burned. Now it was a bright thing that could illuminate his personal darkness almost as well as Judith once had. He turned back to the counter and started chopping at the first thing that came to hand. More cucumber. Yes, well, we all know what that means, he thought, and thank you very much Doctor Freud.

'And that puts you in a very powerful position, doesn't it?' Judith said. She grabbed a tea-towel and walked across to him, drying her hands on the way. 'I was wrong, so I've got to suffer in silence.' That's right, Fitz thought at her. That's just too damned right. She pushed her way between Fitz and the counter. 'Well no,' she said. She was as close to tears as Fitz had seen her in a long time. Tough. 'I don't want half a relationship. I want us to sleep together,' she added loudly, then continued in a parental careful-the-kids-might-hear undertone. 'I want sex.' Fitz didn't say anything.

71

He suddenly understood why they called it the heat of anger; his face was burning and he felt as if the blood had turned to lava in his veins. *Be quiet, Judith*, he thought at her. *One more word and I'm going to say something we're both going to regret.* But she wouldn't be quiet. 'I like sex, for God's sake,' she said.

'Yeah, we know that,' Fitz said, cutting her off before she'd even finished speaking. Got to lighten the atmosphere somehow he thought. Cool the blood, calm the brain. 'Naughty Fitz. You're supposed to be mature.' He could see her in his peripheral vision. She seemed amused. Good. Maybe they'd get out of this alive after all. 'House trained,' he said, and thought: Like a puppy. Well, I'm not a fucking puppy. The anger was back and there was no point in trying to hold it back. 'You should be able to talk this through like a rational human being.' He was surprised at how bitter his voice sounded. Not that he was angry, but that he had let so much of the anger show when he hadn't meant to. Before, it had always been a sideshow, something to amuse himself during the long lonely hours trapped in the prison of his own skull. But this was real. This was real. 'Well I'm not a rational human being,' he said. 'I'm blazing.' He jabbed the knife in the air. 'I'd like to cut that bastard's balls off.'

He sighed, long and ragged. Then he did the only thing he could, in the circumstances. He poured himself a glass of the Bull's Blood he'd found conveniently open.

'Glass of wine, dear?' he said, as if nothing in the world were wrong. For a moment a smile seemed to hover around Judith's mouth. A moment later, he realised she was actually trying to stop herself from crying. And a moment after that, she had left the kitchen, and he was alone with his wine.

EIGHT

Napoleon Bonaparte appeared at the top of the stairs that led down to the basement of St Hilda's Hospital, and if looks could kill the whole of the Russian army would have been dead in their boots. As it was, the Russian army were nowhere in sight, and he had to make do with killing Bilborough and the rest of his team, which was fine, since he was actually Senior Pathologist Geoffrey Harrington.

'I'll give you ten minutes,' he said. His knee-boots clattered on the steps as he came down them, and he moved stiffly because of his tight white breeches.

Bloody man, Bilborough thought. Didn't he think they'd all like to get home? But no, they didn't count. They didn't have swanky parties to go to. They only had pregnant wives to worry about, and –

He wasn't going to think about that. He'd promised himself he would concentrate on the job – on that poor little tyke in the other room. Penhaligon and Beck were both trying not to smile. Fitz was just standing there, with a neutral expression on his face. He looked terrible, Bilborough thought. That was OK. Just as long as he could do the job.

As the pathologist got to the bottom of the stairs, Fitz stepped up to him. 'Look,' he said in a confidential undertone, 'I'm a psychologist. I can help.'

Beck and Penhaligon laughed outright. Bilborough found he was smiling, and hated himself for it. It's all right, he told himself. Just because there's a dead kid next door doesn't

73

mean we can't have a good laugh now and again.

Harrington wasn't amused. He pulled off his tricorn hat and said, 'This way.' He went through to the morgue, and everyone followed.

'How was Moscow?' Beck asked his retreating back, then giggled at his own joke. So did Penhaligon.

Bilborough scowled.

Inside the morgue, they gathered round the body. It was white as uncooked dough, and clay was smeared over the mouth and nose. A noose, stiff with mud, was still tied round its neck. Its jeans were pulled down to its ankles, but a sheet had been pulled up round its waist, hiding its genitals. Its. Bilborough couldn't think of it as a child, much less as Timothy Lang. Christ, you couldn't. You'd go mad.

They were all quiet. No-one was laughing now. Harrington glanced at the body.

'You dragged me down here for this?' He sounded outraged.

'We think it's murder,' Bilborough said, irritated. Why else would they have sent for him?

'You think it's murder? What's this? And this?' Harrington pointed to the body's – to Timothy's – forehead and chin.

Bilborough didn't know what he should be looking for. Why did the pathologist think he'd been asked in anyway?

He looked away, sickened. God, he'd been scared he was getting cynical, but at least he still knew he was looking at a body that had once been a child who talked and laughed and read poetry and wept. All the pathologist saw was a lump of meat that meant he'd been dragged out of a good party.

'Breaks in lividity,' Fitz said from somewhere off to the side.

'Caused by?' The damned pathologist sounded like he was testing a bunch of students, Bilborough thought. Arrogant, jumped-up –

'Pressure,' Fitz said. His voice was grave. 'He was left face down after he died.'

Thanks Fitz, Bilborough thought. Thanks a million. For once he meant it. He looked at the big psychologist. There was no trace of amusement on his face, only compassion. Yet Bilborough knew that at any minute he'd come out with some wisecrack or other. He didn't know how Fitz switched it on and off like that, or whether he thought it was a good thing or not.

'Bruises to the front and sides of the throat. None whatsoever at the back,' said the pathologist. He glanced at the body, then back at Bilborough. 'He's been strangled, left face down and then strung up.' Simple, his expression said. You'd have to be damned thick not to see all that straight up. 'He's been dead about two days, as a first approximation.'

'Thank you,' Bilborough said, fighting hard to keep in control.

'And you're a DCI?' said the pathologist, as if he'd proved some obscure scientific theory.

Bloody hell, Bilborough thought. He knew what the man was thinking: what they always thought – promoted too young, over his level of competence, can't do the job, can't make decisions. 'I thought it was murder, and I wanted it confirming. You've confirmed it. Thank you.' He had difficulty keeping his voice level. 'You can get along to your party now.'

The pathologist scowled. He turned and headed towards the door. As he took his tricorn from the attendant, Fitz called, 'What are you going as?'

Beck giggled aloud. Bilborough glanced at Penhaligon. She was smiling. He realised he was, too. The mood in the room was far lighter than it had been. He glanced at Fitz. The psychologist was staring sombrely at Timothy Lang. He did care, Bilborough thought. They all cared, however they showed it; and they were all on his side. He would have to try and remember that, in future.

● ● ●

75

Fitz settled himself on the edge of a desk, next to Penhaligon. He folded his arms across himself, letting his cigarette dangle loosely in his fingers. Behind them, the noise and bustle of the station were muted by a half glassed-in partition.

There was a bank of black and white TV screens directly in front of them. Bilborough and Beck were questioning the witness, Francis Bates, but he wasn't co-operating. Fitz made him thirty-fiveish. He had mousy hair, and he was quietly spoken. Cheating on his wife probably gave a dangerous edge to his life, just that pinch of spice that would remind him he was more than a machine for going to work and paying the bills. He'd never leave her, of course. He'd need to take a decision to make that happen, and Fitz didn't think decision-making was Francis Bates's strong suit.

'Just like being at the movies, hey Panhandle?' Fitz asked during one of the frequent lulls in the on-screen conversation.

'All we need is the popcorn,' she agreed. She was holding a shorthand pad and Biro, which she had chewed almost to bits. Oral fixation, Fitz thought, off-handedly.

'Or a hot-dog?' he asked, enjoying the private joke, knowing she'd never make the connection from pen to fixation to phallic symbol. Then again, the fact that he'd thought of it might just mean he fancied her something rotten. Which he did of course. The light turned the tiny curls that had escaped her ponytail to red gold. He found himself staring at the delicate line of her jaw. 'What's your favourite movie, Panhandle?' he asked by way of changing the subject.

She shushed him. Bates was talking again.

' – a man, jogging, that's all,' he said.

'Your girlfriend didn't mention a jogger,' Beck said. Sharp as knives, that Beck.

'She was in the car. I was having a pee,' Bates said. The tinny TV speakers robbed his voice of most of its emotion, but Bates didn't sound defensive. The way he'd dropped the mention of the jogger into the conversation made it seem unlikely he was lying.

'Can you describe him?' Bilborough asked.

'Thirty-odd, average height. It was dark!' Now Bates did sound defensive.

Bilborough stared at him. He sounded relaxed enough, Fitz thought, but he was sitting awkwardly, slumped back but with his head craning forward and with his arms crossed, making a barrier between him and the man – or Fitz suspected, him and the world. Fitz was worried about him. Panhandle had told him how he'd seemed to lose control when he was questioning Amanda Perry; then Fitz had seen it himself with the pathologist. Not that he had much room to talk about self-control, Fitz thought. The difference was, he understood why he got angry, and he used it; channelled it creatively, whatever. Bilborough didn't.

'Nothing else?' Beck asked.

Bates paused for a moment. The tiny TV picture made it hard for Fitz to be certain, but he seemed to be trying to think. 'Track suit top . . . it had a hood.'

'Then what happened?' Bilborough prompted.

'I got back in the car. We started to mess around, and she took off, into the wood.' He paused. 'I chased her for a bit.'

'Chased her?' Bilborough asked. He still looked and sounded guarded. If I were you, Bates, Fitz thought, I'd be careful. He peered at Bilborough. I'd be very careful indeed. He took a long drag on his cigarette and let the smoke hit the back of his throat. Now, what could be upsetting Bilborough?

It couldn't be the way the case was shaping up. True, they didn't have very many leads, but they'd hardly begun the investigation. The pathologist had upset him, but the half-arsed little popinjay had been well out of line, and everyone knew it. Taking the piss out of him had been as much public service as it had been good clean fun.

77

So, back to Bilborough. His wife was pregnant. Maybe it was as simple as anxiety over the pregnancy mixed up with seeing Timothy Lang dead. Close. Sex and death: you always came at least close if you got those two involved. But there was something else, something he couldn't quite place. He'd get it eventually, though.

'She likes that kind of thing,' Bates said. He sounded embarrassed.

'What kind of thing?' Bilborough asked.

Bates glanced down at the table. 'Rough.'

Beck leaned forward a little in his seat. Fitz wondered idly what kind of magazines he kept under his bed, but Bates continued speaking so he had to drop that line of thought.

'We were just about to start when we saw it – '

'A thirteen-year-old boy,' Bilborough said. His voice was dangerous. Here we go, Fitz thought, and had to remind himself that Bates was the one he was supposed to be analysing. Bilborough and Beck would have to wait for another day.

'I didn't know who he was, how old he was. We just ran – '

'You left a thirteen-year-old boy swinging from a tree.' Bilborough brought his hand up to his mouth, as if he were trying to shield himself from looking at Bates.

'She's married.' Bates sounded defensive. 'I'm married. I've got kids.' He was pleading now. Fitz realised the man was terrified they would tell his wife, or that the media would find out. He'd be spinning scenarios about how that could happen every time there was a let-up in the conversation. If Bilborough really wanted to find out more, or to make sure Bates co-operated, he'd give him time to think, maybe hint that they might need to check his story with his wife.

But Bilborough didn't as much as pause. 'You could've phoned anonymously.' He sounded like he was spoiling for a fight.

78

'We did.'

'*She* did. Twelve hours later. You left his parents clutching at straws for twelve hours.' Bilborough's voice was flat. 'If it had been left up to you, you wouldn't have phoned at all.' Bates looked at the table, looked at the side wall, anywhere but face the withering contempt in Bilborough's eyes. 'Your missus finding out about your bit on the side – that means more to you than the death of a child.' Bilborough broke suddenly. He lunged out of his seat at Bates. His hands slammed down onto the table. 'For Christ's sake, what kind of a man are you – '

'Hey,' Beck said. Bilborough ignored him. 'Hey, hey.'

Whatever else Beck said was lost as Bilborough shouted, 'He could have been alive. Didn't that enter your head?' He got up and moved away from the table. Doesn't trust himself, Fitz thought. 'He could have been alive – you could have saved him – ' He thrust his finger at Bates, who sat staring at his clenched hands.

Ah, Fitz thought. This is it –

'We've got what we want,' Beck said. 'All right – '

For once, Beck had a point. That meant Fitz was free to think about Bilborough, who was completely ignoring Beck anyway. 'It's human nature.' He stormed towards the back of the interview room. 'If a child's in trouble, you don't go away from him, you go to him.' His voice was angry, and more than that, desperate. It was as if some basic tenet of his belief system had been challenged, Fitz thought. Bilborough spread his hands wide, almost as if in supplication. 'If you don't do that you're not human, you're some kind of bloody animal – ' His face was flushed, his voice thick with emotion.

'Boss – ' Beck said, cautiously, though he made no move to stop Bilborough.

'We were there.' His finger jabbed the air. 'We were there waiting with them, you tosspot.' Fitz remembered Penhaligon telling him how badly Bilborough had handled telling the Langs. Another piece of the puzzle clicked into place. Bates stared straight ahead, as if he already knew what Bilborough was telling him. 'You prick. You bloody animal.' Bilborough shoved his face right up close to Bates's. 'Twelve. Bloody. Hours. And then they're told. You prick – ' he went on, after that, until he ran out of things to say and Beck persuaded him to leave.

Through it all, Bates just sat there, saying nothing, staring at his hands.

Penhaligon sipped her mug of tea and leaned against a desk in the duty room. She felt gritty-eyed. The long night's vigil with the Langs was finally beginning to catch up with her. That was the same for all of them, of course, except Fitz. He looked dreadful anyway. She wondered again where he'd picked up the scratches on his face.

As for Bilborough, she'd been seriously worried about him before they got him out of the interview room. It was the baby on his mind, she supposed. He looked pale and shaky, and his eyes were red-rimmed. The harsh strip lighting didn't help.

He'd asked for suggestions as to how they should continue the investigation. Beck had leapt in, of course, full of it as usual.

Now, he held forth to her and Bilborough as if he were lecturing trainees at Hendon. Fitz had settled himself on a seat further back, out of Beck's line of sight. As always, the seat seemed too small for him. He wrapped his hand round his plastic coffee cup. The steam rose off it slowly. Penhaligon realised she hadn't been listening to a word Beck had said.

' – we don't do anything until a full post mortem,' he said. 'Then, we say it's murder, stick the family on telly – '

God, Penhaligon thought. Hadn't he seen how hard the first appeal had been on them? Sit here, read this, don't look straight at the camera, lovie. Oh, and if you have to cry,

80

don't streak your mascara, Julie, there's a sweet. Penhaligon had been with them in the studio. She'd wanted to thump the make-up artist before they were through.

'I'd like to speak to them first, please,' Fitz said, from behind Beck.

'I'm talking,' Beck said, suddenly teacherish. 'Appeal for this jogger to come forward. Meanwhile, we talk to every kid in the school.'

'What do you think?' Bilborough asked Penhaligon.

Caught off guard, she said what she'd thought earlier, while he was bawling at Bates. 'I think you should go home.'

Bilborough stared straight through her. Whoops, she thought.

'I'd like to look round the house first thing in the morning, please,' Fitz said.

'The family have been through enough,' Beck said.

'You're putting them on the telly. Is that supposed to be some sort of relaxation therapy?' Fitz said, raising his voice.

Beck was speaking again. She struggled to concentrate on what he was saying: ' – a comfort for them. Seeing themselves on telly.'

He said it as if it were one of the great truths of the twentieth century. Moron, she thought at him.

She was suddenly sick of Beck, sick of the stink of stale cigarettes and cold machine coffee that pervaded the incident room, sick of Bilborough waiting for her to screw up.

We're all tired, Penhaligon thought. Edgy. We ought to go home and get some sleep; but she, at least, didn't want to sleep. She knew she'd dream of Timothy Lang's body turning slowly as he hung in the moonlit woods, of his marble face staring up from the morgue slab; but in her dream his eyes would be open, blue eyes staring up at her, demanding that she get involved, let herself be hurt by his death. She could not do that. Must not. Bilborough had, and

81

he was coming apart because of it, she thought.

'Can I speak to you a minute?' Bilborough's voice cut through the sudden, tense silence Beck's pronouncement had left in its wake. He started in the direction of his office without waiting for a reply.

Trouble, Penhaligon thought. She followed him into the office.

'Shut it,' he said curtly, nodding towards the door.

Definitely trouble, she thought as she pushed the door to. She turned back to face Bilborough. Before she could move or speak he had crossed the room and was standing far too close to her. He was furious. For the first time in her life Penhaligon appreciated the meaning of the word 'overbearing'. She was tall, but Bilborough was taller. He stared down at her so she had to crane her neck to meet his eyes.

'Don't you ever do that again. Don't you ever – ' he said.

'Do what?' Penhaligon said, belatedly, though she knew.

' – suggest that my private life's interfering with my work. I've seen you in tears. I've seen you sobbing your bloody heart out and I didn't say – '

'I'm sorry,' Penhaligon said. It was true. When Giggs was murdered she had been distraught. But Bilborough wasn't listening.

' – it to you, so how dare you say it to me?' he said in a furious undertone. He jabbed his finger at her in that familiar gesture of his. Penhaligon suddenly understood how Amanda Perry and Francis Bates must have felt when Bilborough had let loose at them.

'I am sorry,' Penhaligon said, wondering how many more times he would make her say it. There had been times recently when she had had to struggle to remember that underneath it all, she actually liked Bilborough. This was one of them.

But he backed off. He didn't exactly smile, but his face relaxed. He went over to his desk and got a photo, which he tried to pin up with the others above the interview room monitors. He fumbled and tried again; this time, the photo slipped out of his hand. He stared at the floor where it had fallen. He didn't bother to pick it up. Instead he twisted round and said over his shoulder as if nothing had happened, 'I'll phone her in a minute. See how she's doing.'

Penhaligon nodded. 'Right,' she said.

Bilborough turned round and walked towards her. He made an odd, awkward gesture with his hands. He sighed raggedly. 'We're not sleeping. That's why . . .' his voice trailed off into another sigh. Penhaligon was shocked to notice that he was almost shaking. She hadn't realised quite how bad he was. 'She's a week overdue. Her blood pressure's up and down every minute.' He swallowed hard. Penhaligon thought he might be about to cry. 'They wanted to take her in and induce it, but she wanted it natural.' He looked at Penhaligon. She nodded and thought. Please don't let him cry. I don't think I can cope if he cries. But he didn't. Instead he went on, 'Natural means up every half hour for a piss, every hour for cramp, every two hours waiting for contractions.' He paused again. 'I said to the nurse, "Take me in. She's only having a baby. I'm having kittens." '

NINE

Judith found Fitz in the kitchen. She'd been so engrossed in the television that she hadn't realised he'd come in.

He smiled at her tiredly. The artificial light did nothing for his pallor. 'I'm starving,' he said by way of explanation.

It was hardly surprising, Judith thought, considering that he'd been dragged away from dinner before they even got to the main course. She watched as he loaded cold chicken and salad on to his plate.

'Is there any wine left?' he asked. 'Not that Spanish crap – something decent?'

'Bottle of white open in the fridge,' she said.

He wasn't even going to tell her what this latest case was all about, and she wouldn't ask. She hated it, hated him getting caught up in sordid police work. She realised she was twisting her wedding ring round on her finger. He was watching her do it, and she knew he'd come up with some complicated reason for it.

She went through into the front room, where Mark was lounging on the sofa, watching the late-night horror film. Judith hadn't been able to summon the strength to argue. She supposed she was lucky he wasn't throwing popcorn at the screen – his empty Pepsi can hadn't yet made it to the rubbish, and he'd finished it a couple of hours ago.

On screen, someone's head exploded. 'Aargh,' Mark cried, clutching his face theatrically. 'It's the invasion of the stewed tomatoes – '

Judith picked up her magazine and pretended to read. Three new window treatments vied for her attention with an

84

interview with Harrison Ford and an article on *Where to Find the Best Divorced Men.* It was truly riveting, she thought, as she watched Fitz come in, bearing a loaded tray.

He sat down, carefully balancing the tray on his broad knees. His hands engulfed his knife and fork as he started on his meal.

'Bad for you, that,' Mark said.

'What is?' Fitz said, round a mouthful of chicken and lettuce.

'Eating after nine o'clock at night. Anyway, you eat too much – '

'Mark – ' Judith said, warningly.

'Do I now?' Fitz said. His voice held that hint of danger that meant he was about to launch one of his diatribes.

'Yeah,' Mark went on. 'You know what they say – eat fast, die young – '

'Mark!'

'Leave a fat corpse,' Fitz finished for him. He took a long swig of wine, then dabbed delicately at his mouth. 'Pass the butter, dear,' he said to Judith.

In anyone else, Judith thought, it would have been a case of putting himself down before someone did it for him. With Fitz, it was more likely revenge – stopping Mark from having his bit of fun at his father's expense. Then again, maybe not. With Fitz it could be hard to tell, even after all these years of marriage.

'You know, Mark, I long for some sign of affection from you,' Fitz said. 'I mean, I'd love to think that little piece of barbarism was just your way of telling me you worry about me.'

Mark stared at him as if to say 'fat chance'.

'Then again, I'll never know,' Fitz said. 'Or maybe I will.' He paused. 'You see, Mark, after we're dead I believe that our lives will be shown again – ' he dropped into his fake-American accent, ' – in that great movie theatre in the sky – '

85

'Give over,' Mark said. He looked genuinely uncomfortable. Judith tried to concentrate on Harrison Ford's early life as a carpenter. Ignoring Fitz was the only way she'd found to deal with him. He was like a toddler having a temper tantrum. Pay no attention and he'd stop. Eventually. At least this time he wasn't doing it in public, he was just trying to alienate his son.

'Yes folks,' Fitz went on, 'everything you've ever done, shown in glorious Technicolor and Surround-sound. All your friends will be there. All your enemies.' He lowered his voice. 'Just imagine it, Mark. That time you shat your knickers when you were three. That cassette you nicked when you were thirteen – remember that? Such *appalling* taste. The night Helena stayed here when we were away in Scotland – '

'What!' Judith said. She hadn't known about that.

'Found a used condom in his waste-paper basket, dear,' Fitz said. He turned to Mark, who had flushed bright red. 'Not our brand – '

'Fitz, how dare you – ' Judith said. This was outrageous, the worst thing he'd ever done to her. In front of her *son*, for God's sake. She'd have left, but she felt welded to her seat. She had to know what else he said to Mark.

'Well anyway,' Fitz went on, 'as I was saying – '

'I don't have to listen to this,' Mark said. Good for you, Judith thought. But he made no move to leave. It was Fitz's best trick, this way he had of making people listen to him.

'Ah yes. The bad as well as the good will be shown up there on the great celestial projector. I mean, there was that month of Saturdays you spent helping old Miss Tyler clean her attic ... which brings me to the difference between heaven and hell. Do you know the difference, Mark?

'You're going to tell me anyway,' Mark said. He was staring at Fitz the way a cobra might stare at a mongoose: he knew he'd met his match.

From time to time – as now – it occurred to Judith that

there was a difference between her arguing with Mark and Fitz doing the same thing. When she did it, it was because she had a serious point she wanted to make: usually, that he ought to get himself a job, or at least help around the house more. When Fitz did it, it was a way of establishing communication. For all his incisive understanding of other people's emotions, Fitz found talking about his own feelings almost impossible. He couldn't do it head-on, he had to take some roundabout route, and even then he only arrived at it obliquely. His son was much the same. The only difference was that Mark didn't have any problem expressing anger. Fitz was at least consistent. He let his anger out, but only at targets that didn't matter much to him.

The business with Graham had been different. The business with Graham would be something Judith would regret for the rest of her life.

'The difference between hell and heaven,' Fitz said. He lit a cigarette, as if to define the subject at hand. 'In hell, everyone will know what you did, but not why. And they'll interpret even your purest motives as being tinged with selfishness ... if not downright wickedness. They'll say, "Bet he thought that old lady was a secret millionairess", "Bet he thought Angelina Humphries would let him cop a feel if he helped her with her geography" – aah, you didn't think I knew about that, either, did you?'

'That's it. I've had enough,' Mark said. He stood up.

Fitz carried on regardless. 'See, in heaven, it's different. In heaven, they'd see the good behind the bad. They'll know that when you took that cassette, you only did it so you wouldn't feel left out at school.' He tapped the ash off his cigarette. 'They'll know that when you yell at me, it's only because you wish your mother and I – '

'Fitz, that's enough,' Judith said, loud enough to drown him out. Mark took the opportunity to leave the room. 'You shouldn't do that to him,' she said. 'It's bad enough with strangers, but your own son – '

87

'Is big enough to take it,' Fitz said. 'Or big enough to learn to keep his mouth shut.'

'Yes, well we know where he gets it from, don't we?' Judith said.

'Thank you,' said Fitz. He stubbed his cigarette out. 'Now if you'll excuse me, I'd like to get some sleep.'

'There is a bed upstairs, you know,' Judith said. She thought that if she put it that way, without any sexual pressure at all, maybe he would sleep with her – and maybe this time, it would be for the whole night through.

'There are three, in fact,' Fitz said. 'Unfortunately, people will be sleeping in all of them.'

All right then. Maybe she would have to be more direct. 'Ours is big enough for two.' She paused. She could feel her pulse beating at her temples. 'What I said earlier – you don't . . . we don't have to make love – '

Fitz nodded. 'Just as well. I've no intention of doing so – '

'Please – ' she said, and thought, dammit, I promised myself I wouldn't beg. Not this time.

'Remember last night?' Fitz said. 'I wouldn't want to be responsible for the outcome.'

'That's just your problem, isn't it Fitz?' Judith said, knowing even as she did so that she was lashing out at herself as much as him. 'You never will take responsibility for anything – '

'Is that what you think?' His voice was low and dangerous. Then he laughed suddenly. It wasn't a pleasant sound. 'Frankly – ' he was using the American accent again. ' – frankly, my dear, I don't give a damn.'

He stood watching her. Judith wished she could think of some snappy quote to come back at him with, but really there was nothing left to say. In the end, she left without saying anything, and went upstairs. He didn't follow her.

Andy sat watching the television. It wasn't turned on. His mother was in the kitchen. She was defrosting the freezer. Ten o'clock at night, and she was defrosting the freezer.

His father was sitting in the chair opposite him. He had a can of Foster's in his hand. Another – the last of a six-pack – balanced on the arm of the chair. The empty cans stood carefully around the base of his chair.

'I'm going out,' Andy said. He had to go and talk to Melanie. He'd put it off as long as he could. Christ only knew, it didn't seem so important now, not with Tim dead. But the house was like a mausoleum. He couldn't stand it.

'Don't go,' his father said. 'She needs you here – '

Andy ignored him. He wasn't going to be guilt-tripped. Not by the old man. It wasn't his fault Tim was dead. Had killed himself. Had been murdered. None of the words sounded right.

' – I need you here, son.'

Andy stared at his father. Son? When did you ever treat me like a son? he thought. Or Tim either. So what if he was a rotten little pansy? He still deserved better than what he got from you.

He got up and headed towards the door. His father caught up with him in the hallway, as he was putting his jacket on.

'We ought to talk about it.'

Andy ignored him, and felt for his keys in his pocket.

'That's what they say, don't they? Shouldn't bottle it up – '

'That's a load of bollocks, if you ask me,' Andy said. He had the keys, and a pocketful of loose change. 'I'm going to see Melanie. You can tell Mum, if you like.'

His father came unsteadily towards him. 'You shouldn't feel guilty about it, Andy.' His eyes were shiny with uncried tears. 'He wasn't like us – '

'He was a bleeding little queer,' Andy said. 'I thought it before and I still think it now.'

His father grasped at the banister for support. 'Don't,' he said. 'You shouldn't talk like that – '

'Why not?' Andy asked. 'You said the same.' His father

seemed to shrivel. Andy didn't know why he was saying it, why he needed to hurt the old man. Except that it was true. They'd all known that Tim wasn't quite right. 'You did.'

'If I did,' his father said, and stopped. He seemed at a loss for what to say next. 'If I did, I didn't mean it. You know I loved that boy.'

'Yeah,' Andy said. He turned and went out the front door, letting it slam shut behind him.

The night air was cool on his face, but it didn't cool his temper. You certainly gave Tim more time than you ever gave me, that's for sure, he thought.

'Mike told me about Tim,' Melanie said. She sipped her Coke. No Bacardi tonight. She wasn't in the mood, she said.

Andy nodded. 'When did you see him?' He sipped his Snakebite. It was his third. Getting pissed seemed like a good idea, maybe the only good idea he could possibly have.

They were in the Rising Sun. They didn't go there often – it was full of old people, and it didn't have a pool table or even a juke box, just a dartboard. The only surprising thing about it was that it didn't have sawdust on the floor.

'He came by at work. He said you'd been down to the workshop – '

'Yeah,' Andy said. His drink tasted disgusting. He didn't care. 'What happened?'

'Nothing happened. He told me you were in a right mood – ' she finished her drink, fished the lemon out and sucked it. Andy watched her. God, he didn't want her to dump him.

'I didn't mean that. I meant, what did he say to you about – ' he couldn't find the words. Not to her face. 'You know . . .'

'We don't have to talk about that now,' she said. Her face had the same odd expression it had had that morning in the kitchen.

'We do,' he said. He swished the last of the Snakebite round in the glass and considered getting another round in. But it would only give her the chance to change the subject.

90

'All right then,' she said. 'I went back to the pub last night – '

'I know.' He'd been angry about that once, but now it seemed a long time ago and not at all important.

'Sorry,' she said. She picked up a beer-mat and started shredding one corner of it. Her nails were long and pearly pink, and they picked at the cardboard. 'We were talking – ' There must have been something in his expression, because she added quickly, 'Not just me and Mike. Ali was there, too. Anyway, I said you'd gone home because you were upset about Tim, and he made some crack about him . . . you know.'

'Yeah.'

'I told him to stop. You know I always felt sorry for him – ' Andy could only nod. He wished he'd listened to her then. 'And he said that I obviously had nothing to worry about, with you.' She grinned, but she didn't seem amused. She started folding the edge of the beer-mat back and forth. 'I should have left it alone, but I didn't. I asked Ali what he meant.' She was angry now. He knew her well enough to recognise it, though her voice was quite calm. 'In the loos, I asked her. And she said that Mike told her we're sleeping together.'

'I'm sorry, ' he said.

'She said Mike had been getting at her to do it with him – because if I'm doing it with you, why shouldn't he expect the same?'

'I didn't mean it – '

'Well, I don't see how you could have told him accidentally – ' her voice had gone ice-cold. She tore the beer-mat in two.

'He sort of assumed, and I didn't – ' What the hell could he say? He drained his glass. It was very empty, not even a tiny little bit left in it. 'Want another drink?'

'No. I want to know how you told him without meaning to.'

'Told you, I don't know,' Andy said. He slammed the glass down on the table. He stood up. 'I am getting another drink,' he announced.

'I don't think you ought to – '

'Don't you bloody tell me what to do,' he said.

Melanie stood up. 'I'll leave you to it then,' she said. She pushed her way free of the table.

'Mel, don't,' he said when she was halfway to the door. 'I'm sorry.'

'So am I, Andy,' she said. Her eyes were glinting with tears, just like Dad's had been. Christ, did he have to make everybody cry? He'd certainly made Tim cry often enough. 'Tell your mum I said I'm sorry about Tim, will you?'

Andy nodded. 'Will you phone?'

'Yes,' she said, but she didn't sound very sure of it. And then she was gone, and the door was swinging shut behind her, and Andy was alone in the pub.

He went to get himself another drink.

It was gone midnight by the time Penhaligon got home. She opened the door quietly, so as not to disturb Peter. The hall was quiet and dark, but there was a line of light from under the living-room door. Penhaligon stepped inside. As she turned to close the door, the handle slipped from her grasp and slammed shut.

'Damn,' she muttered as she tried, ineptly, to double-lock the door. Somehow, she just couldn't get the key to turn.

When she turned around, Peter was standing in the living-room doorway. 'You're late,' he said.

'Our mis-per turned into a murder enquiry.'

'Christ, you don't turn up when you say you're going to – you don't even phone to let me know – and then you start spouting jargon at me when you do turn up.'

'Peter, I have spent most of the night waiting with the kid's parents,' Penhaligon said. She started off calmly enough but as she spoke she relived the horror of it, and it made her angrier and angrier. 'I've had to tell them he's dead,' she was almost crying, almost shouting. But only almost. 'I've had to look at him strung up in the woods and then on a mortuary slab. And I don't need this.'

Peter didn't speak. She went into the kitchen and opened the fridge. She had to eat something or she wouldn't sleep, and then she'd feel rough in the morning. There was a bit of cheese, a couple of slices of ham. That would do. She took them and opened the bread-bin. It was empty. 'There's no bread,' she said. It was the last, the absolutely last, straw.

'It was your turn to shop,' Peter pointed out.

'Yes, well somehow I didn't find time,' Penhaligon said, thinking guiltily of the half hour she'd spent sitting in the cafe that afternoon. 'Telling the parents seemed just a bit more important than making sure we're stocked up with wholemeal – '

'There's some casserole in the freezer,' Peter said. 'I had mine earlier.'

'Kind of you to think of me,' Penhaligon said. 'I don't suppose it occurred to you to leave it in the fridge – faster to heat through, you know?'

'I didn't know when you'd be in. You didn't call.' He turned and went into the front room.

Bloody man, Penhaligon thought as she got the casserole out and put it in the microwave. She'd been perfectly happy living on her own. She should never have agreed to him moving in.

The microwave pinged. She put the casserole into a bowl and took it through into the living room. Peter was watching MTV. Penhaligon didn't recognise the band, but they were far too loud whoever they were. She sat down and started to eat. The casserole was delicious.

'Is it OK?' Peter asked.

Here we go, Penhaligon thought. Puppy-dog time. It was always like this. They'd row, and she could predict to the minute when he'd want to make peace. Usually she'd let him, but tonight she was just too tired to bother. She finished eating and put the bowl on the coffee-table. She still hadn't spoken.

'Oh come on, Janie,' Peter said.

'Personally, I'm fine.'

'Look, I'm sorry I snapped. I'd fallen asleep in here, and the door banging woke me – '

'Yes, well some of us only got two hours' sleep last night – '

'Don't be like this.' He turned the TV off with the remote control. 'All I wanted was a nice night out at the cinema, like we planned – '

'I should have phoned. I didn't phone. I'm sorry.' She didn't sound sorry, not even to herself. He knew what the job was like. It wasn't her fault if he wouldn't make allowances for it.

'Look, I know you're tired – '

'Don't condescend to me,' she said. She knew that wasn't fair, that she'd already said as much herself. But she didn't care. 'I have to put up with it from Bilborough, and Beck's too pig-ignorant to know better.' She stared fiercely at the blank television screen, wishing Peter hadn't turned it off, but she couldn't be bothered to lean over and take the controller off him. 'You, I don't have to take it from.'

'I was just thinking, tomorrow when you go in you could book some holiday – '

She'd forgotten about that. The brochures were in her bag. She'd thought about saying so, then realised she'd have to admit she'd had a proper lunch hour – in which she could have phoned him, if only she'd thought of it. Suddenly it was all too complicated. Going away with him was the last thing she wanted. 'Oh, stuff your bloody holiday. I'm going to bed,' she said, and stood up.

She went to the bedroom and undressed in the dark. Her drum-kit was a vast silhouette in one corner of the room. For a second she thought about pulling the dust-sheet off it

94

and pounding out all her frustrations on it, as she had before Peter had moved in. It was more consideration for the neighbours than for Peter that stopped her. She settled for punching her pillow instead. The damn thing was too soft to be a worthwhile opponent, and her fist made a wimpish thudding sound on impact. It was a good enough second-best though – just like everything else she settled for these days.

Damn.

She sighed and slid between the cool sheets, wondering what Fitz was doing at that moment. She was still awake an hour or so later, when Peter finally came to bed. He wanted to make love, but she pretended to be asleep.

TEN

Andy had had enough. His head felt like it was full of molten lava, and his mouth tasted like something had died in it. He'd fallen asleep with the light on, and now it was hurting his eyes. Somewhere, some stupid birds were singing at full volume. He wanted to stick his head under the pillow and go back to sleep, but he felt too sick even to do that.

Besides, sometime last night, while he was still drunk, he'd realised that someone was going to have to pay for what had happened to Tim.

He felt like he'd thought about it all night long, though he knew he'd slept because he'd dreamt of running through the woods, of hands reaching out to grab him by the throat and squeeze the life's breath out of him. He was Tim in the dream, but he was also himself, trying to push his way through the branches before the man got to his brother; then he was Tim again, staring up at his killer – at Andy – who was staring down at Tim's frightened face, and yet he was also racing through the woods to try and get to him in time to save him.

The dream had faded quickly. He'd forced it away, by getting up quickly. Jeans on, Doc Martens on. He'd planned what he would do the night before.

Someone had to pay for Tim, and he knew the police wouldn't make it happen. They were just pissing around. What did they care? They said it was murder. Andy knew better. Tim had killed himself. Whatever Mum said, that had

96

to be the way it was. He hadn't been able to take the bullying, the comments he got every day.

If only he'd turned round and laid into one or two of them, they would have backed straight off. But Tim wasn't like that. He was too gentle. Too good for them.

That was what he'd thought last night. It was the drink talking. Andy thought as he pulled his tee shirt over his head. But there was a bit of truth in it. It was easy to call him a little queer, a faggot. But deep down, Andy knew that whatever else Tim had been, he'd been a good person. Kind to Mum – kinder than Andy was, a lot of the time. Bright, too. He'd have stayed on for A-levels for sure. And he was tougher than he looked. Tough enough to take all the crap the kids at school threw at him without breaking or losing his temper. Until now.

Andy knew who the culprits were. Maybe they hadn't put the noose round Tim's neck, but they were to blame just the same.

No point telling the police. They'd just say they were only interested in finding the murderer. Oh yeah. What they wanted was to tick a little box on some form or other. Improve their clear-up rate, that was what they called it. Case closed. You you and you – you get your promotion this year.

But care about Tim? No way.

So Andy would have to see to it.

Andy put his crash helmet on as he went down the front path. Just as he got to his bike, a car pulled up. The door opened just as he revved up, and the red-headed woman officer got out. The fat guy was with her.

'Have you got a minute, Andy?' the woman called.

Sure, he thought. But not for you. He went.

Andy brought the bike screeching to a halt right next to the main entrance of the school. He glanced up at the building as he locked his helmet onto the bike. It was a concrete and glass brick: he could see the kids moving up around it through the plate glass walls of the main stairwell.

He hated the place. He'd hated it from the second he'd first stepped inside at eleven till the moment he'd left when he was sixteen.

He still remembered his way round, though. He went straight in and up the stairs. Round and round the spiral. The clatter of his feet echoed on the wooden steps. A few little girls – first or second years – giggled behind their hands at him. The boys stood back. Sensible, he thought. You learned when someone wanted a fight in this place. Learned, or had your head kicked in, and then learned.

He heard someone mutter something about getting a teacher.

Fine, that was fine by him. He had a few things to say to the teachers. But Rope and his crony Mulligan came first. The rest could keep.

He came to a classroom door and bashed through it. There was a bunch of little kids being taught by Cassidy. Hopalong, everyone had called him when he first arrived. Andy had other names for him. Wimp. Dickhead. Him and the words he was going to have with Mulligan and Rope. Well, Andy would have words with him. Later.

He turned and walked out of the room. Cassidy's voice followed him along the corridor: 'Andy! What are you doing bursting into my classroom?'

Andy ignored the voice, ignored the stares of a few straggling kids who hadn't managed to change rooms yet.

He crashed through the double doors of another class-room. The room inside was shadowy. The curtains had been drawn and a slide projector was running. Andy looked round. There was Rope, with Mulligan right by his side as usual.

Good. Andy made it through the class in three strides. The projector went kerchunk and the picture changed from a

98

shot of amoebae to one of ferns. More useless crap that would be sod all use to anyone when they tried to get a job.

He glanced round. Jessup, the geography teacher, had only just realised something was wrong. He'd managed to get to his feet, but there were half a dozen rows of chairs between him and the front of the room. This is what you get for skiving off to have a snooze at the back of the room, you old bastard, Andy thought.

He barged through the front row of kids to get to Rope. People started yelling. He heard someone shout his name, and someone else call Rope's. Mulligan tried to grab him, but he bashed the kid aside. Then he had Rope. He hauled him out of his seat into the space at the front. He rammed his knee into Rope's groin, but missed and got his belly instead. Rope doubled over. Andy smashed his fist into him, and felt it connect with bone. Nose job. Good. Rope tried to slide out from under, but Andy managed to get in one more good punch. Then he grappled the kid and brought him down. He slammed Rope's head into the floor, once, twice, three times –

Someone grabbed him by the arms and yanked him back. Andy twisted round. Cassidy. Andy surged forward, trying to break free. No go. He rammed his elbow back into Cassidy's midriff, but the teacher was too quick for him.

'Get him off,' Cassidy yelled. 'For Christ's sake what do you think you're doing?' he said. He hauled Andy away, spun him round and shoved him back.

Andy slammed into the projection screen. It crashed back under his weight. He squinted against the dazzle of the projector light. Cassidy released the pressure, then pushed Andy against the wall again.

'What good will that do?' Cassidy yelled. Kerchunk. The slides changed. The light flickered from light to dark to light again. 'What good can that possibly do?' Kerchunk. 'Now just calm down. All right?' He was shouting.

Andy was still riled. He could feel the blood thundering

in his ears. You next, Cassidy, he thought. You damn well next.

It was worth it. It was worth being frogmarched through the hall and down the stairs by the copper. It was worth being giggled at by the damned kids, just to see Rope staring at him, terrified. Just to feel that crunch of fist on bone.

The copper got him halfway down the stairs before he spotted Cassidy again. He was talking earnestly to a woman copper. Probably explaining that there were 'extenuating circumstances'. Bleeding-heart do-gooder. He'd probably said that the last time Rope had sent Tim home with a split lip. If it hadn't been for him and his extenuating circumstances –

'You did nothing,' Andy yelled at Cassidy as he came level with him. 'You knew what was going on and you did nothing.' The copper hustled him by, but he twisted back to shout, 'It's down to you. You and every teacher in this shithole.' The copper yanked him down the stairs. He yelled louder. 'You knew what was going on and you did nothing.' They were almost at the bottom of the steps, but there was one last thing he had to say. 'He trusted you. He told you everything. You never lifted a finger.'

ELEVEN

'You want the truth?' Mr Lang asked. Fitz sat opposite him, almost immobile. 'You'll despise the truth.'

They were back at the Langs' house. The place had the feel of a mausoleum about it already, Penhaligon thought. The front room was as neat as it had been the night before, but in the kitchen the dishes were piling up in the sink because no-one could be bothered to wash up. Not too many of them, though. She would have laid odds that Mrs Lang hadn't eaten since Timothy had failed to come home. She wrapped her hands round her mug of tea and watched Fitz and Mr Lang. They sat at the dining table, talking in undertones.

Penhaligon had never seen Fitz like this before. The bantering, judgemental, mad-at-the-world man she thought she knew had gone. That man had been too big for this neat suburban semi, with its bric-a-brac and its British Home Stores lamps and its Marks and Spencer's houseplants. Now the man seemed not smaller, but comfortably large, filling it up with the warmth of his grave presence.

'You'd have preferred it to be suicide,' Fitz said.

Mr Lang nodded. How did he know that? Penhaligon wondered. How?

'He was always a victim. Murder, he's a victim to the end.' Mr Lang's voice was a monotone. He sounded cried out. 'Suicide, well, that's some kind of courage he's shown.'

Courage? Is that what it is? Penhaligon thought, and remembered her father, his skin turning slowly yellow with

101

the Paracetamol poisoning that had killed him, and the skin of his face drawn tight over the bone with pain. She supposed it might be.

'I didn't hope. I didn't pray. I knew.' Mrs Lang stared steadily at Fitz. 'I knew it wouldn't be suicide.' Her hands were finally still. Penhaligon thought, It's the not knowing that does that, that makes you seek out something, anything to pass the time. She knew more about that than she wished she did.

'Because suicide's a bomb under the kitchen table, every member of the family cut to pieces.' Fitz's voice was a gentle undertone. It was hard for Penhaligon to believe that this was the same man who teased her, bullied suspects, embarrassed his wife in restaurants. 'He wouldn't do that to you?'

Dad, Penhaligon thought. Oh, Dad.

'He loves me,' Mrs Lang said. Loves, present tense, Penhaligon thought. She understood that, too.

I love you, Dad, she thought.

'Have you got a son?' Mr Lang asked.

'Yeah, eighteen,' Fitz said. 'Eighteen years old, not eighteen sons.' He smiled slightly, the first hint of the old Fitz that Penhaligon had seen in all that long morning.

The smile died in the face of Mr Lang's unremitting sorrow. 'You'll know then. Your son's born. One day you'll watch him play football for the school, take him to Old Trafford, buy him his first pint. Not Andy. Anything I wanted, he did the opposite.' Fitz nodded. He seemed sad. Penhaligon wondered if he were thinking about Mark. From what Fitz said, his son seemed to hate and despise him in equal proportions. Then again, maybe Fitz's psychologist's training had taught him not to think about his personal life when he was with a client. Penhaligon couldn't tell. This new Fitz was almost a stranger to her. Mr Lang went on,

'But that were OK. Tim was born. I'd do it all with Tim.' He sighed deeply, as if he were trying to stop himself from crying. He paused. He seemed to be trying to find words for something he'd never thought about before. 'But Tim turned out to be a girl,' he said at last.

Penhaligon wondered if he meant Tim were gay. Maybe that would be hard enough for him to think about. But the way he'd said it seemed to imply something different, something less usual. She'd have to remember to ask Fitz about it.

'Guilt,' Mrs Lang murmured. Her voice was dull. 'They told me it was murder.' She wouldn't meet Fitz's eyes. Her gaze flittered all round the sitting room, from the knick-knacks on the sideboard to the mirror over the fireplace and back again. 'I felt relieved. The blame lay somewhere else.' She looked at him then, as if begging for understanding, or perhaps forgiveness. 'I didn't think about Tim, what he went through. I do now. But then – when they told me – I didn't think about his pain and his fear. I just felt relief.'

He has to say something, Penhaligon thought. She'll hate herself until she dies if he doesn't. But Fitz didn't say anything. Not then.

'Guilt,' Mr Lang said. He glanced at Mrs Lang. She was sitting on the sofa next to Penhaligon, who was holding her hand. He looked back at Fitz. 'I wanted a crisis. We rowed over Tim. Separated over Tim.' Again, his gaze drifted towards his wife, but she was staring fixedly at the blotchy pink patterned wallpaper. ' "Just give me a nice little crisis," I thought, "and I'll go back and . . . sort everything out, and everything'll be OK. We'll be together again." Well, I've got my crisis.'

'There's always guilt,' Fitz said. Mrs Lang sat opposite him again. She stared at him with blank, hopeless eyes. Even the chestnut lights seemed to have gone out of her hair. 'I've spoken to dozens of parents who've lost children. They've all been blameless; they've all felt guilt. If only they'd done this, if only we'd done that. If only you'd made Tim put on his coat, delayed him by two minutes – ' Mrs Lang's mouth worked as if she were trying to swallow. Penhaligon knew that Fitz was saying what was in the woman's heart. How does he know? she thought again. Oh, Dad. ' – two seconds, he'd never have been in that place at that time. He'd never have met his killer.'

Penhaligon thought, He met his killer in a little brown bottle of pills. I couldn't have stopped him. He would have died anyway. The Chorea would have got him.

She looked at her hands, then at Mrs Lang. She should cry, Penhaligon thought. It would be better if she cried. But Mrs Lang didn't cry. Fitz went on, 'May I read you something?' Mrs Lang nodded.

'It's a father talking. "She was young, vulnerable. Pictures used to flash before my eyes; my daughter lying dead in a ditch. I told myself all fathers thought that way, all fathers saw these pictures. But then it happened. It's as if I willed it to happen. I saw those pictures in my mind and I willed it to happen." '

There was a pause. Light glinted on the tears that leaked from Mrs Lang's eyes. She didn't speak or make a sound. Penhaligon, watching from the chair, remembered wishing her father were dead. Anything to get it over with. She'd hated her mother for wishing he were dead before his time, but she'd wished it herself, in the secret places of her heart. And then he'd taken the Paracetamol, and they'd found out too late for the doctors to do anything about it.

'You know just what he means, don't you?' Fitz said. He was speaking to Mrs Lang, but the words seemed to twist a knife deep in the hidden places of Penhaligon's heart, so that the last awful secret she kept hidden there could finally leak away. Mrs Lang was crying now, really crying, making little mewing sounds as she sobbed. Fitz took her hand. 'Guilt soon goes. Grief remains, but grief is your friend. It lets you mourn. Remember. Cry.'

I'll cry, Penhaligon thought. Now now. Not soon. But I will cry.

The phone began to ring. Eventually, Penhaligon thought to get up and answer it.

'I never knew,' Julie said, after Fitz and Penhaligon had left. 'I mean, you should have said – '

Steve stared at her blankly. He's *old*, she thought. There were ten years between them, but it had never bothered her before. Tim's death had aged him, though: etched lines of despair deep into his face, put bitterness into his eyes.

'What?' he said, so long after she had spoken that she thought he hadn't heard.

'I never realised how much you wanted to come home,' she said. The sunlight shafting through the windows showed up a smear on the glass. She would have to do something about that. Later. Later would do.

'How could you not know?' Steve asked. He stood up, but then he just stood there, as if he didn't know what he should do next.

'I don't know,' Julie said. 'Maybe I didn't want to know.'

He's going to go, she thought. She didn't want to be alone, not in this house, when everything she saw reminded her of Tim.

'I'll make a cup of tea, shall I?' she said.

Steve nodded.

White, two sugars: that had been how Tim had liked it. When he had been at primary school, he had been the first one home. They would sit drinking tea in the kitchen, and talk. Sometimes, she would buy buns, just for the two of them. It was their special time, their secret time. She had talked to Tim like no-one else – certainly like no-one else in the family.

105

She realised, suddenly, that tears were leaking down Steve's cheeks. She went to him.

'I did care about him, you know,' he said.

'I know. I know.' She put her arms around him, and then he was holding her and kissing her. She broke away. 'We shouldn't,' she said. 'Not now.' But somehow what they should or shouldn't do didn't seem to matter, not when the only comfort she could find in the world lay in his arms.

'I'll wait here for you,' Fitz said. They were parked near the crematorium gates.

'Get a cab, Fitz,' Penhaligon said. 'The boss might need you.' He just looked at her. 'Charge it to expenses,' she said, and when he still didn't move, she fumbled in her purse till she found a five-pound note. 'Here,' she said, pushing it into his hand.

'Oh come on,' he said. 'It isn't the money. You should know me better than that.'

Penhaligon smiled, though she had felt like crying ever since they had left the Langs.

'You'll want me here later,' Fitz said. He wasn't teasing. 'Trust me.'

'I'll see you in a bit,' Penhaligon said, and got out of the car.

She made her way through the crematorium gates, past the Chapel of Rest and then into the Garden of Remembrance. There were some seats under a colonnaded walkway along one side. In the centre there was a square filled with neatly pruned rose bushes, each with a small brass plaque beside it. Gravelled paths led between the plants, and up to an arched gap in the hedge that opened on to another garden.

It was somewhere about here, Penhaligon thought. She hadn't been back since the funeral. She walked along first one path, then another, stopping occasionally to look at the plaques. *Valerie Montague, 1947–1991. Howard Nguema,*

1982–1990. God, she thought. Only eight years old. *Phyllis Thomson, 1914–1991.*

It was no use. She had no idea where her father's rose bush had been planted, though she remembered the funeral with greater clarity than she wished.

The flowers had been laid out in a great Technicolor swathe under the walkway. She had watched them, watched all the sad-eyed murmuring mourners as if they were extras in a bad movie. Her mother had cried. Penhaligon hadn't. She had simply waited for them all to go, and then she had stood looking down at the rose bush for a long time, until the vicar had asked her if she were all right.

But now she couldn't even remember where it was. She shut her eyes. She might not be able to remember, but she was trained to observe. There had been blossom petals in drifts around the bush. A ragged-edged shadow falling obliquely across it – there had to have been a hedge at her back. And the vicar – he had come from her left, through the gap in the hedge.

She was in the wrong garden. She went through into the next one. There was a cherry tree in one corner, just in front of a line of bushes. She hurried to that corner. The bushes there all looked the same, and any one of them could have been her father's. She couldn't tell. It had been nothing to look at, not much more, really, than a bare forked stick. It could have grown into any of these plants.

I have to find it, she thought. I have to. But it was impossible to tell which, if any of them, it had been. Perhaps it had been none of them. Perhaps she had imagined it all, the funeral, his face staring up at her, his teeth bared to bite back the pain, imagined her anger at him. She could hardly breathe at the thought of it, as if her throat were choking off words she needed to say. She had said so much, and so little. Surely there could be no more to say?

I didn't imagine it, she thought. It was here, somewhere in these gardens, and if I look long enough I'll find it.

She felt as if a hand were pressing against her chest, stopping her from breathing.

What would Fitz say about that? She could imagine his lazy Scottish drawl: *What have you got to lose from seeing the rose bush, Panhandle?* *Nothing*, she thought at him fiercely, but the Fitz in her head told her firmly that if she saw it, she wouldn't be able to pretend. *Pretend what?* she asked him silently. He shrugged shoulders as massive as mountains. *You tell me, Panhandle*, he said. *But if you can't remember, you must need to forget. What would you like to say to your father?* he asked, remorseless as ever the real Fitz was. *Nothing*, she whispered aloud. *Must be something*, Fitz-in-her-head answered. *Or you wouldn't be choking on unspoken words.* He smiled one of his sly smiles, and was silent.

I'm sorry, she muttered, sullen as a child; *I'm so sorry I was angry.* She'd raged at him for trying to kill himself, raged at him again for taking the pills. 'Such a stupid way to do it,' she'd said. Paracetamol. Slow. Painful. Irreversible. The liver failure had left him jaundiced-looking and feverish to the touch. There was something else she said to him, or wanted to say; but there had been so many things left unsaid it was hard to remember any one in particular.

She'd promised herself she would cry, but the tears just wouldn't come. She wanted to cry. She ought to cry. Fitz had said so, and when was he ever wrong?

It was pointless. She thought, I'll just look at his rose bush, and then I ought to go. She bent to look at the brass plaques. *Kevin Andrews. Anne Sullivan. Richard Dennison.* But not Robert Penhaligon. This was the place. She was sure of it. She stood looking down at the plaques, as if she could make her father's name appear on one of them by force of will.

Eventually, she walked away. There was a gardener fussing around by the colonnade. He smiled at her as she got near.

108

On impulse, she said, 'I was looking for my father's rose bush, but I can't find it – '

He asked her if she was sure she'd looked in the right place. She lied and said she was.

'I don't mean to be rude, but are you sure the extension fee was paid, miss?'

'I don't know,' Penhaligon said. 'What is it?'

'Well, see, the bushes are removed if the families don't pay for their upkeep. We have to do that to make room for the, er, new ones.'

Penhaligon nodded. 'I see,' she said.

It made sense. She even thought she remembered her mother saying something about it. The bloody bitch.

'Are you all right, miss?' the gardener asked, echoing the vicar's words of so long ago.

'I'm fine,' Penhaligon said. 'Fine.'

But she wasn't. She felt sick. By the time she'd turned away from the man, she felt as if something inside her had broken, and before she'd got beneath the shelter of the colonnade she was sure she was going to be sick.

She sat down. Shit, she thought. It was as if he had never existed. Gone. Nothing to prove to the world that he had ever walked in it. Except her. But when she died, there'd be nothing left of him, not even a memory.

She began to cry. The tears seemed to come out of nowhere. She didn't want them. If she once started in earnest, she might never stop. Dad, she thought. She wanted to touch his hand, to hear his laugh on a sunny day, to hold on to him and never let go, and know it didn't matter because he was her father, and she never had to be tough DS Penhaligon with him, one of the boys, a woman with balls.

She was sobbing. Her chest ached from it, and her throat burned. He was gone, gone forever and it was no use saying – as the counsellor she had seen had said – that he would live on in her memory. She wanted him alive, now, in front of her. Not dead, laid out like any punter in the morgue,

109

waiting for the autopsy. She had stood there, looking down at him, thinking, God, Paracetamol; of all the stupid . . . and she had whispered something at him, not knowing that her mother was close enough to hear it. They'd rowed. She'd said something and they'd rowed because of it.

Her mother had said, 'You two-faced little cow.' Very up-front. Not like her mother's usual icy indifference. What had she said that had been two-faced? 'You two-faced little cow. You're no better than I am – '

She remembered. Oh Jesus, now she knew what she had said. She didn't want to remember, but she couldn't put it back in the box. She whimpered. It was as if she were there, looking down at him, with his skin like yellow wax; and she said, 'Why didn't you ask me, Dad? I could have told you an easier way to do it.'

It wasn't the words that hurt. It was knowing that she had meant them.

She buried her head in her arms, and for the longest time there was nothing in her world but the tears. When she was done with crying she could hardly see, her eyes were so sore; but that was OK. She just wanted to sit there for a while and pretend nothing mattered.

'Here,' said Fitz's voice beside her. She turned. He held out a handkerchief.

'I wanted to kill my father,' she said.

'Guilt, Panhandle,' Fitz said. His voice was unexpectedly gentle. 'The same kind of guilt the Langs feel, as anyone feels when someone dies.'

'No,' Penhaligon said. She hoped he wasn't going to lecture her, or even counsel her the way he had the Langs. She'd already heard that speech once today, after all – even if it was a very good speech. 'He tried to phone me. I wouldn't talk to him.' Her hand kneaded the tissue. 'Didn't dare. He would have told me . . . Then, afterwards, I forgot.' Suddenly she was crying again, crying a storm of tears and she didn't care that Fitz was watching.

110

'Breathe, Panhandle,' he said. 'That's it. Keep breathing. Don't try and stop it.'

She could hardly hear him over the sound of her sobbing, but eventually she was done. 'I forgot that he'd tried to phone. I was so angry with him for not telling me. It was my fault.' She stared at him. There was no hint of reproach in his eyes. 'I told myself that if I'd known, I could have tried to stop him. But that isn't how it was. When it happened, you know what I thought? I thought I should have helped him do it. Given him an easier death. And then I forgot that I'd thought it.' There, she'd said it. It was real now that someone else knew about it. She'd never be able to forget it again. There was one more thing, though, and this time she really had to struggle to find the words. 'All the time I've blamed my mother for burying him before he was dead. I hated her for it, but I'm far worse than her – '

'Love, Panhandle,' Fitz said. 'Love is like guilt. It comes in many guises. Don't mistake it for hate.'

He took her hand. There was nothing flirtatious in it. They just sat for a while, and when Penhaligon was ready, they left.

TWELVE

Penhaligon dropped Fitz in town. He'd said he was happy to make his own way back to the station, and she had a couple of quick chores to do.

She went into the first newsagent's she came across and picked out a card for her mother. Something tasteful, she decided, something with a pretty bunch of flowers on it. She picked one out at random – tulips in pastel pink – and wrote it out while she stood at the counter.

It was hard to know what to say after so long, when the last time they spoke they had had such a terrible row. In the end, she just put, 'Mum, It would be nice to hear from you, Love, Jane.'

Maybe her mother wouldn't even respond. But she had to try.

Her next stop was the travel agent's. At some point during the drive from the crematorium, she had realised that she had lost too many people. Her father had died. She had argued with her mother. She didn't want to lose Peter. Maybe a holiday would be just the thing to recapture whatever elusive quality had brought them together in the first place. If it didn't work, she would know that she had tried her hardest.

She pulled the brochure out of her handbag and made a fast decision. Kos. The Hotel Agora, and damn the expense. Hurriedly, she filled out the forms for her and Peter, and put the deposit on her credit card. She was going to be paying for this for a long time to come.

● ● ●

The natives are restless tonight, Beck thought as he drove up to the station entrance. He smiled to himself. A crowd of people had gathered round the gates.

In the back of the car, Andy Lang was a sullen, brooding presence. Beck didn't blame him for trying to beat crap out of the lads who had bullied his brother. What else was he going to do?

Beck slowed the car to a halt. He'd have to talk to them. There'd be no getting through them otherwise. They pressed round the car. Their voices babbled questions at him. He spotted a shorthand pad, a cassette recorder. Reporters, he thought.

'If you want my autograph you can form a line, all right?' he said. He grinned to himself again, and drove through the gates.

Beck marched Andy into the station. A faint whiff of bacon from the canteen hung in the air. Get this over with, he thought, then a nice cup of tea . . . they turned the corner and headed towards the custody desk. There was a knot of figures around it – a couple of arresting officers and a pair of lads.

'Tom Rope, 145 Huntley Road, Hulme,' one of the boys said, apparently in answer to an unspoken question.

Andy broke into a flat run.

Shit, Beck thought, and charged after him. Too late. Andy had grabbed one of the boys.

'I want a word with him,' Andy yelled. 'The little bastard.'

Beck was half minded to let him go at it, but he pitched in and hauled him off. Someone swore. Fists flailed. Beck shoved Andy in the chest and forced him towards the door. The two arresting officers pushed the boys back, out of harm's way, and between them they hustled Andy off down the corridor.

'Put him in a cell,' Beck called to them.

113

'Number Three,' the duty officer added, completely unfazed by all the fuss.

The two bullies stood near Beck. He was between them and Andy, who was, in any case, rapidly disappearing down the corridor between the two officers. Little toerags, Beck thought.

One of them – Rope, Beck thought – darted sideways. 'Shithead,' he bellowed down the corridor.

That's it, Beck thought. He turned and faced the lad.

'Yeah,' Rope said, as if Beck was some smaller kid in the playground, or maybe a teacher everyone knew was soft. His whole stance said, 'Want to make something of it?'

Beck didn't bother answering. He grabbed a handful of the kid's shirt, then yanked his arm up behind his back in a text-book come-along. He moved at speed down the corridor. The kid's nose and mouth were crusted with blood, so Beck reckoned Andy must have got at least one good one in. Good for Andy.

'I'm going to put you in a room with Andy,' Beck said. 'Just the two of you.' He knew about bullies. He knew about the fear that drove them on, and he knew how to deal with them.

'I didn't mean it, right,' Rope said. 'I was lying.' His voice had gone high with fear and, just maybe, pain. Good, Beck thought.

One of the arresting officers pushed past on his way from banging Andy up. Beck caught his eye. The man winked.

'You bullied Tim for years,' Beck said. They were almost at Cell Three. 'Now you can show big brother how it's done.'

'I'm scared of him, OK?' Rope said. 'I'm – '

The battered metal door was right in front of them. Beck let go of Rope's shirt, but held on to his arm. He pulled the hatch in the door down and forced Rope up close to it. Andy lunged for Rope as soon as he saw him. He yelled something incoherent. Beck pulled Rope back at the last moment. Andy stuck his hand through the hatch.

Beck slammed Rope against the wall, not too hard. 'Shut up,' he said. 'You're a big bully, aren't you?'

Teach the kid a lesson, that was the thing. Put the fear of God in him. If it could give Andy a little bit of comfort, that was a bonus.

'Yeah,' Rope agreed. No big deal, Beck thought. He'd probably have agreed that up was down if he thought it would make Beck let him go.

'And a coward.' Beck could almost feel Andy looking at him through the hatch, urging him on. Just one good hard slap to make sure the kid remembered the way things were . . .

'Yeah,' he said. His voice was hardly louder than the mewing of a kitten.

Beck let him go. He shoved him in a holding cell and slammed the door. An hour in there would sort the little sniveller out for sure.

He grinned as he went upstairs to see Bilborough. That was the way to deal with jumped-up little so-and-so's like Rope and Mulligan. If someone had been a bit firmer with them, Timothy Lang would have had a better time of it. Might even be alive today. In fact, Beck thought, he might just have saved a life – the life of the next kid Rope and Mulligan would have picked on. Only now they wouldn't dare.

Bilborough was in his office, doing some paperwork. He looked rough. He looked up when Beck went in.

'Boss, did you know there's a crowd of people outside the station?' he asked. He knew what Bilborough was like when the pressure was on. There was no point going the long way round something when the short one would do as well.

'I knew there were some people, yes,' Bilborough said.

'Well, it's a bit more than that – I had to talk my way through them – '

'But you managed?' Bilborough tapped the end of his pen on his notepad.

'Well, yeah. But that's not the point – '

'What do you want me to do, Jimmy? Send the boys in mobhanded wearing riot gear? Gas the lot of them?'

Now that was a bit much, when he was just doing his bit. 'I just thought you ought to know, boss – '

'Yes, well thank you. I'll get a couple of men out there – '

'I'd make it more than that, if you want my opinion.'

'When I do, I'll remember to ask,' Bilborough said. He started to write again.

Jesus God, Beck thought. I know he's tired. I know he's worried. But there are limits. There are definitely limits.

As he started to open the door, Bilborough said, 'Jimmy?' Beck turned. 'You might have a point.' It was the closest Bilborough would get to an apology. Beck knew him well enough to know that. 'But with these community policing initiatives they've been sending round lately . . . I move in too quick we could have a riot on our hands – '

'Yeah.' Beck nodded. It was true, but he still didn't agree with Bilborough. The longer that lot stayed out there, winding themselves up, the more likely something was to set them off. He remembered something Mr Allen once told him, that if you were going to have to make a move in the end, you were probably best off to do it straight away. 'The Chief Super said – '

'Sod the Chief Super,' Bilborough said. He slammed the pen onto the desk. He took a deep breath. 'No, look, forget I said that. Whatever Mr Allen would say, this is my shout, get me? And I say we keep an eye on the situation but we do nothing yet.' He scowled. 'When Fitz and Penhaligon get back, I want to see the three of you, OK?'

'You're the boss,' Beck said. He left the room thinking, Your shout, is it? Your neck, more like.

It was quite amazing how many people wanted to look at furniture in their lunch hours, Penhaligon thought as she walked into Crown-Lee Home Furnishings. She threaded her way between the lounge furniture on one side and dining-room showcase sets on the other. She looked around, but she couldn't see Peter, just several couples examining the three-piece suites and a woman looking at carpets.

Where had Peter said they'd put him this week? She had to think quite hard to remember that he was supposed to be in the children's department. That was bad. Maybe he had a point. Maybe she should take more of an interest in his work.

She found him eventually. He was showing a young couple a range of nursery furniture. The woman was heavily pregnant. Her husband was getting positively lyrical about the benefits of solid pine wall fitments.

Penhaligon kept her distance, but stood where Peter couldn't fail to see her. He looked straight at her for a couple of seconds, then went back to his customers. Fair enough, Penhaligon thought. She sat down on a typist's chair at a desk nearby.

Ten minutes later, she was still waiting. The husband had gone on to discussing wipedown surfaces. Even his wife was beginning to look bored. Penhaligon looked at her watch. God, there was going to be hell to pay. She stood up. Peter glanced in her direction. She tapped her watch. He made a so-what face at her.

She went and stood nearby. Peter ignored her. ' – with an APR of only twenty-three per cent – ' he said to the couple, flourishing some leaflets in front of them.

'At that rate the kid'll be in secondary school before we've paid for the cot,' the woman said.

'It'll last a lifetime, though.' That was the husband. He rubbed his hand appreciatively over the wardrobe door.

'*How* many kids are you wanting?' the woman asked.

'Excuse me – ' Penhaligon said. She was being stupid, she thought. She should tell him at home later on, not now, when he was obviously busy.

Peter glared at her. He made an excuse to his customers, and hustled Penhaligon off to one side. 'What?' he whispered.

117

'I came to say I was sorry about last night,' Penhaligon said. 'I didn't realise how busy this place is.'

'Well, contrary to popular belief, I do actually work for a living. I just don't make a fuss about it '

'Look, I said I'm sorry. Doesn't that mean anything?'

Peter glanced over at his customers. They were talking to one of the other assistants. 'Damn,' he muttered. He started over to them.

Penhaligon made a sour face at his retreating back. Him and his bloody commission. 'Peter – ' she said.

He looked back at her. 'We'll talk about it tonight,' he said.

Penhaligon nodded. They probably would. But she was beginning to regret paying for the holiday already.

Penhaligon slowed her car as she got close to the station. There was quite a crowd of people now. She recognised one or two of them – neighbours, at a guess. Mr and Mrs Lang weren't there. Neither was Andy. That was sensible. Hanging around the station would only upset them.

'What's going on, Constable?' said a voice from out of the crowd; it sounded vaguely familiar. Penhaligon wound her window down. A microphone pushed through it. She glanced to the side. The journalist she had seen hanging round the Langs' house was among the people crowding round the car.

'That's Detective Sergeant to you,' Penhaligon said. 'And no, no comment.'

'How are the boy's family taking it?' It was the same woman.

Bloody ambulance chaser, Penhaligon thought. She pushed the microphone out and rolled the window up, then drove forward slowly. The crowd parted reluctantly in front of her.

Inside, she met Beck just as she was going to put her things in her locker. 'Where have you been?' he demanded. 'The boss wanted to see us all half an hour ago.'

118

Shit, Penhaligon thought. 'Sorry,' she said. 'Be with you in a second.'

'Get a move on,' Beck said. 'I'll get Fitz.'

They waited in Bilborough's office for a good ten minutes before Penhaligon showed up. Beck sipped his tea, but he watched Fitz out of the corner of his eye the whole time. The big man sat making notes, as if nothing unusual had happened. Didn't he realise that it was obvious what was going on? The pair of them, both late back, carefully not showing up together. What Beck really wanted to know was how Fitz managed it: first that classy wife of his, and now Penhaligon. She was far too good for the likes of a fat, arrogant bastard like Fitz. Well, they both were.

Penhaligon arrived eventually. 'Sorry,' she said, almost before she was in the door.

'Good of you to make it,' Bilborough said. Beck grinned.

'Sorry,' Penhaligon repeated. 'I had to – '

'I asked Panhandle to go back to the Langs' and get my dictating machine,' Fitz cut in. 'I left it there. Good job you've got her well trained,' he added, directly to Bilborough.

'I – ' Penhaligon started.

'You can give it to me later, Panhandle,' Fitz said.

I'll bet she can, Beck thought.

'All right, all right,' Bilborough said. 'I just wanted to make sure we're all up to date on what we've got so far. Jimmy?'

'Andy Lang's banged up. So are the pair of little toerags he saw to – '

'OK. Fitz and I will talk to Lang after we're finished here. Get rid of the other two. Jane?'

'Nothing much – only that there's a crowd of people outside the station – '

Bilborough pulled a sour face. 'I've been through this with Jimmy. I'll let you know when I want something doing about it, right?'

'Yes, boss. One more thing, though. This morning at the Langs'? I was listening to Mr Lang talk to Fitz – ' she glanced at him. Something is definitely going on there, Beck thought. 'He said something about Tim being a girl.' She frowned. 'It just seemed an odd thing to say – '

'So the kid was a little queer,' Beck said. They hardly needed Fitz to point that out. 'The lad Andy had a go at told me the same thing – '

'Ahh, I see you're wearing your Mr Enlightened of the Year crown, today,' Fitz said.

'You'd know I suppose – '

'Hold it,' Bilborough said. 'Just hold it the pair of you. Jimmy, I want to hear what Fitz has to say. Fitz?'

'Timothy could have been homosexual. In that case, he might have known his attacker – he might have been meeting him, for example. But he might have been a trans-sexual – '

'Wore his mum's knickers, you mean,' Beck said.

'No, Mr Enlightened, that's precisely what I don't mean.' Fitz paused. He took a sip of coffee. 'Lots of straight men wear women's clothing. They get a kick out of it, but that's all. They don't want to be women, or go to bed with men.' He looked straight at Beck. 'I'm surprised I need to tell you this,' he said.

'Unlike some people, I don't get my kicks out of filth – ' Beck said.

Fitz just smiled.

'So what did Mr Lang mean?' Penhaligon asked, looking at Fitz.

Jesus, Beck thought. Well, it wasn't that surprising she'd want to know. She probably liked it when he talked dirty to her.

'If Tim was transsexual, it means he felt like a girl – '

'Don't we all?' Beck said. He realised Fitz would take that the wrong way, and added hurriedly, 'In the summer. Heat gets the old hormones going – '

120

'Quiet, Jimmy. I want to hear what Fitz has to say,' Bilborough said impatiently.

'He'd want to wear women's clothing – '

'Told you – '

'But not to get a kick out of them – because he felt comfortable in them. He'd want to do things girls did, whatever he felt those were. But none of that means he would necessarily fancy men – '

'Oh, come on,' Beck said. He was suddenly sick and tired of Fitz's dirty little fantasy world.

'Plenty of men undergo gender reassignment – '

'Gender reassignment – ' Jesus, you give it a fancy name and that makes it all right, does it, Beck thought. 'Christ, that is sick,' he said.

' – and end up with female partners.' Fitz lit a cigarette. 'And vice versa, of course. Then again, some of them are *also* gay – but not all of them. So they start out male, with male partners. And end up female, with a male partner.' He gave one of those secret little smiles of his that Beck hated. 'Certainly gives you something to think about, doesn't it?'

'I'll tell you something, Fitz.' You're a condescending bastard, that's what, Beck thought. But he said, 'Some of us don't need to think about it. Some of us know where we stand already.'

'I said that'll do, Jimmy,' Bilborough said.

'Where does all this get us, Fitz?' Penhaligon asked.

'I haven't got enough to go on to tell whether he was transsexual or not – ' Bloody hell, Beck thought. Someone get me a tape-recorder. *Doctor* Fitzgerald finally admitted he doesn't know something. Fitz went on, ' – a family like the Langs – they'd probably think using deodorant made him gay. The men, anyway – '

'You might be able to tell more after we've spoken to Andy?' Bilborough asked. 'If he was gay, we might be in luck. He might have known his killer.'

'Uh-huh,' Fitz said. 'But a boy, thirteen? I'd lay odds he was more confused than anything else.'

He glanced at Beck and smiled again. Now what the bloody hell did he mean by that? Beck wondered.

THIRTEEN

Cassidy read to the class. No-one whispered. No-one poked a neighbour or stared out the window. There was no air in the room.

'I give this heavy weight from off my head. And this unwieldy sceptre from my hand.' His gaze drifted to an empty desk. Timothy's desk. 'The pride of kingly sway from out my heart; With mine own tears I wash away my balm.' He faltered to a stop. His gaze returned to Timothy's desk. 'With mine own hands I give away my crown, With mine own tongue . . .'

He faltered again. Stopped. He put the book down gently on his seat, took his jacket and, without a word, walked out of the classroom.

Later, Cassidy sat in his flat. The noise of a pneumatic drill from the roadworks outside competed with the roar of the traffic.

There was a half empty bottle of whisky on the desk in front of him. He stared at the pile of books next to it. Only one was open. His gaze moved from it to the pen in his hand. He put the Biro down on the open page. He took a long swig from the bottle, and loosened his tie.

The noise from the drill was unbearable. A strangled sobbing noise came from Cassidy's throat. He went to the window and shut it, then went to the gas fire and turned it on without lighting it.

He went into the kitchen, and turned every knob on the

gas cooker full on. The gas jets, unlit, roared. He stared wildly round the room. Another sobbing noise escaped from his throat. He grabbed a towel and dumped it in the sink, then soaked it thoroughly. He wrung it out and wedged it along the bottom of the door. For a moment he sat, slumped on the floor. Then he opened the oven door. He drew his knees up to his chest, and rubbed his hands up and down them. Up and down, up and down. He made a mewling noise, like the sound a distressed child might make.

The roaring of the gas jets died.

After a moment, Cassidy used the cooker to haul himself up. He went to the cupboard and opened it. The gas meter had run out. He felt in his pocket for coins, and found none.

Still whimpering, he left his flat.

FOURTEEN

Beck took Rope and Mulligan out of the cells. They were very quiet as he hustled them into the station yard.

Rope looked up at him sullenly. There was a big blob of dried blood under his nose, and come tomorrow he wasn't going to be able to see much out of his left eye.

The crowd outside the gates was bigger than it had been before. Journalists, some of them. Trouble-makers. Ten of them to each one that had some business being there.

'In the car,' Beck said. What did the kid expect? Sympathy?

He put his hand on the kid's head so he wouldn't bump himself on the door frame – it wouldn't do if he suddenly started claiming the police had done him over – and pushed him into the car.

The crowd surged forward as the car moved off, but they were careful not to cross the line into the station.

Mulligan and Rope gave Beck the finger through the back window, now they were safe from him. Little shites, he thought. He'd no doubt they'd see that pair again, after they left school if not before.

He watched a while longer, to make sure the crowd let the car through. He'd have to tell the boss about that. Surely now he'd want something done?

But when Beck went inside, he found that Bilborough was interviewing Andy, and had left strict instructions he didn't want to be interrupted unless there was an emergency. Well, Beck thought, it wasn't that yet. And he was hardly going to go over the boss's head by involving the brass –

125

not when he himself had said it was his job to decide how they played it.

Beck went and got himself a coffee. He sipped it, counting his blessings that he wasn't a uniform and didn't have to go out and face the crowd.

The interview room was hardly the most inviting place to try and talk: white tiled walls reflecting harsh fluorescent lighting, chipped Formica on the table and stained linoleum on the floor.

Fitz wanted a cigarette. He played with his Biro instead. He kept forgetting it wasn't a cigarette, and every so often his hand strayed towards the lighter that lay nearby on the table.

Bilborough lounged against the wall. Though he seemed relaxed, Fitz knew that he was strung out. There was still something there that Fitz didn't quite understand, but it would have to wait. He'd be content if Bilborough helped get the truth out of Andy.

The lad sat well back in his chair, arms by his sides. The books, Fitz thought, would tell you his posture was open, inviting friendly overtures. Well, sod the books. The lad radiated hostility, and the only thing he was inviting was a fight: come on, take me on, if you can.

Well, his father had wanted a boy's boy, all right, and he'd got it. Only they'd never been close.

What had Mr Lang said? 'Anything I wanted, Andy'd do the opposite.' When his parents split up, Andy had stepped into his father's shoes. He'd have done that whether he was asked to or not, but Fitz could almost hear Mr Lang's flat, matter-of-fact voice: 'Take care of your mother the way I would. You're the man of the family now.'

And what pressure had that put on Andy? Not just looking after the mother, but Tim, too. Tim who his teacher said was effeminate, his father, in that telling phrase, 'a girl'. Fitz wondered if that were true, or whether it had been

126

imposed on him from outside – those wide blue eyes, that corn-silk hair. Put those looks together with a quiet, bookish nature and you might very well come up with something that would quickly be branded effeminate – or, the word his father had avoided, homosexual – even if the lad had a different girlfriend every week.

But at the moment that didn't really matter. What mattered was the accusation's effect on Andy. He was a big, good-looking lad. Bright, too, though, as Fitz had suspected, he'd done badly at school. Andy Lang? Trouble, the teachers had said. Not big trouble, not call the police trouble. But if there had been a fight, Andy would be hanging round the edge of it. Smoking in the bogs. Wagging lessons. All, Fitz would have laid odds, to distance himself from his bookish, so-called effeminate little brother. Anything to make himself look big, look tough, keep him in with the ruling clique. He wondered idly how old Andy had been when he lost his virginity. Ten to one he'd started saying he'd done it years before the actual event.

He had a sullen, trapped look about him now. Fitz wasn't at all sure there was anything to be gained from talking to him. But Bilborough wanted it done, and God only knew, Bilborough paid the bills. His thoughts skittered wilfully to Judith, to that letter from the bank and the row it had caused.

'Why did you go for those two boys?' he asked, to concentrate his mind. It was a forthright, almost innocent, question. Andy ought to go for that; he seemed to set a great deal of store by straightforwardness. A reaction, Fitz thought, to the kind of dishonesty that went on when a couple start to split up. Again, his mind skittered towards home, this time to his son, Mark, and his loudmouthed hurtful comments. If Mark were telling the truth, he despised Fitz, hated him even. Fitz told himself he didn't believe it, but the comments hurt none the less. Concentrate, he told himself. Andy. That's the thing.

Andy jerked his head towards Bilborough. 'Look, I've already told him why,' he said. If he noticed that Fitz was distracted, he didn't let on.

'Tell me,' Fitz said. He was bored, that was the trouble. God. Timothy Lang lay dead on a mortuary slab, and he, *Doctor* Fitzgerald, had the gall to be bored.

So do something about it.

'They used to pick on him,' Andy said. Flat statement, voice matter of fact, body language relaxed: it was probably the truth, Fitz thought; but it didn't get them very far; he could have guessed as much. Time to push, just a little bit. He tapped the pen on the table. This was better. There might be a chase here. 'Tim asked for help, didn't he Andy?' Fitz noted the slightest tightening of the mouth, a slight tensing of the shoulders. Nothing gross, no refusal to meet his gaze. The lad was bright. 'You didn't give him any.' Andy licked his lips. 'Now he's dead, you feel guilty.' That hurt. He stared up at the ceiling.

Andy knew about guilt, Fitz thought. Otherwise, he wouldn't have been able to meet Fitz's gaze even for a short while. So why would he feel guilty? The parents. It had to come back to the parents. Taking the mother's side. Refusing dad, maybe at first out of a genuine lack of interest, but later as a means of showing where his loyalties lay.

'Look, it was happening in school – ' his head came up. He glared at Fitz, challenging. He wasn't beaten yet. 'The teachers there. They should have done something about it, you know what I mean.'

'And they didn't,' Fitz said.

'No.'

Andy felt guilt all right. Fitz was sure of it. He hadn't been exaggerating when he told Mrs Lang all parents felt guilt when a child died, especially if murder was involved. It wasn't different for siblings. But Andy was hiding something, some special, secret cause for regret. Did you

128

kill him? Fitz wondered: some brotherly quarrel turned especially nasty, out there in the woods? But he dismissed it immediately. Andy wouldn't have fought Tim. He would have considered it beneath him, something you just didn't do – like fighting a sister.

'You're lying,' Fitz said, after a moment. A few pauses in the conversation wouldn't hurt. They'd give Andy time to squirm.

'Look,' Andy said. He was suddenly furious. He leaned across the table. His lips peeled back into something that was very nearly a snarl. 'Cassidy "had a word". Gobshites like that don't understand "a word".' Andy glared at Fitz, then at Bilborough. Finally, he slumped back into his seat.

Cassidy, Fitz thought. Interesting. Why him? Why not Tim's form teacher, or head of year? Out of the corner of his eye he saw Bilborough's face tighten almost imperceptibly. Whatever was working on the man, he wasn't letting it get between him and the job at this moment. But Bilborough could wait. So could Cassidy. For the moment Fitz was more interested in Andy's reaction. He'd relied on the teachers to do something he couldn't do himself. No, Fitz thought. Not couldn't. Wouldn't. The question was, why not.

'Why didn't you do something?' he asked. His voice was intense. He allowed himself to move just a little towards Andy. The lad might not know how to interpret the action consciously, but his subconscious would recognise it, and it would make him uneasy: Andy was used to being a dominant male, toughest guy around. Now there was a much bigger, much more dominant male, and one that had just acted aggressively. Andy wasn't used to that, not with his father missing from home. Discomfort was the only possible reaction.

Fitz was rewarded by the sight of Andy shifting slightly in his seat. Time to up the ante. See you and raise you, he thought. He raised an eyebrow at Andy.

129

'I've already told you . . . it was happening in school.' He glanced wildly at Bilborough. 'The teachers there should've sorted it out – '

'Bzz,' Fitz said. He wanted to keep Andy off guard. The lie detector impersonation usually did the trick. 'Lie,' he said in case Andy didn't get it.

'Look, it's their – '

'Bzz – '

' – fault. They should – '

' – lie – '

' – it out. It's not my responsibility.' He was really upset now, Fitz thought.

'Bzz. Lie. Bzz. Lie,' he said, just in case Andy was in any doubt about what he thought.

'Piss off!' Andy shouted. He looked at Bilborough for sympathy. He ran his hand through his short mousy hair. It wasn't warm in the room, but a bead of sweat clung to his upper lip.

The door clicked. Out of the corner of his eye, Fitz saw Bilborough look round, but he kept staring straight at Andy. He wasn't letting the lad off the hook now.

It wasn't that they were going to find out much that would help with the investigation, not unless Andy knew more about Tim's friends than Fitz thought he did. Even then, they might not be relevant. No, Fitz had to get Andy to admit the way he'd let Tim down because otherwise the guilt would fester like an unlanced boil for years. He'd meant it when he told Tim's parents that guilt soon went: it did, if there was nothing real to feel guilty about. But that wasn't the case here. He could feel the weight of Andy's culpability the way a boil would drag at his skin, building up, building up . . . lance it now and it would be painful and messy. Let it go and the poison would enter the bloodstream, tainting everything Andy did, every relationship he ever had. In the end, of course, he'd seek help – probably with some half-arsed, semi-qualified psycho-babbling jargon-infested idiot like Graham.

Fitz didn't like Andy over much – he was too much the macho bullshitter for Fitz's taste – but he wasn't about to let that happen to him.

He noticed that Bilborough had left the room.

'I've just left your mother.' He couldn't keep the anger out of his voice. Andy grinned. Not amusement. Embarrassment, maybe. A challenge for certain. 'If you'd helped Tim, you might have saved her some of this pain.'

Andy's grin widened, but his knuckles went white as he clenched his fists. He might blow ... pay or play, Fitz thought. He was almost shouting now. He'd sat with the Langs all morning, and suddenly he didn't give a damn about Andy and his future guilt, but only about Mrs Lang and the terrible weight of grief she was having to bear. 'Don't say you don't feel guilty about that, Andy.' Andy looked ready to punch the living daylights out of something. Or possibly to cry. 'Your mother breaking her heart. All that grief.'

'I've got mates. They took the piss out of Tim all the time.' His voice was raw with fury. 'He was a little faggot,' Andy said. *Was*, Fitz thought. Not *Is*. No confusion of tenses there, Fitz thought. No trying to keep Tim alive in his mind.

'You're saying I should've stood up for Tim against my own mates?'

Yeah, Fitz thought. Like you should have stuck up for your dad when your mother started putting him down. His own thoughts added the phony American accent: *and Doctor Fitzgerald, why is it so important to help this boy you hardly know?* And without the accent: *Because, Fitz, I can't get close to my own son any more. Surrogate fatherhood's the best I can do.* He heard Bilborough come back into the room. Something clicked. Bilborough. Fatherhood. Guilt. He tagged the association and left it alone for later.

'Well, that's bollocks – all right?' Andy said. He was

131

•

spoiling for a fight. Bilborough jerked his head towards the door. Fitz frowned and stood up. He wanted to smile at Andy – to let him know that he was on his side, however it looked. But he didn't. If he was going to help the lad, he couldn't let him off the hook yet.

Bilborough sat down. As Fitz headed towards the door, he heard Andy say, 'Yeah.' He was aggressive, all psyched up with his opponent of choice disappearing from sight.

'Tell me all you know about Mr Cassidy,' Bilborough said.

By the time they let Andy out, he'd started to believe he'd be drawing pension before he saw daylight again. But once Bilborough started asking about Cassidy, things got a lot easier. For one thing, Fitz wasn't there, stirring it up every time he said anything. And for another thing, Cassidy was such a wanker that Andy had no problem telling Bilborough exactly what he was like.

After that, Bilborough had made some poxy speech about how you couldn't take the law into your own hands, and how if he ever did anything this stupid again, there'd be Big Trouble.

At the end of it, he stood opposite Andy, leaning on the back of a chair. 'But,' he said, 'taking everything into consideration, if you are prepared to promise that nothing like this will happen again, I'm prepared to caution you – '

'You mean I can go?' Andy sprawled back in his chair. No point letting the bastard know he'd been worried.

'You'll have to sign the caution – ' Andy nodded. He'd have signed anything short of his own death warrant if it meant they'd let him out. 'All right, then,' Bilborough said. 'Andrew Lang, I am formally cautioning you . . .'

Andy tuned his voice out. It was just more of the same, anyway. They stuck a piece of paper in front of him, and he signed it. Then they gave him his stuff back, and he was allowed to go.

132

Melanie was waiting for him in the reception area. He hadn't expected that. She stood up when she saw him. He tried to smile, but couldn't quite manage it. Then he realised that Bilborough was watching him from the corridor, and forced himself.

'Hi,' Melanie said. She sounded shy.

Jesus, he thought. The last time she saw me I was nine-tenths rat-arsed and I wasn't exactly nice to her. She put her arm round him. He realised that he was almost crying. But only almost. He palmed at his eyes. 'Mike tell you what happened?'

'Yeah,' she said.

'Might have guessed.' He laughed, though there was nothing very much funny going on. 'He always did have a big mouth.'

'Yeah,' she said again. 'Come on. There's a whole bunch of us, outside. Waiting to find out what's going on.'

There were quite a lot of people outside the gates. Before they got to them, Andy said, 'About last night – '

'Don't worry about it,' Melanie said. She squeezed his hand.

Somehow, they never did talk about it again. They joined the crowd. Mike was there.

'Hey,' he yelled. 'Who's a ruddy little hero then?' He slapped Andy on the back, and Andy shoved him back. After that, he was trying to answer fifteen questions at once. Some of them were from journalists, some from neighbours, and some from people he didn't know at all.

When the fuss had died down, he realised he hadn't thought about Tim since Fitz left the interview room.

133

FIFTEEN

Fitz always felt uncomfortable in Panhandle's car, as if it were too small to hold him. The handbrake bit into his thigh, and he was sure that at speed – for instance, at the crazy speed Panhandle was making now – one day the passenger door would fly open and he would go crashing out onto the road. Damned cheap modern cars. Give him a good old Morris Minor any day.

Balls.

That wasn't it. It was having her close to him, so close he could almost feel the heat of her body, imagine that the handbrake digging into him were her hand, locked in some moment of pleasure. He glanced at her. The morning rain had given way to watery sunshine, and it turned her hair copper. Her perfume was sharp, citrus. He wanted her, dammit.

Go on, he thought to himself. Say it, Fitz. Say, Panhandle, will you let me screw you into the ground one of these days?

It would be a pure motive, all right. Pure lust, nothing more.

Not that he couldn't love her. There was always that possibility, in the future. But he couldn't love her and Judith at the same time, and he was by no means done with Judith. Not yet. Probably not ever.

So asking Panhandle to go to bed with him would be pure: no love offered, neither implied nor explicit. Except . . .

Except that it would be no such thing. He'd be doing it to

get even with Judith. You've slept around, I've slept around. Now do you see how it feels? Do you feel how the knife turns every time some stray memory makes you flash on the thought of me in bed with her? Do you feel that moment of anxiety when you realise she's younger than you, maybe got nicer tits, better legs? That nagging, gnawing, urgent question – is she better than me? Did you do it just the once or did you fuck all night long till you couldn't move for weariness and only your fingers moving through the tiny copper hairs on her arm let her know you were still awake . . .

Oh no, Fitz, he said to himself. Not a pure motive at all, and if you had any sense, you'd make sure you were never alone in a car with Panhandle. Not in a car. Not in a room.

He looked out the window at the playing fields and the buildings beyond. Within moments they gave way to a housing estate. She was going too fast, too fast for him. He realised he'd moved as far over toward the door as he could get.

Damn Cassidy, he thought. If the man wanted to kill himself he should have had the decency to –

'This morning, with Mr and Mrs Lang?' Panhandle said, breaking his train of thought. She shifted a sweet round in her mouth. Oral, Panhandle, Fitz thought. Very, very oral.

'Yeah.' He couldn't bring himself to look at her.

'I thought you were brilliant.'

Oh no, Fitz thought. He stared through the windscreen at the white line unrolling in front of them. Not compliments. Not now.

He had to say something. 'You should hear my pillow talk,' he said.

They got closer to the city centre. Office buildings and shopping complexes squeezed in on them. Panhandle turned a corner. A fire engine and a couple of marked police cars huddled at the base of the Arndale Centre. Uniformed officers kept the public back – the desire to conquer death,

Fitz thought: stare it in the face then walk away, as if practising so that in that final moment when you stare down into the abyss, rather than falling you'll dance lightly along the edge, leave death cursing behind you and walk back to your warm, safe life. But you won't. You'll go down into it, like all the billions before you, and no amount of ogling road kills and pissing on forest fires will make one whit of difference.

He got out of the car and tilted his head back, back, further back till he was dizzy with the effort of trying to see the top of the building. There *he* was. Not much more than a speck, legs dangling over the parapet of the building.

Bloody Cassidy.

'Are you all right?' Penhaligon asked.

'No.' Fitz couldn't look away from Cassidy. 'I'm afraid of heights.' Reluctantly, he looked down. He leaned on the car roof and said to Panhandle. 'That's a lie. Nobody's afraid of heights. They're really afraid of themselves, what they might do.'

Panhandle smiled. God, it was good to be so open with someone. He thought of her, in the car, the warm sharp smell of her. The noon light turned her hair almost orange. She squinted into the sun. Her eyes were cool blue, but there was nothing cool about her expression.

Don't say it, Fitz thought. Don't say a word, because if you do you're walking on the edge of the abyss and it isn't death you'll be staring down: it'll be losing Judith, losing everything that makes it all worth anything.

But somehow his mouth was opening and the words were spilling out, and they weren't anything he wanted to hear. 'Listen, if I do survive this will you let me take you out, get you pissed and make a pathetic attempt to seduce you?' It was OK. She'd think it was a joke for sure.

Wrong again, Fitz thought. She didn't speak. She didn't need to. The look on her face said it all.

• • •

136

The Centre was taller than any building had a right to be, but that was OK. Fitz was fine as long as they were going down the escalator to the lower ground floor and then up in the lifts that went straight through the shopping centre and the office levels to the roof. He was fine as long as he had concrete around him, concrete and metal and no treacherous slippery ledges, or dizzying drops as sheer as a cliff face.

The lift journey took too long. Fitz refused to think of the number of storeys, or to allow his brain to work out the number of feet . . . say fifteen feet per, plus maybe two for the ceiling voids. Seventeen, then, times maybe twenty? And then there was the shopping centre underneath. God. Four hundred feet, give or take a yard. From outside it had looked more like half a mile.

And then, far too soon, the journey was over and the caretaker, a young guy in surprisingly smart green coveralls, was leading them up through the access door, and he was outside. Four hundred feet, Fitz thought. A ridiculous height for a building.

He stepped outside. The world was suddenly bigger than it ought to be, as big as it would be if you stood on the wheatfields of mid-America, with nothing at all between you and the horizon. Fitz's mouth went dry. His heart hammered.

Good old fight or flight reflex, he thought. Well, there was nothing to fight up here, and up here flight wasn't something he wanted to contemplate.

It's OK, he thought. There's fifty feet of concrete between me and the edge, and even then there's a parapet. Unfortunately, that was where Cassidy was. Fitz glanced at Panhandle. She smiled back at him encouragingly.

He started to walk forward, as tentatively as if there were a chance that at each step the floor might fall away beneath his questing foot.

He forced himself to concentrate on Cassidy. He was sure the man was doing this because of Tim, but that only pushed the question 'Why?' one stage further back.

Maybe he'd killed the lad and now he felt guilty. That was the easy answer, the one Bilborough would latch on to. But maybe it wasn't correct. maybe Tim's death had simply forced Cassidy to reassess what was happening in his life – to stare into his personal darkness – and maybe he hadn't liked the answer he saw there.

Finding the answer was a secondary objective. The first thing Fitz had to do was to get Cassidy down – preferably without killing himself along the way.

He got to the parapet. It was maybe a yard wide and came up almost to his crotch. You can't fall, he told himself. You'd have to get up on it and jump. Cassidy had got on to it, and now he sat there, legs dangling into space. He didn't react to Fitz's arrival.

Fitz said nothing. He needed a moment to gather his wits and his courage, and to quell the queasy feeling in his stomach. How many times had he said he liked to live life staring into the abyss? How many times had he derided others for not daring to do the same?

He stood very straight, and looked down without moving his head. He couldn't see much, just a section of sky and the top of the building opposite. He forced himself to lean forward. There. Just a little further.

All the clichés were true. The world turning, the people crawling round like ants, the cars like toys. The urge to jump swept over him. To fly, for an instant, free of the heavy weight of being Fitz. He thought, I'll count to a thousand, then I'll do it.

By the time he got to fifteen, he remembered a conversation he'd once had with a pathologist. The woman had told him that if you're going to jump, you should dive headfirst. That way, you die on impact if not before. Feet first, your thighbones get driven up into your rib case and beyond. Messy, especially if you happened to be awake at the time.

'Stay away from me,' Cassidy said.

138

'I will,' Fitz said. This was as close as he intended to get to heroics. He'd broken his own rule when he'd tried to talk Sean, the kid who had murdered Giggs, out of blowing himself to kingdom come. It had been too damned close, and it had confirmed all Fitz's opinions about what heroes did. They died, that's what heroes did.

'If you come near me, I shall jump, and I'd much rather jump in my own time, so please don't come near me,' Cassidy said, staring straight ahead. His voice lacked all emotion, but Fitz didn't think he meant it. The longer they sit, the longer they have to worry about how much it'll hurt. If they really mean it, they do it in the first few seconds. Or they hang themselves. That was Fitz's theory, though he'd seen no research to back it up.

'OK,' Fitz said.

How many times had he prided himself on staring into the face of the abyss? How many times had he said he wasn't like the little people, with their little lives, running scared from their mortgages and their mediocre hopes and their fears of ageing and dying? He wasn't like that. He lived life large, and if he sometimes alienated people because he made them aware of their smallness, that was part of the gamble.

Only when Judith had left, he'd realised what staring into the abyss meant. He'd known fear and failure and he'd known why he lived the way he did. Because those other things weren't real risks. He gambled, but he chose the stake and the odds. He drank, but he knew how to deal with the hangover. He upset people, but never the people that really mattered.

Until Judith had said she'd had enough. The worst part was acknowledging he was out of control. She'd asked him to promise he would stop. He'd refused, not to hurt her or even to provoke a reaction, but because he knew he couldn't keep the promise and he wouldn't lie to her.

He stared down. The world swung beneath him. The urge to jump came over him again. It wasn't a suicidal impulse.

He didn't want to die. He just wanted to feel the air buoying him up, the wind on his face.

It would be, he thought, a moment of grace in a disgraceful life. But that didn't mean he had to do it. If he could control that impulse while looking straight into the depths of the abyss, maybe he could control the drinking and the gambling. Maybe he could win Judith back for real.

Besides, he was supposed to talk Cassidy down, and he could hardly do it from a point three feet behind the man's right shoulder.

Carefully, having great regard for his bulk and the slipperiness of the still damp roof, Fitz lowered himself on to the parapet. He lay full length across it and stared straight down at the pavement.

He could just make out some of the upturned faces of the people below. Fall from this height, you wouldn't just land messily, you'd splash.

'Forty or fifty feet's enough, you know,' he said by way of opening the conversation. 'Why so high?' But he knew why. If you were a man like Cassidy, you'd lived a quiet fearful little life – from school to college and back to school again – so if you decided to end it of course you'd grab the last chance you'd ever get to feel that adrenalin rush. You'd craved it, and feared it, and now there was no point running from it any more. At worst it would kill you. 'Too much time to think,' he went on. No reaction from Cassidy. Maybe he thought he'd done all his thinking. What was the worst thing that could happen? What would shock Cassidy into realising what he was doing? 'You might change your mind on the way down.' He allowed amusement to colour his voice.

Still no reaction. So. There was still the Timothy Lang card to play, but for it to be effective he needed to get Cassidy off guard. He allowed himself to free associate for a moment. 'Lemmings,' he said. 'We laugh at lemmings, you know, for throwing themselves off cliffs – ' He allowed

140

himself the luxury of looking up. He couldn't – he just couldn't – look at that vast drop and think of something leaping into mid-air. Not and stay sane. ' – but I have a suspicion that the lemmings will have the last laugh, because one day – what's your first name, by the way?'

Cassidy didn't answer.

Fitz looked at him. The man hadn't moved. How the hell he could sit staring a hundred feet straight down and listen to chatter about lemmings was beyond Fitz, but he was doing it just the same.

'Nigel,' Cassidy said at last.

'Nigel.' There must be worse fates but Fitz couldn't imagine one. 'God, I'd be suicidal.' Cassidy stared straight ahead. 'One day, Nigel, a lemming will fly.' Out of the corner of his eye Fitz saw Cassidy look down. He'd be thinking of what – the lemming, the flying, the smash landing? Or a boy's face contorted in agony, and then his legs swinging slowly in the air? 'Tim Lang didn't kill himself, by the way. He was murdered,' Fitz said, very quickly.

Cassidy turned and stared at him. Ah, Fitz thought. That got to him. In that instant, his understanding of the case crystallised: Cassidy had done it. The only question that remained was whether it had been deliberate or an accident.

'Pigeons did it, you know,' Fitz went on. Keep him off balance. 'Millions of pigeons over thousands and thousands of years, thudding dead to the ground.' For once Fitz didn't stop to analyse, though there was a part of his mind that logged the fact that Cassidy had scrambled back onto the parapet, the agonised, flinching expression on his face, and the almost imperceptible tic under his right eye, with remorseless precision. Later. Later.

For now Fitz went on, 'And then, one day a pigeon flapped and didn't hit the ground quite so hard. And the day after that, one of them flew as it followed its instincts.' Cassidy was staring at Fitz the way he'd look at a madman.

141

But his gaze still kept drifting to the edge of the parapet and beyond, as if he thought he might find salvation there. Or absolution.

Fitz considered for a second. Time to convince Cassidy he was wrong. Only one way to do it: up the ante, put everything he'd got into the kitty. Time to fold or show your cards, Cassidy. He didn't think Cassidy could see him, let alone raise the stakes.

'Come on,' he said. He clambered to his feet. 'Let's do it. Let's follow our instincts. Let's fly.' He meant it. For one, glorious, insane second he actually meant it. He felt his toes hanging over the lip of the parapet and he didn't care. 'Let's fly to the top of the world, ma,' he bellowed to the world at large. He heard Cassidy scramble to his feet. 'Come with me,' he said.

Cassidy grabbed him. 'For Christ's sake,' the teacher shouted. For a split instant Fitz pulled against him, so that Cassidy had to haul him back. 'For Christ's sake.'

Then suddenly it was Fitz turning, Fitz shielding Cassidy from the drop, because the man was shaking, staring down into the street and almost crying.

After a minute, he broke away. Fitz watched him for a second. He went over to a corner and threw up noisily.

Fitz stared down at the street, at all the little people wandering around down there. He made a fakey, American-style salute, and then he walked away.

SIXTEEN

Penhaligon watched Fitz cross the roof. There had been a moment when she had thought he'd do it for real. Another when she thought he would slip. She thrust her hands deep into her jacket pockets. Idiot, she thought, and wasn't sure if she meant Fitz for the way he behaved, or herself for worrying about it.

Cassidy lagged behind. Bilborough would want him brought in for sure after this. She didn't think Cassidy was stupid enough to do a runner. All those people in the shopping centre, though . . . it would be very tempting. She pulled her radio out of her pocket and asked for a uniformed escort out of the building.

Fitz got to her well ahead of Cassidy.

'What did you think you were playing at?' she asked. 'You could have been killed.'

'Didn't happen that way in the movie,' he said. She frowned. 'Butch Cassidy and the Sundance Kid. When they jump off the cliff. Though I have to say Nige Cassidy and Doctor Fitz doesn't have quite the same ring.'

Penhaligon poked him in the chest. 'Yes, well he isn't Paul Newman and you certainly aren't Robert Redford,' she said.

'Really?' Fitz said, all wide-eyed innocence. 'I must remember to tell my hordes of female admirers that.'

Cassidy arrived. Next to Fitz he seemed dull and mousy, and smaller yet because he was hunched over as if he were walking through driving rain. He looked as if he wanted to say something, but for a long moment he didn't speak.

143

Eventually he said, 'I . . . I just wanted to say thank you.' He wouldn't look straight at Fitz.

'No problem,' Fitz said. 'Cats rescued from trees, little old ladies helped across roads – ' he paused. 'Criminals caught.' He dropped into a dramatic, phoney American accent. 'This must be a job for . . . SuperFitz!'

'Come on,' Penhaligon said. She turned and went inside.

The lift was quite small. Cassidy's breath reeked of alcohol. Penhaligon hated it. She tried to edge away from him, but there wasn't the room. Funny how, with all Fitz's drinking, she'd never noticed it smelling. But then, with Fitz it would have been different.

She was intensely aware of Fitz's gaze on her, of the way he studiously looked away every time they came close to making eye contact. If Cassidy had noticed – God, how could he not notice? – he showed no sign of it.

No-one said a word until the lift reached the lower ground floor. They came out into the stylish, marble-walled lobby. Penhaligon kept close to Cassidy, her shoulder almost touching his. No point in taking chances. Fitz walked just a little way behind, where Cassidy could hear him easily but not see him. It would make the man uneasy. Penhaligon wondered if Fitz chose that position deliberately, or if unsettling people just came naturally to him. She suspected the latter.

The glare and bustle of the shopping centre lay ahead of them. There were two constables waiting nearby, not quite lounging against the wall. They put their helmets on and fell in behind Penhaligon's little group, then walked two or three paces behind.

'You asked about his mother,' Fitz said.

Penhaligon picked it up. ' "How's his mother handling it", you said.'

'Yes,' Cassidy said. If he still felt any gratitude towards Fitz, his tone didn't reveal it.

144

'His mother. Not his parents,' Fitz said.

They came out into the shopping mall. The bright lights of the store fronts beckoned: fast food, fashions, furniture. People hurried past, mothers with children, single men, elderly women. One or two stopped and stared at them openly. More glanced as they went by, then looked away hurriedly. It was the presence of the uniformed officers that did it of course. Without them, there would be nothing to mark their little group out as special.

'Well, his parents have split up.' Cassidy sounded almost impatient, as if he were telling them something obvious. Maybe it was obvious to him, or maybe he just wanted them to think it was.

'How did you know that?' Fitz asked.

He and Penhaligon stepped onto the escalator at exactly the same time.

'Well, I taught him.' Cassidy was very matter of fact about it, as if he were used to answering questions like this. It took Penhaligon a second to work it out. Then she realised he sounded as if he were making a report in a social workers' case conference. That wasn't so unlikely, not in a big secondary school like Sydney Road.

Fitz followed them onto the escalator. 'Yeah, well, you taught hundreds of kids. Do you know all their family backgrounds that well?'

The escalator swept them upwards. Penhaligon looked over the handrail at the crowds of people below. For the moment she was content to let Fitz do the talking. Cassidy might talk more if he thought he was just having a chat with him.

'No,' Cassidy said. He suddenly seemed ill at ease. He rubbed the back of his neck with his hand, and tried to turn away from Fitz, but he was blocked in by the side of the escalator.

'But you know Tim's?' Fitz shot back.

'Yeah.'

145

Penhaligon had a dozen questions she wanted to ask, but she made herself wait. There would be time later, and at the moment Fitz seemed to have something on his mind.

'So you knew Tim particularly well.' Fitz didn't make a question of it.

'Yeah.' Cassidy was definitely on the defensive.

'Yeah? Then why did you lie to me?' Fitz asked. Penhaligon turned to look at Cassidy. To hell with subtlety. She wanted to see his reaction. He turned away from Fitz. Couldn't look him in the eye. 'I found a copy of Wilfred Owen in Tim's room,' Fitz went on, enunciating each word with exaggerated care. 'Did you give that to him?'

'I might've done.' He was definitely shifty about it. Later, Penhaligon realised that was the moment she decided he was definitely guilty.

'Oh come on,' Fitz said impatiently. 'You give a book of poetry to a thirteen-year-old boy, that's intimate.' He smiled. Penhaligon knew that smile. It meant he was at his most lethal. They came to the top of the escalator. She stepped off. So did Cassidy. Fitz followed, still talking. 'You would remember that.'

Cassidy came to an abrupt halt outside a health food shop. Penhaligon stopped at one side of him. Fitz came round the other, so he was boxed in. 'Look,' he said, 'I did a stupid thing. I'm sorry.' Penhaligon stared at him. 'I'm a bit depressed, and a bit drunk.' He looked from her to Fitz and back again, almost challenging. But only almost. 'If you're going to charge me with something, charge me. But I'm not going to answer any more questions about Tim.'

'What shall we charge you with?' Penhaligon asked. It was time she took more of a lead, she decided.

It was noisier up here. Somewhere, a bunch of little kids were having a good time, judging by the way they were shouting.

Cassidy started to move off, though not as if he were trying to get away. Penhaligon and Fitz moved with him, still close in. The uniformed officers followed.

'I don't know,' Cassidy said. 'Anything. Trespass. Wasting police time. I don't know.' His voice trailed off into the general noise of the shopping centre. He sounded almost desperate, as if he wanted to be arrested. To stop himself doing it again? Penhaligon wondered. It wouldn't be the first time a murderer had had that much insight.

Cassidy moved a little way ahead of them. Penhaligon allowed it. There was no way he could get away, and he might loosen up a bit if they eased off.

'Murder?' Fitz asked.

Cassidy slowed and looked round sharply at him. That got you, Penhaligon thought. The harsh electric lighting made his skin look pale and accentuated the deep shadows under his eyes.

'You like to keep fit,' Penhaligon said. He didn't look fit.

'Yeah.'

Penhaligon thought of him laying in to the punchbag in the school gym. How many punches like that to kill a thirteen-year-old? But he hadn't pummelled Tim to death. He'd strangled him. If it was him, she told herself firmly. He might yet be innocent. 'Burn off all that anger – stops you taking it out on the kids,' she said, quoting back what he'd said in the gym.

'I was joking,' Cassidy said. His defences were well up now.

Penhaligon switched the subject. 'Do you jog?' she asked as if she were making dinner-party conversation.

'Yes.' He was obviously irritated.

'Were you jogging three nights ago?' Penhaligon asked. Cassidy muttered something, as if he were buying time while he worked out his answer. Here we go, Penhaligon thought. 'Were you jogging three nights ago?' she asked quickly. The trick was to force an unconsidered response.

She was suddenly aware of Fitz. Though he seemed more interested in the shops they were passing, she knew he'd be noting every word, and storing it up for later use. Or misuse. She wondered what he'd think of her questioning technique.

'No.' The reply was equally sharp.

'Where were you?' Penhaligon asked.

'At home.'

'Alone?' she asked. Her voice went unintentionally coquettish. She glanced sideways at Fitz. He didn't seem to have noticed.

'My girlfriend. She was with me.' He sounded uncertain. He looked back at Penhaligon.

Convenient, she thought.

'Do you believe him?' Fitz asked, proving he'd been listening.

'No,' Penhaligon said. She enjoyed doing a double act with Fitz like this. They were good together, and they both knew it.

'She thinks you killed Tim.'

'I didn't.' Cassidy sounded determined, as if he could make them believe him by sheer force of will.

'I asked you if you lived alone,' Fitz said. 'Do you remember that?'

'Yeah.'

'But I'm thinking of getting married.' Penhaligon picked up the question. It was time to put a bit of pressure on.

'It's true. I am thinking of getting married.' Cassidy sounded affronted. Maybe he thought they were going to accuse him of lying to them. Penhaligon had no idea what Fitz had in mind, but she was prepared to run with it, sight unseen.

'Yes, but why articulate it, hmm?' Fitz asked. He flapped his hand around extravagantly. 'A simple yes or no would have been enough unless you think something's implied by living alone.'

'Such as?' Cassidy asked.

'You said, "I was at home with my girlfriend." Not, I was

148

at home with Jo or Lesley or Sammy.' Fitz was about to pull off one of those feats of deduction that Penhaligon never quite understood. She had to stop herself grinning. It was ridiculous. She almost felt proud of him, for God's sake. Sure enough, Fitz went on, 'You said, "I was at home with my girlfriend." What's your girlfriend's name by the way?'

Cassidy stared at a shop window, at the floor. Anywhere but at Fitz or Penhaligon. 'Lesley,' he said at last.

'Lesley,' Fitz said, with the air of a conjuror pulling a rabbit from a hat. 'How did I guess?'

'I've no idea,' Cassidy replied, managing to sound like a member of the audience who was determined not to be impressed by the trick.

'You wouldn't say, "I was at home with Lesley", because,' Fitz paused dramatically, 'Lesley could be a man and that's the very last thing you'd want anyone to think.'

Cassidy said, 'You think I'm gay.' He sounded offended by the very notion.

Penhaligon spotted Beck coming up behind them. She hoped Fitz got this over with quickly. She knew what Beck thought of queers – they were never gays or homosexuals to Beck, always queers – and it wasn't nice.

'No!' Fitz said. 'You think you're gay.' He spotted Beck. 'Ahh, Super-sleuth,' he said, by way of introducing him to Cassidy. 'Do you know this man can fill in the *Sun* crossword in under three days?' The uniformed officers behind Beck turned away, though whether they were embarrassed or just bored, Penhaligon couldn't tell.

For a minute Beck looked as though he might try and make something out of it. He took a deep, audible breath and stared at the floor. Then he seemed to think better of it, and said to Cassidy, 'I'd like you to accompany me to the station, please.'

Not this time, Penhaligon thought. He'd bully Cassidy all the way to the station, then take the credit for getting him there. 'We'll bring him in,' she said.

He glared at her. 'The boss said . . .'

The boss said, the boss said. He might as well have come right out and made it 'My best mate said'. She glared right back at him. 'No, we'll bring him in.'

For a moment, he held her gaze. Go on, she thought. Make something of it. Right here in public. I dare you. But Beck looked away.

'You're going to wish you'd jumped,' he said to Cassidy, and walked away.

SEVENTEEN

Julie didn't want to wake up, but there was someone hammering on the door. She tried to ignore it, to turn over and go back to sleep, but something heavy was lying across her arms.

She opened her eyes. The late afternoon sun barred the bed. Steve was lying next to her, with his arms wrapped around her. They had made love for the first time in over a year. Tim? she thought, and was too disorientated to understand why his name should come so easily to mind.

The banging was still going on. Tim, she thought again. They might have found out what had happened to him. She had disentangled herself from Steve and pulled on her nightdress before she remembered that Tim was dead.

'What is it?' Steve asked sleepily.

'Don't know,' Julie said. She had just realised that the noise was coming from the kitchen, not the front door.

She bolted downstairs, leaving Steve to follow. She paused as she went into the kitchen. A figure was silhouetted against the frosted glass of the outside door.

'Wait.' Julie said. She opened the door cautiously. A woman in her late twenties stood there. Her face was oddly bland: perfectly made up, but not a face you would remember. The same went for her clothes, which were slightly up-market of Marks and Spencer, but not much. She might have started the day looking smart, but she had evidently spent a lot of time in the rain.

'Mrs Lang?' she said. She thrust her hand at Julie. She had something box-shaped in her other hand, but it was pressed against her side so that Julie couldn't make out what it was. 'Victoria Kingsley. I'm a journalist, Mrs Lang. I wondered if I might talk to you, just briefly?'

Julie stared at her. Kingsley withdrew her hand after a moment or two, when it became clear Julie wasn't going to shake it.

'What the bloody hell?' Steve said from behind Julie. 'Haven't we enough problems without the likes of you – '

'I know this is a trying time for the both of you,' Kingsley said, 'but most people find it a comfort to talk about, you know, what's happened – '

'You – ' Fury made Julie incoherent. She had had to talk to so many people, and now this little snip of a girl dared to come here.

' – because otherwise all sorts of things might get printed . . .' Kingsley paused, just for a second. 'Things that don't quite represent your true feelings. I'm sure you've seen the sort of thing?'

'Which paper sent you?' Steve demanded. 'Come on, I want to know the name of your boss – '

'For instance, I'm sure my readers would be interested to know how you feel about Mr Cassidy – '

'What?' Julie said. She suddenly realised that the thing Kingsley was carrying was a dictating machine, and that it was already running.

'What do you mean, "Cassidy"?' Steve said.

Julie turned to try and warn him about the tape machine, though she wanted to do it without speaking if she could. But he was flushed with anger, and she knew she had no chance of keeping him quiet.

'Well, there's obviously been some kind of involvement,' Kingsley said. She smiled. Julie had seen that smile on the faces of children who had swiped the last sweet in the bag. On the face of a grown woman, it was especially unpleasant. 'Why else would he have tried to commit suicide?'

'Suicide?' Julie said. For a second, completely irrationally, she thought Kingsley was telling her that Tim had killed himself after all. 'He didn't – ' Then what she had heard sank in. 'Are you trying to say that man killed our Tim?' she demanded. 'Are you? Are you?' She was shaking with rage. She took a step or two forward. Kingsley backed off.

'I'm sure you can make your own mind up, Mrs Lang,' the other woman said. 'But – '

'But nothing. You come here, sneaking around, making accusations. Lying – ' She'd had enough. All she wanted was to be left alone, to grieve for Tim, and this woman dared to intrude on that – to make money out of her private misery. 'Well I won't have it,' she said. 'I won't.'

'Take it easy, Julie,' Steve said. He put his hand on her shoulder. 'You've got a bloody cheek, you have – '

'You really are taking this the wrong way – ' Kingsley said. She stepped forward, so her foot was across the threshold.

' – there's a copper right outside the front door – ' Steve said.

'Don't you dare,' Julie said at exactly the same moment.

' – but you know that, sneaking round the back to get at us.'

'Look,' Kingsley said. 'I'm just trying to make this easier for all of us. You'll have to talk to one of us sooner or later. It might as well be me – ' but she did step back again.

'I'd sooner drink lye,' Julie answered. 'I've nothing to say to you.'

Kingsley paused. She looked at the ground for a second. When she looked up her expression was softer. 'I'm sorry,' she said. 'We've got off on the wrong foot. You have to understand I'm new to this, and my boss, well, he's a bit of an ogre. I didn't mean to hassle you, but if I come back without a story – '

'That's your problem, not ours,' Julie said. She suddenly remembered that the tape machine was running. What had she said? She couldn't remember, but she was sure that this Kingsley woman would twist it out of all proportion. She was suddenly tired of being quiet and brave, tired of crying and tired of feeling guilty for everything she'd done in the

153

thirteen years of Tim's life. 'I'll tell you what's going to happen,' she said. 'You're going to hand over that tape and you're going to leave. And if you come within a hundred feet of me again, I'm going to slap you so hard you won't know what month it is, never mind what day.' She'd been speaking very fast. She stopped for breath. 'Got me?'

'Now look,' Kingsley said. 'I'm just trying to do my job. I've broken no laws and – '

'No laws? I'll show you laws,' Julie said. She reached out and grabbed the tape recorder before Kingsley could react.

'Julie!' Steve said.

She ignored him, and before Kingsley could do anything about it, she opened the machine up and took the cassette out. She pulled the tape out – yards and yards of shiny brown tape – and hurled the cassette away across the garden. It felt wonderful to be doing something, instead of sitting moping.

'Here,' she said, shoving the recorder at Kingsley. The younger woman gaped at her, but only for a second. A loud bleep broke the silence. Kingsley took a portable phone out of her jacket pocket. She spoke into it briefly, then listened for rather longer.

'Sorry I can't stay,' Kingsley said. 'It's amazing what you can pick up on police-band radio. Trouble at Anson Road.' She smiled at Julie, the first genuine-seeming smile she had spared them. 'I just thought you'd like to know – see, I'm not a total bitch.' She turned and headed down the path to the garden gate.

'I'm going,' Steve said.

'What?' Julie said. The rush of energy had left her, and she felt as bewildered by Kingsley's sudden departure as she had by the reporter's arrival.

'You heard. Anson Road. Something's going on. I want to know what it is.'

Julie watched him go. She thought perhaps she ought to go with him, but all she wanted to do now was sleep.

● ● ●

Community policing had a lot to answer for, Beck thought. While he'd been out of the station the crowd at the front had grown much larger. People surrounded the car on all sides. Their bodies blocked the light and made the inside of the car very dark, and even with the windows shut tight he could hear them shouting.

If he'd been a different kind of person, he decided, he would have been quite frightened. As it was, and being himself, well, he could understand it.

Mind you, if he'd been the Chief Super, he'd have had them dispersed long since – Bilborough's shout or not.

The trouble was, they weren't going to let him get through. He moved the car forward very slowly, hooting the horn as he went, but it was useless. He realised after a minute or two that they thought he was bringing someone in.

He'd about had enough, actually, what with Penhaligon coming it in the Arnedale like she'd made Chief Super while he wasn't watching. All right then, he thought. He slammed the palms of his hands down on the steering wheel then opened the door.

He got out.

Immediately, the muted sound of shouting turned into a roar of voices. He stared around at a blurred confusion of faces. Fists waved in the air. A baby wailed. The mike boom came jolting down near him, and a flashbulb popped.

He couldn't make out what any single voice was saying.

Christ, he thought. Make this quick. You had to show strength though. Couldn't let them see they had you on the run. He closed the car door before he tried to speak to them.

Pick a ring-leader, one person you can deal with. That was what the training manuals said. Before he had a chance to do even that much, he realised that Timothy's father was standing close by. Next to him, bull-necked and red-faced, was his neighbour Lindsay. He'd seemed OK while he was helping on the search party. Now his face was contorted with rage.

Beck tried to say something, anything to calm things

down. He couldn't even hear his own voice, let alone anyone else's.

'There'll be a statement later,' he said, but his words just blended in with the Babel of sound around him. He made a motion with his hands, trying to make the crowd see with their eyes that they would have to be quiet if they wanted to hear him. 'Just be quiet for a second,' he bellowed, and miraculously they were, at least enough so Beck could make himself heard if he shouted. 'I understand how you're all feeling, but I want you all to go home, all right?'

Beck turned to get back into the car. Lindsay reached for him. Beck paused. Any minute now he'd have a riot on his hands, unless he could talk them down. I should get a bloody medal for this, I should, he thought as he turned to Lindsay. The man had a wad of chewing gum in his mouth. His breath stank of spearmint.

'We pay your wages, right?' He jabbed his finger at Beck. 'We got kids, they play in the woods.' He was playing to the gallery, making sure everyone in the crowd heard what he was saying. 'We want to know what the bloody hell you're doing about it.' He paused. 'A bit of information, you know what I mean?' He shoved Beck on the shoulder, not hard enough to hurt but enough to push him backwards.

The crowd roared. Beck snapped. He came back just as hard. He thrust his finger in Lindsay's face, wishing just for a second it could be a fist. 'You do that once more, I'm going to have you arrested, understand?'

The crowd were starting to turn ugly. A chant was starting somewhere towards the back. 'Oh yeah,' Lindsay said. It was a direct challenge, no doubt about it. Don't be stupid, a small voice in Beck's head said. Radio for assistance. No shame in that. Before Beck could make his mind up, Mr Lang got between him and Lindsay.

'My son's dead,' he shouted. There was a lull in the noise. 'I'm getting information off the bloody press.'

'His son – ' Lindsay put in. The shouting started again.

156

'I don't think that's right, do you?' Lang finished at a yell.

No, well, I never said I did, thought Beck. He was suddenly tired of the whole damned thing. 'Just let me through, all right?' He started to open the car door. Riot or not, he'd had enough.

The noise was thunderous. He couldn't hear anything Lindsay or Lang were saying even though they were standing right by him. There was no point even trying to talk to them through that.

There was going to be no getting through unless he said something. He could see that. Besides, they'd know soon enough. 'All right, I'll tell you,' he yelled. He could hardly make the words out himself, but they were enough to quieten the crowd. 'We've picked up a shirt-lifter.' The thunder of voices turned approving. 'We're bringing him in, OK?'

'Ah great.' That might have been Lindsay. It wasn't Lang. He was standing dead still with a bleak, slightly bewildered expression on his face.

'Who is he?' someone shouted.

'Where's he live?' yelled another voice.

Oh no, Beck thought. You don't get another word out of me. He got in the car and started her up. The crowd let him through.

'I'm not gay,' Cassidy repeated for the umpteenth time.

'We'll talk about it at the station,' Penhaligon said.

'Am I being arrested then?' he asked. It was the closest he'd come to a conversation since he got in the car.

'You know that phrase you sometimes see in the papers – "a man is helping police with their enquiries"?' Fitz said. He twisted round to look at Cassidy, who nodded warily. 'Well, that's you.'

Cassidy seemed to take a minute to digest that. 'I want a lawyer,' he said.

'You'll get one, if you need it,' Penhaligon said as she

hung a right into Anson Road. As she did so a crowd of people ran towards the car from the front of the station.

God, she thought. The crowd had been nothing like this big before. Nor as angry. She just had time to wonder how they knew Cassidy was being brought in.

The first person spat on the car even before he was within range, and then suddenly they were surrounded. A gob of spit landed on the windscreen, then another and another. People were hammering on the roof and doors.

Penhaligon drove faster. She could shake them off, maybe. But they kept pace. Someone was clinging to the bonnet. There was a solid press of people behind him, and to both sides.

Blam, blam, blam went the fists on the body of the car.

The crowd began to chant: 'Die bastard, die bastard, die, die, die.'

She was going to kill someone if this kept up. She slowed right down and picked up the phone. She had to shout to make herself heard. '. . . to Control . . . Urgent assistance required . . . there's a hostile crowd – ' Jesus, she thought, don't they know there's a crowd? ' – We're outside the station now.'

The car began to rock in time to the rhythm of the chant, which was picking up speed every second. 'Die bastard, die bastard, die, die, die.'

'Jesus Christ,' Cassidy muttered.

Penhaligon blasted the hooter again. There wasn't much else she could do –

Fitz was fiddling with the doorhandle. 'The great British public in a fit of moral outrage,' he said. He almost had it open. 'The great British public smelling blood.'

He really meant it, she thought. He probably thought he could talk the mob out of tearing Cassidy into bite-sized pieces. Bloody arrogant idiot. 'Don't be so stupid,' she screamed at him. 'Jesus Christ.'

'Where are we?' Cassidy demanded. He leaned forward

158

in his seat. 'We're outside a bloody police station.'

Penhaligon ignored him. 'We're staying put,' she shouted at Fitz.

'They'll string me up,' wailed Cassidy.

The windows were smeared with so much spit that all she could see through them was a coloured blur. The car jounced up and down. People were bouncing on the bonnet and boot, battering on the roof. A face flattened itself against the windscreen. The car lifted up and came down hard. She thought, we're going to go over, and –

A hammer smashed through the window next to her. Bits of shattered glass flew everywhere. She managed to get her arm up to protect her face from it. A hand reached in at her. She scrunched up towards Fitz, but the crowd weren't baying for her blood. They wanted Cassidy.

'Christ,' he yelled.

The rear windscreen shattered. Someone reached in and made a grab for Cassidy. Penhaligon heard him whimper. In the rear-view mirror she saw him being pulled out through the back of the car.

'Repeat, urgent assistance required – ' she said into the carphone. She felt her seat jolt as Cassidy clutched at it. Fitz turned round in his seat and grabbed his other arm. For a second it looked like the crowd might win.

'Jesus,' Cassidy screamed. 'Jesus.'

Police officers careened out of the station toward the car. Penhaligon saw a baton rise and fall. A man was hurled off the bonnet to the pavement. A clear space appeared in front of the car. Penhaligon floored the accelerator.

The mob receded in the rear-view mirror. They were trying to get past the police, but the line was holding – no, it was moving towards the gates –

Penhaligon brought the car to a stop. She stared at her hands. They were very pale. and they trembled slightly on the steering wheel. Somebody, she thought, somebody is going to pay for this.

She heard the gates clang shut. A scream of frustration went up from the crowd.

'Come on,' she said, and got out of the car.

Penhaligon handed Cassidy over to the desk sergeant.

'Interview Room One,' he said. She turned away. ' "Thanks a lot, Joe." "No problem," ' he added to her retreating back.

She ignored him. She wanted Beck, she wanted Bilborough, she wanted somebody to tell her what the bloody hell had been going on.

She went up to the duty room. The bellowing of the crowd outside was clearly audible, even though the windows were shut.

Beck entered the room ahead of her. 'All right?' he asked over his shoulder, just as if nothing were wrong.

There was no way he didn't know what had happened. Penhaligon stood in the doorway and opened her arms wide. 'How was that allowed to happen?' she asked. 'A crowd like that outside our own door?'

Beck seemed not to have heard. Penhaligon stared at him angrily for a moment, but he was standing with his back to her, checking something in a notebook.

All right, Penhaligon thought. All right. She slammed into Bilborough's office, an angry little speech already forming in her mind. But when she opened the door, she saw that Bilborough was asleep at his desk.

Oh for God's sake, she thought. She left the room, slamming the door behind her. Tough.

She went back to Beck. She put one hand on her hip. 'You told them he's gay.'

'Gay?' Beck said. His thick black eyebrows lifted in amusement. 'Miserable sod like that?' He turned to face her. 'I told them he's a shirt-lifter.'

'What's going on here?' Bilborough asked from behind Penhaligon.

Here we go, she thought. Somehow, whenever it came

160

down to a situation between her and Beck, Bilborough always made her feel she was in the wrong. Well, not this time.

'I was just about to come in and tell you, sir,' she said, and thought, only you were zonked out on duty, but it won't do me any good to mention the fact. 'There's a hostile crowd outside the station.'

Bilborough looked away. 'Jesus,' he muttered.

'Get on to Brighton Road nick,' he said. Penhaligon wondered if he were talking to her, but then he gestured at Beck. 'A bit of back-up. Discreet,' he added.

'My middle name,' Beck said.

Like hell, Penhaligon thought.

Beck went to use the phone on the other side of the room. Bilborough turned to Penhaligon. 'I'll speak to two of them. In there.' He gestured towards his office. 'In my own time.' You mean, when you've woken up, Penhaligon thought; but she didn't say anything. As Bilborough went into the office he added, 'Pick the biggest mouths.'

He paused by the door to speak to one of the Detective Constables, a woman. 'Why wasn't I told about this earlier?' he demanded.

For God's sake, Penhaligon thought. He damn well knew the crowd was there. She'd told him, Beck – he said – had told him; so now it had turned nasty and he didn't know anything about it. If she challenged him, she knew he'd say he hadn't been kept up to date on the situation – that he would have done something if he'd known how large the crowd was, or what kind of mood it was in.

It wasn't worth the effort.

Go on. Say something, Penhaligon thought at the woman. Say you couldn't tell him because he was dead asleep and you reckoned he'd hold it against you if you drew attention to him by waking him up. Say it! But the woman said nothing.

161

EIGHTEEN

Bilborough hustled Lindsay and Mr Lang downstairs, through the bustle of the reception area. The quiet chat he'd hoped to have in his office had quickly turned into a shouting match. Lang hadn't said much. He'd just stood and watched the officers in the incident room. But Lindsay had done enough talking for two men, and even now he wouldn't just let things drop.

'Will you listen to me, sir?' Bilborough shouted to him as they got near the door.

'I am listening to you,' Lindsay said. He swung round and planted himself in front of Bilborough.

'Stay within the law unless you want to end up in there with him,' Bilborough said. Christ, it wasn't as if he didn't have some sympathy for what they were going through. A lot of sympathy, even. If anyone had done to a kid of his what Cassidy had done to Timothy Lang . . . he corrected himself: what Cassidy might have done.

'Did Cassidy do it?' Lindsay demanded.

Yeah, Bilborough wanted to say. I'd bet my career on it. But instead he said, 'We're conducting our enquiries with vigour. We're optimistic – '

'Did Cassidy do it?'

' – is that clear?'

'Yes it's clear,' Lindsay shouted. Then shut up and let me get on, Bilborough thought, but Lindsay continued, 'I want to know.'

'We're optimistic – '

A WPC came in through the front door. A woman in her

twenties followed her in. She was pale blonde and looked frantically worried.

'Are you going to charge him?' Lindsay shouted.

The woman stopped and gawped at him. The WPC hurried her past.

'We're talking to a man and we're optimistic – '

'Are you?' Lindsay jabbed his finger at Bilborough.

'I'm not going to say any more to you,' Bilborough said. 'I'm going to take you back upstairs and we are going to bang you up, understand me?' He gestured at a couple of constables who were standing by the reception desk. 'Take these two upstairs till they've cooled off,' he said.

The constables moved in on Mr Lang and Lindsay. Lindsay shook his off.

'Don't make it any harder than it has to be, sir,' said the uniform. His tone was firm but non-confrontational.

Good man, Bilborough thought.

'All right, all right,' Lindsay said. 'I can walk by myself.'

Bilborough headed downstairs. He'd only gone a couple of paces when he thought of something. He turned back. 'Hang on you two,' he called. The constables stopped. 'Don't let that pair out except on my say-so. My personal say-so, understand?'

That should do it. He didn't want the mob outside getting any more riled than they were already.

Beck lounged against the doorframe of the interview room, watching Cassidy. He was a loser all right. You could tell from the way he sat slumped over the table, with his long fingers knotted up in front of him.

Arty-farty little English teacher, couldn't take it when the heat was on. Couldn't handle himself when real men were involved. Maybe that's why he went for little boys.

Bilborough hadn't told him to talk to Cassidy before he interviewed the girl, but that was OK. The boss would understand. Unsettle the bastard, that was the thing. Let him know they were on to him and soon the girlfriend would be too. At least, she would if Beck had anything to do with it.

Besides, Mitchell, the uniform on duty, was an OK sort. He lounged against the wall taking slow drags from his cigarette. He wouldn't go shouting it around that Beck had had a word.

'Your girlfriend's coming down,' he said. 'She likes trap two, does she?'

Cassidy's fingers writhed together. He didn't say anything. A muscle in his forehead began to jump.

Suffer, you little bastard, Beck thought. He turned to go. Just one more twist of the knife first. 'Don't turn your back,' he said to Mitchell.

Fitz lounged back in his seat, to one side of Beck and Panhandle. Lesley Anderson sat across the table from them. Her hair and make-up were immaculate. Silver glinted at her ears and throat. She was very pretty, in a high cheek-boned, classically English way. Half the boys in Sydney Road would have the hots for her, Fitz thought. She probably caused more wet sheets than *Playboy*. And that was before you counted the teachers.

He took a drag on his cigarette. The smoke wreathed in the air.

'He says he was with you,' Panhandle said.

'Yeah.' Lesley leaned forward slightly. 'He was.' Her brow creased up. She seemed very sincere. Too sincere, in Fitz's opinion.

'You've remembered,' Panhandle said. God, Fitz thought. She could be so ... severe. Beck caught his eye. By his expression he'd noticed Fitz watching Penhaligon. Fitz made a great play of tapping the ash from his cigarette. No point giving the little shit more satisfaction than he had to.

'Yes,' Lesley said. There wasn't a hint of doubt in her voice.

'He says you went to the theatre.' Panhandle's voice didn't

change. Nor did her body language. She was a good liar. Fitz filed that away in the box in his head marked 'Panhandle'.

Lesley's eyes went wide. She found something interesting to look at in the top left-hand corner of the room. 'You're lying,' she said eventually. 'He hates the theatre.' Her voice had taken on an odd nasal tone.

'He says he cooked you a meal,' Panhandle said.

'Yes he did.' Lesley still couldn't meet Panhandle's gaze.

'What was it?' Panhandle again. Beck shifted on his seat. He wouldn't be able to keep quiet for much longer, Fitz thought. If Lesley broke, he'd want to be able to say he had a piece of it.

'I can't remember,' Lesley said, as if it were a really stupid question. Her hand went to her throat.

'What was it?' Beck asked, right on cue.

Unfair, old boy, Fitz told himself. When Panhandle had picked up the questioning with Cassidy, back at the Arnedale Centre, he'd thought it was a neat piece of work. *Can't have double standards, now can we?* he told himself severely. *Yes I bloody can if I want to*, he answered back. This was Beck he was talking about, and Beck was an idiot. Therefore, anything Beck said was likely to be idiotic. QED.

Lesley still hadn't answered. Her perfect face crumpled in confusion. 'Chicken.' She made a vague shrugging gesture.

'Just chicken?' The questioning had passed back to Panhandle.

'And vegetables . . . broccoli, potatoes, peas.'

'Wine?' Panhandle wasn't letting her off the hook.

'Yeah.'

'What kind?'

'Dry white.' That answer came fast. She'd had time to prepare.

'What then?' Penhaligon was beginning to sound more like a machine gun than a person.

'Listened to music.' Lesley sounded as if she'd like to add, did I do better this time? Is that what you wanted to

165

hear? She was as bad a liar as Panhandle was a good one.

'Classical music?'

'No. It was jazz.' Lesley had an oddly precise way of talking, of hitting the final consonants, especially the t's. She'd been taught to speak properly, Fitz thought. Elocution lessons when she was a child? No, it would have faded by now. Failed actress, maybe? Yet Cassidy hated drama. He wondered what else they didn't have in common.

'Sex?' Beck asked, without preamble. Here we go, Fitz thought. Sledgehammer to crack a nut time.

Lesley stared at him contemptuously. 'No thanks,' she said. Of course, Fitz thought, there was no telling whose nuts would be on the block. He grinned.

Beck didn't even seem to notice. 'Did you have sex?' he said, as if talking to a bad-tempered seven-year-old.

Lesley flushed slightly. The tips of her ears went pink. 'Yes,' she said, hitting the final sibilant very hard.

'What was it like?' Beck asked.

Penhaligon glared at him.

'None of your business,' Lesley said, suddenly all ice-cold imperiousness.

'What would you say if I told you he was queer,' Beck said. He seemed to be enjoying himself.

Lesley looked at him as if he were something she'd found growing mould in the back of her refrigerator. 'I'd say you were the one with the moustache.'

Beck looked away. His expression was almost unreadable. Anyone else and Fitz would have said they seemed ashamed of themselves, but this was Beck and that reason just didn't fit. Fitz dropped the information into his unsolved mysteries mental box, the same one that held his on-going investigation into why Bilborough kept losing it over Timothy Lang.

'Do we have to check all this out, Lesley?' Penhaligon sounded almost bored.

'No you don't,' Lesley answered. She blinked rapidly several times. 'It's the truth.'

166

'You're lying. That's OK,' Penhaligon said. She raised her voice. 'But if we have to prove that you're lying, we will come down on you like a ton of bricks.'

Lesley stared at them like a trapped animal assessing its chances of making a break for freedom. One more little nudge and they'd have her, Fitz thought. Enough sledgehammers, then. Time to get the scalpel out.

'You've been his alibi for years, haven't you, Lesley?' he asked, making his voice gentle, compassionate.

'No.' The perfect mouth puckered round the word. She was upset, but she knew what Fitz was talking about, all right.

'He's gay but he won't come out.' Fitz watched her through a haze of cigarette smoke. Her eyes were hooded, wary. She was in trouble, and knew it. He felt sorry for her, but only up to a point. 'That's understandable – he's a teacher, Clause Twenty-Eight and all that . . .' Sympathy was one thing. Letting her off the hook when she was shielding a murderer was another. 'He needs a woman, a member of staff, to prove to the whole school that he's straight.'

Lesley looked away. She wasn't having any of this. Fitz went on, relentlessly, knowing she'd have to pay attention even if she didn't want to. 'He talks marriage, lets everyone know he's talking marriage. But it is just talk. He never names the day.'

Fitz stared Lesley down. She returned his gaze for a moment, then looked away.

'How long have you known him?' Fitz asked.

'Three years.'

She was scared now, Fitz thought; scared of appearing stupid, of appearing less than perceptive. She was beautiful. He could imagine how it would be: the girls would resent her for it; the boys would assume her looks were all she was good for. When they found out she was brainy as well as beautiful, they'd be intimidated. But she'd been born too late to hide her intelligence the way her mother probably had, so she'd do the only other thing she could, and flaunt it, rub their adolescent noses in it till they smothered; and the habit, once acquired, would stay with her. No, she wouldn't want anyone thinking she'd missed a trick, not Lesley.

'Three years, and all that time, not one suspicion.' Fitz contrived to sound surprised. He took a long drag on his cigarette. The smoke burned the back of his throat. He exhaled slowly, watching her face. That got her, he thought. Maybe she really had suspected Cassidy before this. Maybe not. But now, if she told herself she hadn't she'd feel stupid: and she wouldn't allow herself to do that. 'He tried to kill himself,' he went on.

Lesley's head jerked up. She was genuinely startled, and the way she showed it gave the lie to every other reaction she'd displayed.

'I know what you're thinking,' Fitz said. He was all sympathy. 'You'll have to leave the school.' It was obvious the thought hadn't even crossed her mind. ' "Poor old Lesley," some of them will say, "hanging on to Cassidy like grim death, and all the time blah blah blah . . .",' he let his voice trail off. He gave her time to build the picture in her mind, the teachers whispering in clusters around the kettle in the staff room, then dispersing hurriedly when she came near; the sympathetic glances; even some of the fifth and sixth years sniggering behind their hands. 'Some'll laugh at you – that's OK.' Her expression told him it was far from OK; he'd already known that, though. Time to let the iron show through the velvet. 'But some of them will pity you.' He raised his voice. 'And if you lie to us now, they'll despise you.'

'Were you with him two nights ago, Lesley?' Penhaligon's voice was gentle.

Lesley's gaze flicked from Penhaligon to Fitz and back again. She licked her lips. 'No,' she whispered.

Beck left the interview room a little early. He went and got a sandwich to share with the boss – he'd promised Catriona he'd make sure Bilborough ate properly. Cheese and pickle on white bread, none of your wholemeal rubbish.

168

He found Bilborough working his way through a pile of forms, mostly about incidents with the mob outside the station. Beck pried him loose and convinced him he ought to be watching the interveiws, and none of this 'I'll watch the tapes later', either.

They settled down in front of the monitor just as the Anderson woman was shown out of the interview room.

Fitz looked out of the interview room window. All he could see was grey: grey sky, grey wall, grey pavement. 'How are you and Peter getting on these days?'

'So so,' Penhaligon said. 'Same old Peter, same old rows. Judith?'

Fitz turned. He glanced at the monitor. If Beck had been one whit less stupid, he'd have suspected the man of leaving them alone just so he could eavesdrop on them via the closed circuit television. 'As ever,' he said.

Before Panhandle could reply, Cassidy was brought in. He looked furious. There was a deep vertical line etched between his eyebrows, and his mouth seemed carved in a permanent lopsided scowl.

'Lesley,' he said before he was anywhere near them. 'What did you tell her?'

'Sit down, please, Mr Cassidy,' Panhandle said. She was all business now.

Cassidy sat down reluctantly. 'I know you told her something,' he said. 'I just saw her . . . the way she looked at me – '

Fitz steepled his hands in front of him. 'They told her you're gay.

'I'm not!' Cassidy still managed to sound outraged at the idea, though he must have denied it a dozen times that morning.

Fitz grunted. 'She believed them.' He paused, to give that time to sink in. He was suddenly very aware of Penhaligon sitting next to him, of the exposed length of her thigh under her short skirt. 'I think if you told my wife I was gay, she wouldn't believe you. There has to be suspicion first.'

Cassidy leaned across the table towards Panhandle. 'Shall I prove it to you? Somewhere private?'

In the incident room, Beck and Bilborough looked at each other and sniggered.

Penhaligon stared coldly at Cassidy. If he wanted to get nasty, he was going to have to do it alone. She wasn't going to help him along.

'What were you doing three nights ago?' Fitz asked.

'Ahh . . .' Cassidy searched for an answer. 'I stayed in.'

'With Lesley?'

'Yeah.' Cassidy's hands were folded in front of him on the table. His index finger started to rub, almost convulsively, across the back of his other hand. His watch was large, with an oversized face and a bracelet made of heavy silver links. The cuff of his shirt wouldn't go over it. It wasn't really the sort of thing Penhaligon would have expected someone like Cassidy to wear, but that aside something about it kept annoying her. She'd get it in a minute, she was sure. Meanwhile, she concentrated on listening to the conversation.

'I marked books,' Cassidy said. He stared straight ahead. His hands stopped moving. 'I jogged. I marked some more books.'

In the incident room, Bilborough turned to Beck. 'The fancy man,' he said round a mouthful of sandwich.

'Bates,' Beck said. He ran to the door.

Bilborough stared at the screen. 'What was he wearing?' he muttered to himself.

He was hardly listening as Fitz asked, 'So you jogged through the woods?'

'On the road,' Cassidy replied, his voice almost inaudible because of the distortion from the monitor speaker.

170

'What was he wearing?' Bilborough muttered again. He got up and backed towards the door between the incident room and the outer office. Still looking at the screen, he called to one of the uniformed officers. 'Bob – '

'You live half a mile from the woods?' Fitz asked on screen.

'Yeah,' Cassidy replied.

The officer came over to Bilborough, who said, 'Go in there and ask her to ask him what he was wearing on the night he was running.'

We'll get you, Bilborough thought at Cassidy. We'll get you yet, you murdering bastard.

'So you have used the track in the past?' Fitz asked.

Penhaligon watched Cassidy's reaction. One day, she thought, she'd be able to tell as much from as little as Fitz could. Until then, she'd just have to keep trying.

Cassidy was obviously uncomfortable. 'A long time ago . . . you get a lot of kids in the woods . . .' His hands twisted together. His watch rubbed up against the cuff of his shirt. He started talking faster and faster. 'You're a teacher. You're fair game.' His expression said there was nothing fair about it. 'They shout things out, and it can wind you up a bit. You're jogging to try and relax. That's why I don't use the woods, OK?' His voice had a whining quality that set Penhaligon's teeth on edge. He and his girlfriend made a good pair, she decided.

'Now, why did you try to kill yourself?' Fitz asked, as casually as if he were asking Cassidy whether he preferred his coffee black or white.

Penhaligon missed Cassidy's reply, because just at that moment Bob Henderson, one of the uniformed constables, came in. Bilborough wanted to know what Cassidy had been wearing.

' – I was just a bit depressed,' Cassidy finished.

'What about?' Fitz asked.

171

Cassidy scowled. 'The Exchange Rate Mechanism.'

Fitz smiled, though Penhaligon didn't think it was up to his own standard.

'What were you wearing that night?' she asked. Cassidy looked down at himself. 'While you were jogging,' she clarified.

'Tracksuit. Trainers.' Cassidy sounded tired, as if he'd been asked one too many questions. Tough. Maybe now they'd get somewhere.

'Would you mind if we went to get them?' she asked.

'I would,' Cassidy said. He sounded affronted. He moved his hand across the tabletop. 'Yeah, I would.'

The watch rubbed against his cuff. She had it then. Just for a second she flashed on the thought of him and Timothy, close together. The watch, rubbing up against the boy's clothes, or perhaps his hair, because it was too big to slide under Cassidy's shirt sleeve.

'OK,' she said. 'Did you have that on?' She looked at the watch.

Cassidy looked at Fitz. *What now?* his expression seemed to say. Fitz didn't answer. 'Yeah.' He fingered the watch strap.

'Can I borrow it for an hour or two?' Penhaligon had to strive to keep her voice casual.

Again, Cassidy looked towards Fitz. He almost seemed to be asking if it was safe for him to hand the watch over. Penhaligon thought, maybe it's because Fitz saved his life. Whatever it was, Fitz didn't answer. Cassidy slipped the watch off and handed it to Penhaligon.

'Thanks,' Penhaligon said. Sod Beck and his Superman act. With any luck this would nail Cassidy and there'd be no way he'd take the credit for it.

172

NINETEEN

'Yes I know you're very busy,' Bilborough said into his phone. The Forensics people had made that very clear when he'd asked for urgent treatment of Cassidy's watch. 'Yes I can hold on while you find the report.'

Penhaligon was standing by the window, looking into the duty room. She was smiling to herself. Bilborough could have a good guess what she was thinking about. When wasn't she thinking about Fitz was more the question. He covered the mouthpiece with his hand. 'They've got a preliminary report. Get on to Admin and ask them to find Cassidy a solicitor. Then ask Jimmy Beck to go and bring Bates in – '

'Line-up, sir?' Penhaligon asked. 'Shall I organise some men to go in it?'

All right, he thought. You've proved your point. You're on the ball. 'Good thinking,' he said. 'Oh – and get on to Harrington. Say I need his report now.'

The trick with reluctant witnesses was to shame them into behaving like good little citizens, Beck thought. If you could, you gave them a chance when it wouldn't be too embarrassing. But if they were real toerags, like this Bates, well they really didn't deserve much mercy. You shamed them down any way you could – in front of the neighbours, the wife, the kids, whatever – and by the time you'd finished with them they'd be begging you to let them make a statement, just to shut you up.

Beck knew it worked. He'd done it often enough before.

He knocked on Bates's door. The house looked nice

enough – lacy nets at the windows, hanging baskets either side of the door, kid's bike lying on its side by the path. You'd never have guessed he was playing away.

The door opened. Bates stood there. Shame really, Beck thought. Meeting the wife would have done nicely.

Beck smiled. 'Can I come in?' he asked, loud and clear.

Bates took a step outside. He pulled the door to, but made sure it didn't shut. 'The wife's in,' he said quietly.

Beck raised his voice just a fraction, but enough to let Bates know it could get a lot louder. 'It's about your statement.' He pulled out his notebook and started flicking through. 'You were in the woods with your girlfriend and you saw a man jogging – '

'Yeah.' Bates was uncomfortable. Just as long as he realised the quickest way out of this was straight through the middle of it, Beck thought.

'Who is it?' A woman's harsh voice called from inside.

Christ, Beck thought. If that was my wife I wouldn't just play away, I'd take the bloody ball and leave the pitch.

Bates looked round wildly. 'Christian Aid,' he shouted.

Beck grinned. Bates was definitely beginning to see the trouble he was in. Best make sure of it, though. 'Was he going fast or slow?'

'Quite fast.'

'Well, there you are you see – '

'Won't this keep?'

You don't get it yet, do you my son? Beck thought. 'No. "Jogging" people think "slow". But he was going fast.' You will do though, you will do.

'Yeah.'

' "Running" would be more accurate?'

' "Running from the scene." ' Bates had finally got it. He glanced over his shoulder at the door. No escape there. He looked back at Beck.

'I just want it accurate.' Here comes the kicker, Beck thought. 'Anyway, we want you down the station for an ID

174

parade. You can change your statement then.'

'But,' Bates said, and stopped. 'What am I going to tell the wife?'

Beck grinned as if to say, *We're both men of the world.* 'You'll think of something,' he said.

Cassidy slammed the flat of his hand against the wall of the interview room.

'I taught the boy,' he yelled. He turned round to face the room. He had looked haggard the first time they'd interviewed him, Penhaligon thought. Two hours on – two hours waiting for Forensics to do its stuff with the watch – and he looked goddamn awful. His skin had taken on an odd greyish cast, and the lines on his face were etched deep with fatigue.

'When you teach kids you get close to them.' He seemed to be speaking mostly to Fitz, who was sitting at the table. Interesting, Penhaligon thought. Why him, rather than her or Bilborough? It was just part of what Fitz did, the way he built up a rapport with suspects and witnesses – part of what made him valuable.

Well, she could be valuable too. She glanced sideways at Bilborough, who was standing near the door with his arms folded.

Let him try and say this wasn't all my own idea, Penhaligon thought. Just let him.

Cassidy sat down at the table. 'I've had nits off kids before now, never mind bits of fibre.' He was begging for sympathy.

He didn't get it. Fitz stared back impassively. After a moment he said, 'The thing is, Tim wore a shirt and tie to the school concert rehearsal. He didn't put that tee shirt on until about – ' he glanced at a notepad, ' – five p.m. So that means between five p.m. and the time of his death, you touched him.'

Cassidy's head drooped, just slightly. He rubbed the back of his neck with his hand. We've got you, Penhaligon thought. I got you.

175

'Another thing about tee shirts,' Fitz said. A note of amusement crept into his voice. ' – I've got a teenage son, so I know about these things – you do not put on your best tee shirt to go and see your dad. You save it for copping off. You wear it to impress somebody you fancy.'

Suddenly the room seemed much quieter. It was as if the whole world contracted, until the only people in it were Fitz and Cassidy, the only sound, Fitz's voice. 'He fancied you, didn't he? You were his teacher and very properly you resisted.' Fitz's voice was almost a whisper now. He drew everyone into the spell he was weaving. Cassidy seemed mesmerised by him. 'But that night he came to you. In that tee shirt. A blond, beautiful teenage boy. Those arms, that smile. I don't blame you for weakening. Nobody does.'

Cassidy laughed, breaking the spell. For a second the sound seemed to teeter on the edge of hysteria. The expression on his face was close to crazy. 'I marked books,' he said. His voice trembled. 'I jogged. And then I marked some more books, that's all.' He stared at Fitz. 'That's all.'

The solicitor was a bleeding heart liberal by the name of Shazia Begum. Beck had had dealings with her before. She was very big down at the local women's refuge, and the only surprise was to see her on a case like this.

'He's in here,' he said, jerking his thumb at the metal door of the holding cell. 'You won't need much time with him – he's guilty as sin, mark my words.'

'I'll make my own mind up, thank you Sergeant Beck,' Begum said.

Jesus, what was it with women these days? He'd thought that Asian women, at least, might know their place. You had to hope.

'Yell if he tries anything,' Beck said while the door was open, and added quickly, before it could shut. 'Come to think of it, he isn't going to be interested in you, is he?'

• • •

Waiting for a line-up to start was murder, sheer bloody murder, Bilborough thought. He paced up and down the narrow space behind the two-way mirror that hid the police from the men in the line-up. He was very tired – struggling to keep awake, if he were truthful – and the dim light this side of the mirror didn't help.

Penhaligon and Fitz were deep in conversation down at the other end of the room. He went to talk to them.

'That was a good job, by the way ' he said. Surprisingly, Penhaligon smiled. ' – Fitz.'

'Gee, no problemo, boss,' Fitz said, in that irritating fake American accent he sometimes put on.

Penhaligon was scowling. What the bloody hell had got up her nose? Bilborough wondered as he turned away. Probably thinks she deserves a medal just for doing the job at all.

He stared at the men in the line-up. They seemed like a good selection – Cassidy, with his medium build and mousy hair, had been easy to match; but he was breathing hard and fast, obviously on the verge of a panic attack. Sweat sheened his skin. There was nothing they could do about it, but it was a worry. Bilborough didn't want Begum turning round and saying Bates had picked Cassidy out because of it. He didn't want any screw-ups at all. He just wanted to get the case closed, Cassidy banged up and the paperwork out of the way. Then, he could take some time off, make sure Catriona took it easy, and maybe finally get the nursery painted.

He leaned against the wall. Christ but he was tired. He rubbed his eyes with his thumb and forefinger. They didn't just feel gritty, they felt like he had the whole of Brighton beach stuck behind them.

There was a soft click as the door opened. Light flooded in, briefly, as Beck and another officer brought Bates in and then straight through to the line-up.

Bates walked slowly down the line.

Come on, you bastard, Bilborough thought. Pick him. Just pick him.

177

Bates walked past Cassidy.

No, Bilborough thought. Don't do this. Don't –

Bates turned back. 'This man,' he said, jabbing his finger at Cassidy.

'Yes,' Fitz said.

Thank you, God, Bilborough thought. That's it, all wrapped up. All we have to do is tie the bow –

'This man's here because he taught the boy, isn't he?' Bates went on. No, Bilborough thought. I don't believe it. I won't – 'I know him. He teaches my son and all.' He turned and looked directly into the mirror. 'It wasn't this man,' He gestured at Cassidy. 'It is definitely not this man.'

It can't be, Bilborough thought. It just can't. He looked at Cassidy. The man was almost smiling. It isn't over yet, you bastard, Bilborough thought at him.

'It is out of the question,' Begum said. The scarf she was wearing over her hair fell forward. She twitched it back impatiently. 'Unless, of course, you intend to charge my client?'

Bilborough had requested a blood sample so they could do a DNA profile. It was their best hope of nailing him, unless he confessed. If they charged him, he'd lose his right to refuse to give the sample. But he knew and Begum knew that he didn't have enough evidence to make a charge stick. Yet.

They were in Bilborough's office – Fitz, Penhaligon and Beck, as well as Bilborough and Cassidy's solicitor. The first time Bilborough had met her, she'd been defending a woman who had thrown acid in her violent husband's face. Begum had pissed all over him, found a counter to every piece of evidence he'd produced to show that the attack had been premeditated and therefore not self-defence. He'd made the mistake of underestimating her then. He'd never done so since.

'Look,' Bilborough said, 'we want to test him so we can eliminate him from our enquiries. If he's innocent, he's got nothing to fear from a DNA test. If he refuses – '

'If he refuses it's going to look real bad,' Beck said.

'Really?' Begum asked innocently. Gold flashed at her ears and wrists and nose, but she was wearing western dress. 'Are you aware, Chief Inspector, of the numerous ways DNA testing can go wrong?'

'Oh for – ' Bilborough started.

'She's right,' Fitz cut in. 'A slight change in the temperature the test's developed at, a slightly different length of time, maybe a tiny difference in the substrate – you get a completely different result – '

Thanks, Fitz, Bilborough thought.

'So what,' Beck said. 'We just make sure our tests are done right. No problem.'

'Ah,' said Begum, 'but imagine this situation, if you will. Mr Cassidy is innocent – '

'Is he hell.' That was Beck.

'Hypothetically innocent, Sergeant. Surely even you are capable of imagining that?'

'Don't count on it,' Fitz said. Beck shot him a look that should have had him dead on the floor.

'Anyway, there is some error in the testing, and the result is positive – '

'Now that is highly unlikely,' Fitz said. 'A false negative, that I can understand, but the chances of the samples matching when they shouldn't must be millions to one – '

'I've heard you are a betting man, Doctor Fitzgerald,' Begum looked at him sternly. 'I, of course, do not undertake such activity. The Koran frowns upon it. Nevertheless, I would hesitate to take such a chance with the life of an innocent man. For you see, if my barrister were to go into court in such a case, how would she present it to the jury?' She stared at them all, wide-eyed and innocent. Solicitor? Bilborough thought, she should have been a bleeding actress. 'After all there has been so much in the papers – this murderer caught, this paternity suit settled,

179

that rapist trapped. How are we to persuade a lay jury that DNA testing is less than reliable?'

'That's your business, not ours,' Bilborough snapped. 'We're supposed to get what evidence we can and present it to the Crown Prosecution Service, not make judgements about what's reliable and what's not – '

'I see,' said Begum. 'And that would include taking statements from a suspect without a solicitor present and without the use of a tape recorder?' She seemed remarkably calm, with only the slightest edge to her voice revealing her anger. 'Well, Chief Inspector? Would it?'

'Cassidy was not originally being questioned as a suspect. We were attempting to eliminate him from our enquiries.' Penhaligon, sitting out of line of sight of Begum, raised her eyebrows at him. He had to admit it sounded a bit thin, but all he could do was go for it. 'As soon as we had any real evidence pointing to him as the murderer, we got him a brief.' Begum's gaze challenged him. 'That's all that happened.' Weak, he thought. That last sentence was definitely weak.

'Forgive me,' Begum said, 'but it seems to me that what may have happened is that my client's rights were disregarded. You'll understand if I employ my best efforts to see that doesn't happen again?'

'Oh come on,' Fitz said. 'I know you have a lot to prove – all us men, sitting around in positions of power when you've worked so hard – '

'Doctor Fitzgerald,' Begum said, 'I believe we have had this conversation at least three times before. It may have worked the first time I heard it, but, as you would say, I'm on to you now. You'll have to find another angle – '

'Touché,' Fitz said. He grinned amiably.

'If you'll excuse me, Ms Begum? Fitz?' Bilborough said. His head was beginning to pound. 'I need to talk to my officers.'

They left. Damn, Bilborough thought. The case was

disintegrating around him, and he'd forgotten to call Catriona like he promised. Well, at least he could get one thing right. Jimmy and Penhaligon would have to wait.

Penhaligon had just about had enough. She sat in Bilborough's office and watched him ring his home number yet again. There was no reply. She could hear the phone ringing even from where she was. Beck sat on the next desk. His leg swung back and forth, back and forth. It irritated her, but she knew if she asked him to stop he'd only do it more.

'We can't be sure Cassidy's the one,' she said. 'After all, we know there was at least one other jogger in the vicinity that night – '

'Oh come on,' Beck said.

Bilborough pressed the cut-off button on the handset. He punched another number. The phone at the other end rang out. Penhaligon thought she'd dream of ringing phones when she went to sleep, she'd seen Bilborough go through the ritual so often.

'Look,' she said, 'we've eliminated one suspect; we've found a witness. We're making progress, so – '

Bilborough held the phone away from his mouth. 'How do you know?'

That lost Penhaligon. 'Sorry?'

'How do you know he's not the jogger Bates saw?'

'Bates told us he wasn't,' Penhaligon said, trying not to sound like a school teacher telling a five-year-old how to tie shoelaces for the umpteenth time. She failed miserably.

'He was lying.' Bilborough was just as condescending back. 'Chief witness goes up to chief suspect, "definitely not him". Bollocks.' He paused. 'He just wants to keep himself out of court. Doesn't want some smart-arse barrister asking him what he was doing in the woods.' Penhaligon wondered what made him so almighty knowledgeable. She wanted to point out that despite his rank, he was less than five years older than her. She bit the words back, mostly because she could just hear Beck saying. 'Fancied yourself a high-flier, did you?'

Bilborough spoke into the phone. 'Hello? It's David Bilborough – could you – I've been ringing my wife . . .' Yes, thought Penhaligon. Of course he had been. He had a murder investigation to run, so what could be more natural than to spend half the morning making personal phone calls? She tried to stop herself scowling. Waste of energy; but she just couldn't. She sipped her tea, hoping neither of the men had noticed: Bilborough because he was her boss and she couldn't afford to have him thinking she was being over-emotional; Beck because he was Beck, and he'd ride her about it. Bilborough went on, 'Could you look out of the window and see if the car's there? Thanks.' Still holding the phone, he turned back to Penhaligon. 'Keep away from Fitz. You're starting to sound like him.'

Penhaligon put her mug down on the desk, just a little harder than was necessary. Tea sloshed out over a blank pad. She ignored it. 'What do you mean by that?'

'You know very well what I mean.'

'I don't,' she said, though she had a good idea. Suddenly she realised that if he wanted a fight he was damn well going to get it. 'I don't know what you mean and I'd like you to explain. OK, sir? I'd like you – '

'Come on now,' Beck said. 'Let's just – '

'Nothing to do with you, OK?' Penhaligon said, wishing she had the nerve to tell him to sod off. 'Nothing what-soever to do with you.'

Beck knocked the ash off his cigarette. 'I'd hate to come home to you in a flat week.' He got up and made a great show of going and studying the noticeboard.

'Thanks,' Bilborough murmured into the phone, then put the receiver down. 'She's in the garden,' he said to Pen-haligon, as if nothing was wrong.

Bloody hell, Penhaligon thought. Maybe he was just trying to change the subject. She wasn't having it. This time she

182

really wasn't having it. 'Would you explain, please, sir?'

Bilborough didn't answer. He turned to Beck. 'Do you think he's guilty?'

'Yeah,' Beck said, without any hesitation.

Great, Penhaligon thought. Never mind innocent until proven guilty. Let's just bang someone up so we can go home in time for tea.

'What about you?' Bilborough turned to face her. 'Your gut instinct – is he guilty?'

She wanted to make a fight of it, to say that instinct wasn't the point; gathering evidence and discovering the real killer was the point. Otherwise they weren't just police, they were the judge and jury too. But he'd say she was being naive, like she had been in the Hennessey case, when she'd thought a woman might have been the 'Sweeney Todd' serial killer. And Bilborough was the one who'd write up her recommendation for promotion, when the time came. She couldn't afford this constant in-fighting. Besides, it was a direct question. And her instinct did tell her he was guilty. It was only the method she doubted. 'Yeah,' she said, suddenly aware of the uncomfortably long pause.

'I *know* he's guilty,' Bilborough said. 'Our job is to get all the evidence against that man and hand it over.' Penhaligon said nothing. Nothing she could say would make a difference anyway. 'That's our job. No bloody philosophy, thanks very much.' He picked up the phone again, and started to punch a number while he spoke. 'Whatever's going on between you and Fitz, it's affecting the way you do your work.' He punched the final digit. 'We expect a result, we get sweet FA and you talk about progress?' He suddenly sounded really pissed off. 'I get enough off him. I don't want it off someone on my team.' He leaned across the desk towards her. She suddenly realised that they weren't having a discussion, however heated. She was being read the riot act. In front of Beck. 'And don't give me any crap about keeping my private life separate, because you obviously

183

can't – hello?' He turned his attention back to the phone. 'Me again . . . I'm sorry.' He paused, obviously listening to someone. Penhaligon doodled on her pad and tried to work out how many phone calls he'd made about Catriona since the morning. Five or six at least. Maybe even as many as ten. And he had the nerve – 'Look, I know I'm bothering you, but could you tell her to go in and relax? Tell her I said she's got to go in and relax? Thanks.' He put the phone down. 'A week overdue and she's pulling bleeding weeds.'

Christ, Penhaligon thought. He really doesn't understand what he's done to me. 'I can't keep my private life separate?' It was a real struggle to keep her voice level, but she knew that if she got upset she'd never hear the end of it. 'I haven't been fussing about my wife for the last half hour.'

'I think that's a bit below the belt,' Beck said. Penhaligon glared at him. Of course it was: she was a woman and they were men, so of course she couldn't keep her emotions and her work apart; but if they did it was just the logical – even the caring – reaction to events.

She got up and walked out. There was no winning when they were behaving like this. None at all.

She closed the door carefully, so it didn't slam, and went and sat at her desk. She threw her notepad down. Bloody Bilborough, she thought. Beck had followed her out. He leant over her, one arm on her desk, the other on the table behind.

'She's been pregnant before,' he said. 'They lost it.'

He went back to Bilborough's office before she could say anything. Shit, she thought. Shit shit shit.

The Chief Super's office was, in many ways, just like Bilborough's own, except that it had a window. The big difference was that in Bilborough's office, he was in control. Here, he had to stand and take whatever Mr Allen wanted to throw at him. Like 'I don't know what you thought you were playing at', and 'Community policing

184

doesn't mean no policing', and 'If you'd acted earlier, all this could have been avoided'.

There hadn't been a lot Bilborough could say. Falling asleep was hardly an adequate defence, and he could hardly point out that when he'd wanted to disperse the crowd earlier, it had been Allen's words that had stopped him. He shoved his hands in his pockets and paced the floor, giving himself a few seconds with his back to the man's hard blue eyes. Better not to think about what might happen if he couldn't talk his way out of this.

'I've spoken to some of the ringleaders,' Bilborough said, trying to inject as much confidence as he could into his voice. 'And I've got back-up standing by.' He paced towards Allen's desk. Don't push too hard, he thought. Don't. You'll just seem nervous. 'It's under control.'

The Chief Super's expression was unreadable. 'Can you charge Cassidy?'

'Not yet, no.'

'You know what will happen if you let him go?'

Of course I bloody know, Bilborough thought: Brixton, Bristol, Coventry, that's what happens: riots in the streets and my face spread all over the tabloids as the copper who made it happen. 'I can handle it,' he said, and wished he meant it.

'How's the wife?' Allen asked.

Thank God that's over, Bilborough thought with relief. 'No change.'

'You should be with her, David,' the Chief Super said.

'Maybe,' Bilborough said. He could see where this one was going to lead.

The Chief Super leaned forward. He steepled his hands in front of him. Here it comes, Bilborough thought. 'We can hold the fort for a few days,' Allen said.

He knew it. The few days would turn into a week, and then however long it took to nail Cassidy and deal with the aftermath. It would be nothing official, nothing on his

185

record, but Allen would know. At Bilborough's level, a lot was starting to depend on personal recommendation and having a face that fitted. He had risen fast and far; take an enforced holiday now and he might not get much further.

'Don't do this to me,' he said. 'He's guilty. It's only a matter of time before he coughs.' He stared at Allen, wishing he could say it in a way that sounded less like begging. 'Please don't do this to me,' he said. 'Please.'

The Chief Super tapped the end of his Biro on the desk. 'OK,' he said at last.

Back in his office, Bilborough got himself a coffee and tried to relax. It wasn't possible. They'd missed something. Must have missed something. Maybe Jimmy Beck had a point, maybe they should go and talk to all the kids in the school. One of them might have seen something going on between Cassidy and Timothy. It would be circumstantial evidence, but a bit of circumstantial never did anybody any harm.

He sipped the coffee. It had gone cold, though Bilborough hadn't thought he'd been sitting long enough for that to happen. There was a knock on the door, and one of the Admin staff came in.

'Urgent fax for you,' she said, and dropped a sheet of paper on Bilborough's desk. He picked it up. It was from Harrington at the path lab.

Bilborough scanned the summary at the top of the page: as well as the strangulation, there were scratches and contusions on the upper torso, in the groin area and on the back and buttocks. No semen found in the anus or externally; no blood traces other than the victim's own. Conclusion: Timothy Lang had been sexually assaulted, but not raped, before he died.

Conclusion, Bilborough thought: there's no point insisting on DNA testing Cassidy because we've nothing to compare the results to.

186

TWENTY

'You're letting him go?' Mr Lang shouted. He and Lindsay walked down the station corridor side by side, forcing Bilborough to walk backwards faster than was comfortable.

Bilborough had decided to move them from the interview room, which might be needed at any time, to a holding cell. The two men had assumed they were being allowed to leave, and they didn't want to hear anything he had to say about it.

He backed down the corridor in front of them. He tried to keep his voice reasonable. 'We can't hold a man without evidence and – '

'You must have had evidence to pull the bastard in,' Lindsay shouted.

' – as far as we're concerned the man is innocent – ' Bilborough said, and thought, my arse he's innocent. But it was the official line. 'Though I'm sure we're going to have more questions to ask him.'

'You said you were optimistic,' Lang yelled.

'You two are,' Bilborough said, and suddenly all three of them were shouting and there was no way of telling who was saying what.

'You're staying in the station,' Bilborough said, finally.

'You're holding us and you're letting that bastard get away?' Lang shouted. His finger jabbed at Bilborough.

Go on, Bilborough thought. Just hit me one and get it over. Then I can do you for hitting a police officer and boom, no more problem. He couldn't say that, but he couldn't hide his anger either. 'Look, I have reason to believe a crime will be committed if I let you go. Therefore, you're staying in the station. All right?'

Cassidy was close to breaking. Fitz could feel it in his bones. Fear came off the man like sweat as they got into the van. Fitz considered trying one more time for a confession, but he decided against it. Bilborough needed a result quickly – he'd made that plain; but Fitz thought Cassidy's guilt would work on him faster if he were left alone. Press him and he just might harden up again. Besides, there was no tape recorder in the van: getting an inadmissible confession that would simply be retracted later would be counter-productive.

He settled himself on the narrow seat. The metal bit into his back and thighs. However uncomfortable he was, Cassidy was worse. Silhouetted by the light that fell through the rear window, his hunched, almost foetal, posture was more eloquent than any words he could have spoken.

He was right to be afraid, Fitz thought. Even if they somehow found another suspect, and enough evidence to clear Cassidy convincingly, the shit would stick. He'd already lost his girlfriend – Fitz wasn't proud of that – and his job would almost certainly follow.

He watched Penhaligon and a uniformed officer get into a marked car. It drove off, and a moment later the van lurched forward.

They sped out of the station. Faces appeared pressed up against the rear window. Fists slammed against the sides of the van. Sirens wailed. The van accelerated away from the crowd. Fitz watched as the mass of people receded into the distance.

'I don't believe this,' Cassidy murmured.

Believe it, Fitz thought at him. It's the world you have to live in now.

Judith got home early from work. She made herself a cup of coffee and took it through to the front room, to drink while she watched the television.

First the national, and then the local, news came on. Suddenly Fitz's face stared out at her from the screen.

'– teacher Nigel Cassidy was rescued from a suicide bid by forensic psychologist Dr Edward Fitzgerald,' said the voice-over. The camera panned from Fitz's face in close-up to a longshot showing the height of the Arnedale Centre. 'Police have refused to comment on whether there is a link between the attempt and the murder of schoolboy Timothy Lang – '

Fitz, Judith thought. Oh, Fitz. She could imagine him going up on that rooftop, terrified though he was of heights, just like he'd tried to rescue Sean.

That was the thing with Fitz, the thing she kept losing sight of: he blustered, he bullied, he could be arrogance personified. But when it came down to the line, he was always there, showing his other side, the compassionate, humane, loving side that he tried so hard to hide.

He thought she'd fallen in love with the braggart, the man who pushed at the universe and punctured everyone's pretensions. He was right, but that wasn't all of it. She loved the other side of him as much, if not more.

It was just that lately it had been hard to remember its existence. Well, she thought at his image as he stood next to Cassidy in the street, I'm just going to have to do a better job of remembering. Even when you are driving me to distraction.

Bilborough told Lang and Lindsay they could go. He'd have kept them longer, but he couldn't think of a suitable reason.

Lang walked out of the room. His face was fixed like stone. That one's going to be trouble, Bilborough thought. He rubbed the back of his neck, trying to ease the tension out of it. He'd have to do something. He would, just as soon as he'd phoned Catriona one more time.

• • •

Cassidy's flat was above a butcher's shop. There were roadworks right outside. The noise of the pneumatic drill was enough to drive anyone crazy, Fitz thought. Not clinically insane, just plain, simple layman's crazy. There was a JCB rearing the shovel on the end of its neck, like the skeleton of a *Jurassic Park* dinosaur. A little clot of workmen gathered round it, no doubt discussing the technicalities of digging the next hole, but none of them were actually doing anything.

'Ah,' Fitz said, 'the great British working man, doing what he does best.' Panhandle glared at him, as if to ask why he wasn't taking the job seriously. Much she knew.

'Round here,' Cassidy said, leading them down an alley to the rear of the shop. Some iron steps led up to the front door of his flat.

He fiddled with the door for some time. Eventually he got it open. As he went in, he bent down and scooped up a towel from the floor. He stood there with it, looking embarrassed.

Penhaligon went straight through to the sitting room. Fitz followed her in. There was a faint but unmissable smell of gas. A memory flashed through Fitz's mind: Sean, the boy who had killed DS Giggs, standing in a house that was rapidly filling with gas, clutching a box of matches while all the time the heating timer ticked away to the moment of ignition. The memory was remorseless. He could almost feel the desperate urgency to run away, the blast of heat at his back, the shockwave that knocked him down . . .

Oh God, Fitz thought. First the Arnedale Centre, now this.

'The meter ran out. I had no pound coins,' Cassidy said.

Great, Fitz thought. We aren't just dealing with a suicidal, depressive, child-killer. We're dealing with an incompetent, suicidal, depressive, child-killer.

Cassidy went through to the front room. Fitz followed him. Penhaligon was staring at something on Cassidy's desk, in best detective style. Fitz was more interested in what he could learn indirectly.

He glanced around. And the favourite is Today's Life-style, out of the Reject Shop by Ikea. He'd lay odds on it. The room was tastefully decorated to the point of restraint, from the plain wooden bookshelves to the framed prints on the walls. Only the large white leather sofa that dominated the centre of the room hinted that perhaps Cassidy would like to break out of what he perceived as good taste.

Now, what was he to make of all of this? He'd put money on Cassidy being from a nice, lower middle-class family, probably their first child to go into further education. He'd been bright as a child, but making a living had to come first, hence the teaching. And conformity would come as naturally as breathing. Yet Fitz would also lay odds that Cassidy had wanted to do something outrageous, or at least less safe. He glanced at the bookshelves. Jostled in among the black-spined Penguin classics and the volumes of Faber poetry and plays, there were quite a few little booklets from small press publishers. Fitz pulled one out: *Spirits of the Night* by Nigel Cassidy. *A Dream of Days Unborn*, also by Cassidy. Poems, Fitz guessed, and confirmed it with a quick flick-through one of them. Our Mr Cassidy is a poet in his spare time. I'll bet those kids play havoc with his delicate artistic sensibilities.

He could sense Cassidy standing behind him. The man would be embarrassed and now outraged that they were looking through his things. Any minute now, he'd say 'Do you mind', in that nasal voice of his –

Before he could do so, Penhaligon spoke. She was looking at a school exercise book. 'Is this your handwriting Mr Cassidy?' She turned the book round and pointed at one of the pages.

'Yes.' Fitz couldn't see his face, but he sounded defensive.

'I'm sorry, I'm sorry, I'm sorry, I'm sorry,' Penhaligon read. She flipped the book shut. 'This is Timothy Lang's book.'

'So?' He was very defensive now.

Getting him off guard had worked at the Arnedale Centre. Fitz decided to try it again. Maybe he'd call it the Flying Lemming Strategy. There might even be a paper in it.

Fitz turned to Cassidy. He lounged against the wall as if nothing in the world were wrong. 'Do you remember those Hamlet cigar ads?' he asked. 'I got a great one. A guy tries to gas himself, right?' He glanced round at Penhaligon. She glared at him, obviously not enjoying the joke. Think of it as a double act, he thought at her. 'He's singularly unsuccessful because it's natural gas, right? So he tries to console himself by lighting a Hamlet cigar.' He glanced round. Suddenly he was facing Sean again, and the kid's fingers were moving the match against the side of the box. Laugh at ghosts and they will flee, he remembered, for they cannot stand to be laughed at. It was an old Tibetan saying he'd heard somewhere. Or if it wasn't it ought to be. 'He lights it up. Boom! The whole house goes up. As the dust settles, the camera goes in, finds the packet and it says – ' pay-off time. He made sure the other two were paying attention. ' – smoking can seriously damage your health.'

Neither of them laughed. Fitz suddenly realised that for the last few seconds he had been listening to a low rumbling sound. He turned. The shovel of the JCB smashed through the window. It swung into the room towards him and Cassidy. Bits of glass flew everywhere. The bookcases next to the window crashed down. Paper fluttered upwards. The shovel retreated. It caught one of the bookcases and pulled it through the gaping hole of the window. Then it rocketed forward. Cassidy got his arms up in front of his face, but Fitz could only watch in silence.

He realised, belatedly, that someone, somewhere, was screaming. 'Murderer. Die, you pervert. Die, die, die.'

The shovel tilted up and back. It reversed quickly. This time it caught the window frame. There was a squeal of tortured wood as the frame ripped free of the wall.

'Come on,' Cassidy shouted. 'We've got to get out of here – '

'Don't be stupid,' Panhandle said. She glanced at Fitz. *Don't you dare encourage him,* she seemed to say. 'Whoever that is will tear you to pieces.'

'We could at least go into the kitchen,' Fitz said. She'd been right to yell at him in the car. Trying to get out had been a damn fool thing to do, and when he thought about it, he didn't really know why he'd tried to do it.

They went through. Cassidy started towards the door. Then he seemed to think better of it, and stood uncertainly in the middle of the room. He was shaking, just as he was a little later, when Beck arrived to tell them it was safe to leave.

Penhaligon stood by the car with Fitz and Beck. Cassidy looked ready to bolt, though he no longer seemed on the verge of a panic attack.

Bilborough was dealing with Lang and Lindsay, over by the JCB. The men were being restrained by several uniformed officers, but they were making a good fight of it.

'Cassidy – ' Lang screamed. He got one arm free, and for a moment it looked as if he might get away altogether.

Cassidy jerked round. His mouth twisted into a rictus of fear.

Bilborough yelled at the two men. 'I'm arresting you on suspicion of causing criminal damage and endangering life – '

' – you're dead, Cassidy – ' Lang screamed. He lunged forward, but the uniformed officer pushed him back.

' – you do not have to say anything but anything you do say will be taken down in evidence – '

One of the officers got Lindsay in an armlock and started to drag the man away.

'Tell him he's dead – ' It was impossible to tell whether Lang or Lindsay had spoken.

'Pervert!'

'Do you understand?' Bilborough said, and to the officers, 'Put them in the van.' The men were still screaming abuse as they were dragged off.

Bilborough went across to Penhaligon and the others. He looked exhausted. It can't be easy on him, Penhaligon thought. This case, the Super on his back, Catriona maybe losing the baby. When there was time, maybe she'd say something about the argument.

'What are you going to do about that?' Cassidy yelled at Bilborough. 'What are you going to do about that?'

Fitz was watching him. Penhaligon knew that stare. Something Cassidy had done had led Fitz to some conclusion or other. She raised her eyebrows at him, but before he could say anything, Bilborough spoke.

'Mr Cassidy, I suggest you spend the night in a hotel with DS Beck – ' Bloody hell, Penhaligon thought. *Bloody* hell. She couldn't keep the anger off her face. ' – and Fitz,' Bilborough went on. Cassidy glared at him. 'It's for your own safety. OK?'

Cassidy glanced at the JCB, and the police van that was just leaving. For a moment Penhaligon thought he would argue, maybe start yelling for his brief. But then he seemed to crumble in on himself. 'Yeah. OK,' he said.

Beck touched Cassidy on the arm, with a quick dabbing motion as if he thought he might be contagious. 'We're over here,' he said, and started towards the van.

Penhaligon was still glaring at Bilborough. A minute ago she'd felt sorry for the man. Now this.

'Why Fitz?' Penhaligon asked.

Bilborough didn't even try to answer the question, just turned and walked towards his car.

Penhaligon followed him. 'Sir!' she shouted. It flashed through her mind that she sounded like a whiny schoolgirl. She wondered what Fitz would make of that.

Bilborough turned to look at her, but he didn't stop

194

walking. 'Because Beck'll keep his mind on the job,' he said. 'You won't.'

Penhaligon turned away. Fury washed over her like molten lava.

'Hey, Jimmy!' Bilborough called.

Jimmy, Penhaligon thought, disgustedly. How often did he call her Jane? There was no surer sign of the pecking order. She glanced at Fitz, who was waiting by the car. He gave her one of those calculated glances of his. She looked away. Dammit, Penhaligon thought. The worst of it was having to admit Bilborough was right.

The car smelled of warm plastic and Panhandle's perfume. As Fitz settled into the seat next to her, she fiddled with her handbag. She was obviously furious about the scene outside.

Fitz knew Bilborough had a point. He did distract Panhandle. Sometimes he did it deliberately. He enjoyed distracting her, dammit. Something about the way her eyes widened when she was amused, or maybe it was her smile. But she wasn't smiling now. The trouble was, she knew Bilborough had a point too.

She opened the glove compartment and put her bag in it. A travel agent's brochure fell out.

She stared at it for a second. 'As soon as this is sorted, I'm off,' she said.

'Yeah?' Fitz asked. 'Where?'

'Anywhere. Just as long as there's not the faintest chance of bumping into a copper.'

'Ahh . . . Moss side?'

Panhandle laughed aloud. It had been too long since Fitz had heard her do that. 'I've got two weeks due. I'm taking it.'

The brochure was for the Greek Islands. He thought about Panhandle sunbathing. Bikini or one-piece? One-piece, he decided. She was far too restrained for anything

195

else. Her pale skin wouldn't like the sun, but with care it would take a pale golden sheen; only occasionally the swimsuit would ride up or down a little, and reveal the milk-white skin of her hidden places.

Christ, he thought. Bromide, anyone?

'With Peter?' He had to say something, but he couldn't look at her. Didn't dare. He stared through the windscreen. Bilborough was talking to someone from the fire services. Concentrate on that, he thought. Don't think about her, about the tiny golden hairs on her arms and how the sun would gild them, about slow dancing with her to some crappy muzak in a Greek taverna disco, her body moving against yours, her head nestled against your chest, your hands slowly moving down from her waist to the gentle swell of her hips –

'Probably,' she murmured, her voice slow and slurred.

The slow swelling heat in his groin made thinking of anything but her impossible. 'I'll miss you, he said. Christ, he thought. I have a wife. I love my wife. It didn't matter. 'Can I play the dirty old man for just one minute?' He forced lightness into his tone.

'You've made a career out of it. What's another minute?' She laughed, but the tension in the car was unbearable.

Fitz felt himself floating free, as if nothing they said in this car would matter afterwards, so they could say anything, anything at all. Which was crap, of course, but as long as he could listen to her voice, feel the warmth of her body near his, he really didn't care.

'Yeah,' he said. 'Young women are wasted on young men. You'll be off on holiday with Peter, right?' He thought, I'm making a play for her. I love my wife. I love Judith. I do. But his mouth was stretching open around the words, and there was nothing he could do to stop them coming out. 'You'll want him to rub oil on your back. He'll be reading.' He stared at her for a second. 'He'll do it, but he won't *want* to do it.' He paused. *Stop*, he told himself. *Stop now*. But of

196

course he didn't. 'Now me,' he said, 'I'd rub oil in your back till Boots ran dry.'

Her eyes stripped the clothes from him. She wants me, he thought. He'd known he amused her, that there was an intellectual attraction, but this was different. This was an animal thing, and he wasn't really used to it. He knew that most women saw the size of him and nothing else. Saw the size and were repelled by it. Except Judith – *don't think of Judith*, he told himself fiercely – and now Panhandle.

'Do you fancy a quick one?' she asked, and giggled with embarrassment.

Fitz felt himself go hot. 'Can't,' he said.

'Why not?'

She had to know why not: he was a married man with kids, he loved his wife, he hadn't done with his marriage. 'Minute's up,' Fitz said, as if it were the obvious answer.

She wasn't about to let him off that easy, though. 'That's what you'd like though, isn't it, Fitz? Me on the side and your wife and kids to go home to.'

It was a blow to the belly. To the groin. 'Yes,' he said after a long while. It was his turn to giggle. 'I think most men would.' He chewed his lip. 'In fact, any man who says otherwise is a liar.'

It took her a moment to absorb that. 'Answer this. Not a joke,' she added quickly, 'not a put-down. A straight answer. Yeah?'

'Yeah,' Fitz said. Oh God, he thought. She's going to ask me if I love her. I'm sorry, he thought. Then, to his horror he realised he didn't know who the thought was addressed to, Judith or Panhandle – because in truth he didn't know if what he felt for Panhandle went beyond a great deal of fondness and an ocean of lust.

'Will you come away with me?' she said.

He turned sharply to look at her. 'What, instead of Peter?' There was no need to fake shock.

'Yeah,' she said.

197

'I know what you're thinking – ' keeping his voice light was a real effort.

'Don't tell me what I'm thinking,' Panhandle said.

'You're thinking, I've paid the penance so I might as well commit the sin.' It was intuition. He didn't bother to analyse it out.

'No analysis please,' Panhandle said.

There was silence. Judith, Fitz thought. He tried to remember her eyes, her laugh, the smell of her; but all that came to mind was a blurred impression of weeks and months of rows and shouting. And her with Graham, her legs up round his hips, her little moan of pleasure, the way she liked to nibble an earlobe or a fingertip.

Somewhere a fly droned against a window. I have to say something, Fitz thought. He started to speak.

A rear door opened. Bilborough got in, and slammed the door behind him. 'Drop Fitz at the hotel, then back to the station.'

If he'd noticed anything odd, he wasn't saying.

'Right,' Panhandle said. She glanced at Fitz. Her eyes were very dark. *Later*, she seemed to be thinking at him. He wasn't sure what reply he sent.

Penhaligon was in a real snit, Bilborough thought. He glared at the back of her head as she drove. So she wasn't going to get a night holed up in a hotel with Fitz at the tax-payer's expense. Tough. And she had the damned cheek to accuse him of letting his worry over Catriona get in the way . . . which reminded him that he hadn't phoned home for a while. He'd have to do it when he got back to the station.

The van halted in front of the Royale. Penhaligon parked the car behind it. A bellboy came out and opened the car door. Bilborough watched as Beck got out of the van, looked all round – a bit over the top, but very sound, Bilborough thought – then beckoned to Cassidy, who also

198

clambered out of the van. Fitz hadn't moved.

'Is he paralysed?' Bilborough asked no-one in particular.

Fitz still didn't move. He seemed to be staring at something on the horizon. Eventually he said, 'The answer to your question is "yes".'

What the bloody hell, Bilborough wondered. 'Yes to what?' he asked.

Fitz didn't answer. He just got out of the car and shut the door. Penhaligon put the car in gear. 'I've asked him to come away and roger me rigid for a fortnight.' She paused. 'Sir.' She was smiling. In fact, it was a long time since Bilborough had seen her so happy.

Fine, he thought. Great. 'You're telling me to mind my own business?'

'Yes, I am, sir,' she said mildly.

OK, he thought. If that's the way it is. 'The station next,' he said.

Penhaligon smiled like a Cheshire cat all the way there.

TWENTY-ONE

Fitz followed Cassidy into the hotel room. The man stood in the centre of the room staring around as if everything in it – in the whole world – were strange to him. Perhaps it was, Fitz thought. A week ago, Cassidy had been one more person struggling through the daily round. Then, if Fitz were any judge, a few days ago he'd become a murderer; even then, up until this morning he'd been a reasonably well respected member of the community. But now what he'd done was out in the open.

No wonder he seemed bewildered. He wasn't living in the same world as the one he woke up in.

Fitz glanced quickly round the room. It was a damned sight more luxurious than many the University had paid for him to stay at when he went to academic conferences, which just went to prove that the brute force of law enforcement paid better than brain. Speaking of which . . . he spotted the minibar and went over to it. He poured himself three generous fingers of Scotch. Why not? It was the tax-payer's money, after all.

'This is posh,' Beck said, from behind Fitz's back. Fitz turned round. Cassidy was still standing in the middle of the room, clutching his jacket like a kid with a comfort blanket. His skin was pallid in the electric light, with deep shadows like bruises under his eyes. He looked almost afraid of Beck. Well, no-one had ever said Cassidy was stupid.

Beck jerked his thumb in the direction of the en-suite bathroom. 'There's a bloke in there with a silver cane.' Fitz scowled at him. The idiot probably thought he was softening Cassidy up. 'Taps your dick twice when you've finished.' Cassidy looked away. 'Suit you, that job.' Beck grinned at him. They could have invented the word snide to describe that grin, Fitz thought.

He held up his glass. He swilled the Scotch round, then downed it in one. It burned his throat as it hit. A blend, he thought, and not a good one. Damn cheapskate tax-payers. 'Drink?' he asked.

'I'll get my own,' Beck said. He went over to the television. There was a menu for the private channel on top of it. He picked it up. '*Sauce for Suzy* or *Night of Lust*?' Cassidy didn't answer. That didn't surprise Fitz. Beck would twist anything he said into some piece of foul-mouthed crap. For a second, Fitz almost forgot what Cassidy had done, and felt sorry for him. '*Night of Lust*,' Beck decided for them. 'Suzy's a lesbian.'

He picked up the remote control and went and sat down. Cassidy stared into space.

'Shall I tell you why I can't stand lesbians?' Beck asked. He waved the remote control around.

'Please,' Fitz said. Here we go, he thought. The James Beck Guide to Interrogation: all you have to do is shove the knife into the suspect hard enough, and every time he squirms you twist it. Sooner or later, he'll cough. Trouble was, as knives went Beck's brain was more a rusty penknife than a scalpel.

Come to think of it, Beck would probably think that was a compliment.

'Queers are OK – ' Fitz made sure Beck saw him raise his eyebrows. Beck added quickly, 'As long as I don't turn my back on you, you're OK.' Cassidy flinched. 'Two queers doing it, that's two women going spare.' He clicked the TV on. 'But two lesbians doing it, that's two men going short.'

'You can tell he reads the *Guardian*, can't you?' Fitz said. He wondered if Beck realised just how insecure that made him sound. After all, a man secure in his sexuality and his

201

sex appeal wouldn't worry about a shortage of women –
he'd just assume some other bugger would lose out. Then
again, Fitz thought, if I had that bit of bum-fluff on my head
and something that looked like a hairy fat caterpillar stuck
under my nose, I'd be pretty insecure too.

Beck clicked the remote control. The television flickered
to life. On the screen, a woman slowly unlaced her corset.
Her fingernails were blood-red against the white skin of her
breast.

Cassidy looked away.

Andy had waited with the crowd outside the station for
hours, ever since he'd been cautioned and released. There
were a lot more people now, a lot of local folk but some
journalists too. A few coppers stood around, though there
hadn't been any trouble since Cassidy had been taken out.
One or two of them had tried to talk to Mum, to tell her how
sorry they were. Yeah, right. That was why they'd let
Cassidy go.

Melanie had stayed. She was standing next to him in the
crowd. Mike, too, and some of the others. The fat bastard,
Fitz, had wanted to know why he'd put his friends above his
brother. Well, this was why: you chose your friends, and
they always stood by you, but you had to work at it. Your
family were just supposed to be there, whatever happened.
They weren't supposed to die on you. They weren't supposed to go and get fucking murdered before you could
make things right.

Andy had had a lot of time to think, while he'd been
standing around. He'd watched Mike and Melanie, and he'd
realised that a lot of what he thought he'd seen between
them was just in his head. Pasting Tom Rope, that had been
the right thing to do. Rowing with Mike had been plain
bloody stupid. He wondered if it would have happened if
Tim hadn't been – he forced himself to think the word –
murdered. He felt his fists clench, and his whole body go

rigid with the need to do something, hit something, some-one. Cassidy was going to pay for this.

Melanie slid her hand in his and gave it a little squeeze. She was freezing. They all were. He glanced at his mum. She was pale, with big dark splodges under her eyes, and a pinched look to her face that wasn't just the cold.

He thought about going home and getting a Thermos of coffee to warm them all up. Before he could decide, a cop van came speeding round the corner, with a car right behind it.

The crowd surged forward. Everyone was hammering on the sides of the van. This time, they'd do it right. Turn the van over, get the pervert out and make him pay for Tim. But the van didn't stop. It swept straight through the gates.

People were getting out. Not Cassidy, but Andy's dad, and Mr Lindsay. The car slowed. Bilborough got out. He was in charge. All of this was his fault. The car moved off again, and the gates shut behind it as soon as it got inside. They had him now.

The crowd moved to surround him. 'The suspect is not with us,' he yelled, over all the other yelling that was going on.

To Andy's surprise, Melanie got in front of him. She shoved her finger in Bilborough's face. 'Where is he then?' she shouted, walking towards him so he had to step back-wards.

For a couple of minutes after that, Andy couldn't really hear very much because everyone was shouting. Nobody else seemed to realise that his dad had been taken inside.

'Just go home,' Bilborough yelled. He was nearly at the gates. Any minute now and he'd be gone. He'd have got away with it.

Andy got between him and the gates, so he couldn't get through. 'You're not taking him in there,' he said.

Bilborough was backed up against the gates now. He turned to face the crowd. 'Look,' he bellowed. The crowd became fractionally quieter. 'These two men have broken the law. I can understand why they broke it, but to understand isn't to excuse.'

The crowd surged forward. They were bellowing and screaming. A camera flashed. A tape recorder whirred.

' – wanker – ' someone yelled.

' – justice – '

' – Cassidy – '

' – string him up – '

Bilborough turned to Andy. 'Son, for the last time, let me through.'

This is a police officer, Andy thought. Assaulting a police officer, that's serious stuff. He almost stepped aside; but Melanie was watching him and so was Mike, and besides he had this vivid picture in his head of Tim hanging in those woods, Tim begging Cassidy not to hurt him. He felt the blood roar in his ears. A pulse beat at his temple. 'Look, it's my brother murdered, and you're nicking my dad.'

Bilborough turned back to the crowd. 'They've broken the law,' he yelled. 'And you will all be under arrest if you don't disperse.'

It was too much for Andy. 'You're not listening, are you, you fucking wanker,' he shouted.

Bilborough whirled round. Before Andy could move, he found that his arm was jerked half way up his back. Pain jolted through it right up into his shoulder. He grunted.

'You're nicked, right?' He turned to the uniformed coppers. 'Enough's enough. Get the back-up out here.' He glared at Andy's mum. She looked like she might cry, but she stood aside. One of the coppers opened the gate a little bit.

Bilborough pushed Andy ahead of him so he had to run.

'Andy!' Melanie yelled. He tried to twist round to see her, but it hurt too much and besides, there were too many people.

Then suddenly they were inside, and the gate clanged

204

shut. Bilborough eased up then. Andy turned round, but all he could see were faces pressed up against the bars and hands jabbing through them.

'In you go,' Bilborough said.

Bilborough raged through the station shoving Andy in front of him. Ahead of him, he could hear Lang and Lindsay cursing their arresting officers out. Andy twisted in his grip.

'I haven't done anything,' the lad yelled.

Bilborough yanked his arm hard up against his back. A couple of uniforms stared as he propelled Andy down the corridor. 'I want it dispersed, right?' A uniformed sergeant came out of a side room, laughing and joking with someone inside. Jesus, what did they think it was? A holiday camp? 'I want that mob dispersed. I don't care how you do it, disperse the bastards.'

They turned a corner into the short corridor leading to the holding cells. Lang and Lindsay were just being banged up. When they saw Andy, they started shouting, but Bilborough didn't even try to work out what they were saying. Andy tried to wrench free. Bilborough ran him straight towards the empty cell at the end. One of the uniforms opened the door.

'I've done nothing you soft sod – '

'You've obstructed a police officer, sunshine.' Bilborough let Andy go and shoved him inside. 'Behave,' he shouted as the door slammed shut.

'You've broken my son's arm, you bastard – ' Lang shouted.

'You let Cassidy go – ' That was Lindsay.

'I want a lawyer down here now, and a doctor – '

Bilborough ignored them. He rubbed the back of his neck. Stupid bastards, he thought. Christ, it wasn't as if he couldn't understand where they were coming from – if someone like Cassidy hurt a kid of his, he wouldn't demolish his flat, he'd pummel him into the ground – but couldn't they see they were just making it harder for him to get a result?

He looked up. Mr Allen was watching him from the far end of the corridor. Bilborough was suddenly aware of the uniforms standing around watching him.

'It's under control,' he said. The Chief Super glared at him. There wasn't a hint of sympathy in his eyes now. Bilborough licked his lips. 'I've sent back-up in. It got a bit out of hand, but it's under control.' He paused. Allen didn't say anything. 'It's sorted,' he finished.

A bollocking would have been easier to take. Anything but Allen's quiet outrage. 'You brought those men to this nick?'

Bilborough fought to keep his voice level. 'My officers made the arrest. Taking them anywhere else is bowing to that lot out there.'

Meeting Allen's gaze was harder than facing down the mob outside. Say something, Bilborough thought at him. Eventually he spoke, but not to Bilborough. 'You're needed,' he said to the uniforms.

The men started to run down the hall. 'Come on lads. Come on,' Bilborough said, waving them on. When they'd gone, he turned back to Allen. The Chief Super's expression hadn't changed. Here we go, Bilborough thought.

'You didn't even consider it, did you?' Allen said. It wasn't a question.

'I did, sir,' Bilborough said, trying to keep his voice down.

'The effect it would have.' Allen obviously didn't care who heard.

'I did, sir. They were obstructing.'

'You're not charging him.'

Bilborough answered before he realised it hadn't been a question. 'Yeah,' he said.

'Go up to the canteen,' Allen said.

How much back-up does he think it'll take, Bilborough

206

wondered. 'I've sent the back-up in, sir,' he said.

Allen looked at him as if he were an imbecile. 'You go up to the canteen. Have a cup of tea. Stay there.'

Not this, Bilborough thought. You said you wouldn't do this to me.

'Go and have a cup of tea.'

Bilborough couldn't speak, could hardly move. He heard the blood rush in his ears. Eventually he broke away from Allen's gaze and slid past him into the main corridor.

Somehow, he got upstairs to the men's toilets without screaming. But once he was there, he kicked the door open so hard it slammed off the wall and bounced back. He didn't care about the noise any more, didn't care about promotion, didn't care about any damn thing.

He went in. Easy, he told himself. Easy. He tried to slow his breathing down. He caught sight of himself in a mirror above the sink. His face was almost unrecognisable with anger. It's all right, he told himself. It's nothing, we'll get the crowd under control. Allen'll see I did the only thing I could –

His foot lashed out explosively. It crashed into the door of a cubicle, making the metal ring. Pain jolted up his leg. He felt his mouth curl into a snarl.

Fuck Allen.

It wasn't OK and he couldn't make it be OK, and he didn't want to pretend.

He went into the cubicle and slammed the door shut. Oh Jesus, he thought, oh Jesus. His face was on fire. His eyes burned, thought whether from tears or because of the tiredness he couldn't tell. His breath came out in a long ragged sigh. He put his arms out and used the sides of the cubicle to support himself. It was that or fall down, and if he went down he didn't know if there would be any getting back up.

Penhaligon was thinking about going off duty. But only thinking about it. With Beck and Fitz holed up in the hotel, she couldn't reasonably go home till she was told to. If she'd been Beck, she thought, it would have been different. He'd just have gone, and if Bilborough had said anything, they'd exchange one of those sly little man-of-the-world grins, and that would be that.

If she tried it, she'd never hear the end of it. So she sat at her desk, pretending to do her paperwork and nursing yet another cup of disgusting canteen coffee, and wished Bilborough would crawl out of whatever stone he'd been hiding under since the Chief Super read him the riot act. She was achingly tired, too tired to think straight, let alone write up what had happened at Cassidy's flat.

The phone went. It was the Chief Super. Between her tiredness and the utter shock of him calling her, Penhaligon barely managed to follow what he was saying.

' – so,' he concluded, 'I want those men released, got me, Sergeant? If DCI Bilborough wants to make a fuss about it, you can direct him to me. Is that clear?'

'Yes. Yes of course, sir.' She put the phone down.

God, she thought. Bilborough was in enough of a state without this. Cassidy had to cough now. If he didn't, the boss's career would be on the line.

TWENTY-TWO

Fitz watched Beck go and get Timothy Lang's notebook. Evidently he'd decided it was time to come the heavy policeman. He certainly looked the worse for wear. His tie was loosened halfway down his chest, and his eyes were red-rimmed.

Beck riffled through the book. 'I'm sorry, I'm sorry, I'm sorry, I'm sorry,' Beck read out. 'What are you sorry about?'

Now there, thought Fitz, is a truly incisive question. He settled back to watch a master at work. Well, it was better than watching any more choice excerpts from *Night of Lust* in slo-mo.

Beck waved the book at Cassidy. His black eyebrows arched up. 'You're sorry because – '

'I'm sorry he's dead,' Cassidy said.

'You're sorry because you killed him,' Beck said.

'I'm sorry he's dead,' Cassidy murmured.

'You're lying,' Beck said. He actually managed to get the words out through clenched teeth. Fitz thought it made him look like a rabid rabbit. A balding rabid rabbit at that. 'You're sorry you killed him.'

'I didn't kill him.' Despite Beck's interrogation, Cassidy looked a little more relaxed than he had been earlier. Fitz wondered if letting him rest had been such a good idea; then again, maybe he'd be able to get him off guard.

Beck lit a cigarette. He didn't offer Fitz one. He slapped the lighter down on the table.

'Explain the fibres on your watch,' he demanded.

'I've no need to explain anything,' Cassidy said. He sounded remarkably calm. He was right of course. Nothing he said here would be admissable in court unless he repeated it for a tape recorder.

Beck turned back to Cassidy. 'They prove you touched him sometime between five o'clock and the time of his death.' He moved forward. His face suddenly turned savage. 'You *touched* him.' He made the word itself into an obscenity. 'Did more than touch him.' He jabbed his fingers at Cassidy. The cigarette clenched between them sent rags of smoke into the air. 'Oh, an ordinary common-or-garden rapist, them I can understand – '

I bet you can, Fitz thought. Beck was the sort of man who probably thought rape had something to do with sex. 'You're going a bit too far,' Fitz said.

Beck talked straight over the top of him. ' – but sick bastards like you, shoving bits of metal – '

What? Fitz thought. Where the hell had that come from? He filed it for later perusal. For now he had to stop Beck before the man screwed Cassidy up to the point where they'd never get anything out of him.

'Homophobia – ' he said.

' – into young kids. What kind – '

'It's more than two syllables so you won't understand what it is – '

' – of a hobby is that?' Beck was breathing hard now. 'What possible pleasure can you get from something like that?'

' "Homophobia" – morbid fear of – '

Beck turned on Fitz. 'Look, I know what Fitzophobia is – a morbid fear of men who talk through their arses. Just stay out of this.'

Beck was easy to read, and his past history was writ large in his present behaviour. 'You were about fourteen when you came over here, right?'

Beck looked shocked. Horrified would be an even closer

description, Fitz thought; it told him all he needed to know: he was on the right track.

'This is the suspect,' Beck said, jabbing his cigarette towards Cassidy.

Fitz just gave a secret little smile that he knew would infuriate Beck. Of course he knew Cassidy was the suspect. Why else would he waste his breath winding Beck up, if not to get to Cassidy? Except for the sheer fun of it, of course. Two birds, one stone. Not bad, Fitz thought.

He let his voice drop into confessional mode, only it wasn't his own sins he was reciting. 'New boy in school – a difficult age to make friends,' he said. He let sympathy ooze out of every word. Beck frowned. His thick black eyebrows almost met in the middle. 'The girls would talk to you. New face – girls like that.' He was getting to Beck, and by his reckoning Beck didn't even know why. 'But the boys . . .' he let his voice trail off into a concerned little clucking noise.

He watched emotion play across Beck's bland face. Hostility. Fear. Fear of having his inner self exposed for everyone to see – that was what he'd think. But Fitz knew better. It was much more likely that Beck feared having to admit to himself that what Fitz said was true. Even if he never had to say it aloud, he would know in the depths – nah, Fitz thought, the shallows, surely – of his soul that Fitz had spoken the truth.

Cassidy was watching all this with a bemused half smile on his lips. Something was working through his mind, Fitz decided. Even if he'd wanted to spare Beck, he couldn't have done it. Besides, he'd once had to put Panhandle through the same thing. He'd be damned if he'd be kinder to Beck than he had been to her.

Beck turned to Cassidy, like a man who has had a bad day at work and comes home to kick the dog. He leaned on the coffee table so he could stick his face close up to Cassidy. 'We've got clout,' he said. He wasn't shouting now. His

211

voice was low and menacing. 'When we bang you up you're going to be begging for Section 43.' He thrust his face further forward. 'A bit of protection, get me?'

'I don't want protection,' Cassidy said.

More guilt, Fitz noted. That, if nothing else, convinced him that Cassidy was the murderer. 'The boys ignored you, didn't they, Beck?' If he could put the screws on Beck, Cassidy might recognise a similar pattern in his own past, and start talking. Unless Fitz could shut Beck up, it was the best he could hope for.

Beck looked at Fitz, but he didn't say anything. He turned back to Cassidy. 'You think the screws are going to give you protection? Are they shite.' A little droplet of spittle clung to his moustache.

Cassidy leaned forward. 'I don't want protection,' he repeated.

'One boy in particular.' Fitz looked straight at Beck as he spoke, but all the time he was watching Cassidy out of the corner of his eye. His attention was on Beck, not on Fitz. 'You wanted to be near him. You wanted to hold him. It bothered you – '

Beck talked straight over the top of him. 'Those screws have got kids of their own.' He leaned nearer to Cassidy. His voice was calm – too calm considering the way he'd been raging at Cassidy – but his body was rigid with tension. 'They'll leave your cell door open, turn their backs, the lads'll be in, and they won't be there to shake your hand, you know what I'm saying?'

'You thought you were gay,' Fitz said quietly when Beck paused.

Beck rounded on him. His face was slightly flushed. 'Will you shut it?' he screamed. He jabbed the cigarette at Fitz. Ash flew off the tip.

Here we go, Fitz thought. 'You loved that boy.'

'You are talking crap,' Beck said. But he didn't look away.

212

'It kept you awake at night. "Am I queer? Am I queer? The girls talk to me – they must see it in me. The boys ignore me. I'll prove I'm not queer." ' Beck stared at Fitz. So did Cassidy. He was right then, Fitz thought; it was hardly surprising, considering how many kids went through a period of fixating on their own sex. It didn't say anything at all about whether they'd grow up straight or homosexual. But Beck apparently didn't know that – and neither did Cassidy, by the expression on his face. Fitz pushed on. 'How do you prove you're not queer? You pick a fight. Who do you fight? Whose face do you smash to a pulp?' He paused for a heartbeat, let the thought hang unspoken in the air. 'The boy you love,' he murmured.

Beck stared, mouth open, eyes wide. Cassidy's face was clenched like a fist. Gotcha, Fitz thought.

'Bollocks,' Beck shouted.

He turned back to Cassidy, but when he spoke his voice was conversational. 'He's done this before.' Fitz thought about it. If Beck had been a different kind of person, he might have understood that Cassidy had been laid open at the same time as he had. But this was Beck. He probably just wanted an audience. Beck went on, 'He looks in there – ' he jerked his cigarette towards Fitz's crotch, and then at his head ' – and in there, for something sick, something twisted.' Beck paused. 'And because he's thought it, he says we all have.' He turned to Fitz theatrically. 'Well, we haven't. Most of us are normal.'

Fitz laughed. Jesus, *normal*. As if there were any such thing. And coming from Beck, who was as twisted as anyone walking around without a straitjacket and a section order as Fitz had ever known, it was especially rich.

'Are you giving her one?' Beck asked.

What the bloody hell? 'Who?' Fitz asked, though even as he said the question, he knew the answer.

'Penhaligon.'

For one second, Fitz thought of saying, yes I am. I'm

screwing her senseless every night and then going home and doing the same to my wife. Beck would talk, of course, but then he was probably talking anyway . . . but Fitz thought of Panhandle in the car, earlier. Her face had been so vulnerable; he'd wanted to stroke her face, to run his thumb down her cheekbone and tell her he'd never hurt her; he hadn't because he wouldn't make a promise he couldn't be sure of keeping. But she deserved better than to be used to score points off a little turd like Beck. So he said nothing, simply glared at him.

Beck obviously knew he'd gone too far. Go on, Fitz thought at him. Piss in your pants, why don't you? The big bad Fitz is coming to get you.

Beck didn't hold Fitz's gaze for too long. He threw the cigarette into the ashtray. 'Where was I before I was so rudely interrupted?' He leaned over Cassidy as he had before. Nothing if not imaginative, our Beck, Fitz thought. 'Section 43. If we say yeah, you get it. If we say no, you don't. And if you don't, you end up with your dick in a jar. You understand what I'm saying?'

'Yes,' Cassidy whispered. For the first time, he seemed afraid.

TWENTY-THREE

Bilborough felt like he'd been sitting in the toilet for hours. It had probably been more like fifteen minutes. Not that he was using the loo. He was just sitting on it, fully clothed, because there was nowhere else to go.

The pounding of his heart and the thunder of blood in his ears had finally subsided, but he hadn't been able to face the thought of going outside. It would be all over the station by now. He could just imagine the looks he'd get, the whispers and the way people would hastily change the conversation when he walked up to them.

A cup of tea in the canteen. You're off the case, was what Allen had really meant. He'd tried it earlier, with his 'take a few days off, you should be with her' routine. Christ, Bilborough thought. He should have known that once Allen got an idea in his head he wouldn't be put off as easily as all that. The only question was how long it was going to take for him to live this down – weeks, months, years even, if Allen started talking about it at the polite little dinner parties he loved to hold.

Someone knocked on the door.

'Yeah,' Bilborough said.

'Penhaligon, boss. What are you doing?'

Oh for Pete's sake, he thought. You'd think she'd leave him alone in here, if nowhere else. 'What do you think I'm doing?'

'Your wife's gone into labour.'

Oh Jesus, Bilborough thought. His throat went tight, and he realised he was shaking. Can't lose it, he thought. Can't lose it now. 'Has the crowd dispersed?' he asked.

'Just about,' Penhaligon said.

Bilborough left the cubicle. Penhaligon looked at him oddly as he went to wash his hands. 'Drive me to the hospital, then get on to Jimmy Beck,' he said over the roar of running water.

'Right,' Penhaligon said. She was still looking at him strangely.

'Something I ate,' he said, and thought, Damn. Forgot to pull the chain.

Penhaligon drove as fast as she dared, and even so, Bilborough kept nagging her to go faster.

'It'll only slow us down if we get pulled up,' she pointed out. She watched him in the rear-view mirror. He was a bit of a mess – pale, dark-eyed, almost shaking with exhaustion. She thought about telling him that Allen had ordered her to release Lindsay and the Langs, and decided against it.

Eventually they got to the hospital. He had the car door open before she had even parked. She finally caught up with him as he was trying to find the maternity wards.

'This way,' she said, pointing to the sign.

He nodded and followed her. When they got to the waiting room she found him a chair, then went off to find a nurse in the corridor outside.

'Mrs Bilborough's in the delivery room,' the nurse said. They walked back together. 'We're just settling her in, and then her husband can go in – '

'Here he is,' Penhaligon said. She grinned.

Bilborough was asleep.

A little later, she made the mistake of going back to the station to pick up her things. As she was going past the control room, Louisa stuck her head out of the door.

'Jane? We've got a disturbance at Cavendish Road – '

216

'I'm just off,' Penhaligon said. 'Sorry.'

'It's a Mrs Cassidy. Your suspect's mum. Someone's heaved a brick through her window. I've got Jenny Wright and Alan Carstairs over there, but – '

'But it's our shout,' Penhaligon said. She closed her eyes. Just for an instant she thought – dreamed – about telling Louisa to stuff it. 'OK. Give me the address – '

Jenny Wright opened the door to Penhaligon. 'She's in there,' the constable said, gesturing at a room towards the back of the neat little terraced house. 'She's in a real state, mind you.'

Looking at the gaping, star-shaped hole in the front window, Penhaligon could see why. 'Has she got someone to fix that?'

'Don't think so. She keeps saying, "My son does all that for me." ' Wright shrugged. They both knew Mrs Cassidy's son wouldn't be fixing this problem.

Penhaligon went through into the back room. It was quite dark and cluttered, filled with big old-fashioned furniture and the kind of bric-a-brac that just collects over the years. Mrs Cassidy was a tiny, white-haired old lady, wearing a floral dressing-gown that made her seem to disappear into the armchair she was sitting in. She was clutching a half brick. It had a note tied round it.

'We couldn't get it off her,' Carstairs explained. 'It just upset her when I tried – '

Penhaligon nodded. She gestured at Wright and Carstairs to wait outside. Then she went and sat on the sofa near the old lady. 'Mrs Cassidy? I'm Jane Penhaligon – '

'I don't want you,' Mrs Cassidy said. 'I want my Nigel.' Her fingers clutched at the lacy collar of her dressing-gown. The veins on the back of her hand stood out from the liver-spotted skin. 'He didn't come and see me today.'

Shit, Penhaligon thought. What do I say? Because he's a murderer? Because your darling son strangled one of the kids in his care, then tried to kill himself? She licked her lips. When in doubt, change the subject.

'May I see that, Mrs Cassidy?' She reached for the brick.

'You mustn't,' Mrs Cassidy said. She clutched it with both hands. 'My Nigel, he'll sort it out.'

God, Penhaligon thought. Where are you now, when I need you the most, Fitz? 'Please?' she said. She forced a smile.

'I don't know where my Nigel is. It's Tuesday but he didn't come and see me – ' Mrs Cassidy stopped. She gave Penhaligon a smile of unbearable sweetness. 'It is Tuesday, isn't it?'

'Yes,' Penhaligon said. She tried again for the brick. This time she was able to prise it free from Mrs Cassidy's fingers.

She took the note off it. 'Eye for an eye,' it said, in red felt-tip. 'Die Bitch.'

Anger burned through her. It took all her police training to fold the note back round the brick. She put it behind her, out of Mrs Cassidy's view. Lynching Cassidy was one thing – she could understand that. But this . . . She wondered if any of them had actually seen Mrs Cassidy.

'Where's my Nigel?' the old lady said again. Penhaligon wondered if she'd been senile before, or if the shock had sent her over the edge.

'He's . . . he's helping us,' Penhaligon said. After this, she vowed, she'd never get pissed off with Bilborough when he screwed up breaking bad news. She knew the words she had to say, but it felt as if her throat were closing up around them.

'He's a kind boy, my Nigel is,' Mrs Cassidy said. Her lips trembled. The skin around them was etched with hundreds of tiny lines. She suddenly looked straight at Penhaligon. For a second, the woman she must once have been stared out of her eyes. 'I'm not stupid, you know. They said on the radio. He tried to kill himself, and there was that lad that went missing.'

'I'm sorry,' Penhaligon said. She wanted to go. She wanted to find some dark, quiet spot and sleep forever. She wanted not to have to look at those bright, pain-filled eyes. 'I'm sorry,' she repeated, as if it could make a difference.

Mrs Cassidy started to fiddle with one of her buttons. Her expression said she had gone to some other place. 'I don't understand why they want to hurt him. He wouldn't hurt anyone, my Nigel. He buys me flowers. But he's a bad boy. He buys me chocolates, even though Doctor Evans says I can't have them – ' She looked at Penhaligon. 'Why won't they let him come and see me?' she asked.

Penhaligon swallowed. She didn't know what to say.

'Why?' the old lady repeated. Her hand clutched at Penhaligon's arm. She was trembling slightly. Penhaligon looked away. She'd have to phone Beck and tell him about this. Not that he'd care.

After everything Beck had said about homosexuals, the way he insisted on watching Cassidy take a pee was nothing short of ironic, Fitz thought as he poured himself another drink. Of course he'd claimed it was official policy. Probably thought Cassidy would throw the toilet roll out the window and climb down it and have himself an escape, as Arlo Guthrie had put it in *Alice's Restaurant*. Now there was a movie with no discernible motive, pure or otherwise, Fitz thought. Beck's motives, on the other hand, were pure all right: purely nasty.

He watched as Cassidy came out and settled himself on the sofa. Beck followed him. Fitz drained his glass. He was about ready to start, if only Beck would keep quiet.

Some hope. Beck sauntered out of the bathroom with his hands in his trouser pockets.

'It's your arrogance, Fitz,' Beck said. He was still steaming. He sat down opposite Fitz. 'A nice young bit of stuff like that and you're hanging around her.' He lit another cigarette. 'I wouldn't dream of it.'

Just as well, Fitz thought. You wouldn't stand a chance. But he didn't say that. Unlike Beck, he knew exactly how to aim his daggers. 'Yeah, well at least I've got my hair in the right place.' He ran his hand through it for emphasis.

Beck didn't react obviously. He just poured himself another drink. Can't fool me, Fitz thought. Beck had his arms held in front of him, with his hands down low to protect his balls. By contrast, Cassidy's body language seemed almost relaxed, as he sat bolt upright on the sofa with his arms by his sides and looking neither to left nor right. But that was an illusion. You had to see it as part of the process Cassidy was going through. He wasn't relaxed, he was burned out. His calm posture was the equivalent of a beaten dog rolling on its back to admit defeat: the dog might look like it was playing, but it was actually humiliated.

Fitz riffled through Timothy Lang's notebook. Something he'd seen earlier had held the key, he was sure. He found his place. 'Read it, please,' he said, holding it out to Cassidy.

'I can't,' Cassidy murmured. Given the lack of emotion in his voice, it was almost an act of defiance. It must have taken everything he had left.

'I've had this for years,' Beck said suddenly. He pointed at his moustache. 'I'm not going to shave it off just because a bunch of queers start growing them.' He gestured contemptuously at Cassidy. 'It's beneath me. I'm not that insecure.' He took another drink. 'Do you understand what I'm saying?'

'Keep your hair on,' Fitz said. Beck didn't get it. 'Read it, please,' he said to Cassidy, forcing gentleness into his voice.

'No.'

'Because that's what made you kill him?'

It was a challenge. Cassidy had to realise that. He leaned forward and took the book. 'First Ice,' he said, and stopped. His fingers tightened on the book. 'Tears on the classroom floor. I start to grieve.' Cassidy's voice broke. His mouth

220

worked. Fitz saw him swallow. Then he went on, 'He opens the classroom door, Tells me to leave. First Ice isn't nice.'

God, Fitz thought. The kid had been good. Given time, he might have been brilliant. Only that last line rang false, as if Tim had been trying to force something into the poem that didn't belong there.

All that potential, he thought, all those hopes and dreams and fears, hanging dead in the wood. It was enough to make you weep.

'Why "First Ice"?' he asked.

Cassidy's voice was thick with tears. 'It's a poem. About a girl . . . ' he stopped. For a second it seemed that he would break down, but then he continued, ' – in a telephone box. She's been hurt. I read it to the kids and got them to write about a time when they were hurt.' He did cry then, big gulping sobs that forced the air out of his lungs and made his shoulders shake. He put his hands in front of his face, but he couldn't stop crying.

Hurt, Fitz thought. Oh yes, Timothy Lang had been hurt all right. Treated as a freak by his father and brother, cosseted by his mother, rejected by his teacher – that was the way it had to be, surely? – and, finally, it wasn't just emotional hurt. It was panic and pain and violation. At this man's hands. He couldn't look at Cassidy and not think that.

Beck, sprawled in the armchair, watched with a smug little smile on his face. If he says anything now, I'll kill him, Fitz thought. But Beck said nothing.

' "He opens the classroom door, Tells me to leave." That's you.' Cassidy didn't answer. 'It is, isn't it?' Fitz insisted. Cassidy still didn't answer. For a long, almost unbearable moment, only the sound of his rough sobbing broke the silence. Eventually Fitz murmured, 'Thirteen years old. Beautiful. More a girl than a boy.' Fitz's voice was gentle, seducing Cassidy to enter with him into a dream of what that night might have been. 'You want to hold him, touch him,

221

explore. He's crying. "It's all right, Timothy. It's OK. It's OK." ' Cassidy was rapt. To Fitz's surprise, so was Beck. Time for the dream to turn nightmare. He roughened his voice a little. 'He's screaming. You've gone too far. He'll tell his mother. His mother'll tell the police. The police'll come round to the school.' Cassidy was still with him, but now he looked terrified. Whatever he was seeing, Fitz was glad he couldn't share it. He went on, relentless now, 'One hand's enough. Such a delicate throat. But the eyes won't close. You squeeze and you squeeze and the eyes won't close. You turn him over face down in the mud. You hold him.' Cassidy began to cry again, but softly, as if the fear had taken all his energy; but Fitz was pitiless. 'You run. Where? Home. Pace the floor. "I've strangled him. I've strangled him." A rope. You go back.' Fitz paused. He wanted Cassidy to have time to remember the bowel-loosening horror of that night. 'He's still there. Cold. You pick him up. There's air in his lungs. It gets squeezed out. Sounds like a groan. For one terrible second you think he's still alive.'

He stared at Cassidy. So did Beck. No-one spoke. Cassidy's hands clenched convulsively. He took a long, desperate breath. 'I marked books,' he said at last. 'I jogged.' He looked first at Beck and then at Fitz as if he thought he could persuade them to help him. 'Well, people must have seen me jogging,' he pleaded. 'Then I came home and marked some more books.'

After that, there was only silence.

Catriona screamed. Sweat sheened her skin and her hair hung in rats' tails around her face. Her hand clutched convulsively at his, so that her nails dug into his palm.

Bilborough thought he had never seen her look so beautiful.

The scream subsided into a series of short gasps. I wish she'd at least have gas, Bilborough thought. If he'd had his way, she'd have had an epidural.

222

The nurse dabbed at Catriona's face with a damp cloth. Bilborough wished he'd thought of that.

The midwife moved round to the end of the bed. 'Good girl. Here he comes. Once more. Push now – '

Again the scream. Again the desperate clutching of her hand.

'Pant,' Bilborough said, furiously trying to remember what he'd been told at the ante-natal classes. He wished he'd managed to get to more of them. 'Relax. Relax.'

'He's got a lovely mop of hair,' the midwife said.

She ought to be having another contraction by now. 'Pant,' Bilborough said. 'That's it. Pant now. Pant. Pant – '

But Catriona was breathing normally.

'Come now. Come on,' he said.

Catriona turned to him. 'Will you fuck off,' she screamed.

Bilborough grinned in embarrassment. The nurse and midwife smiled as if it were nothing new.

Catriona screamed.

TWENTY-FOUR

All three of them were exhausted. They sat around the expensive hotel room, and none of them spoke, none of them looked at either of the others.

Fitz was sure that Cassidy was about to break. He couldn't cling to his story much longer, Fitz thought. Choosing the right moment was a delicate matter. Too soon, and Cassidy wouldn't have had time to brood on the terrible picture Fitz had painted for him. Too long, and he'd have had time to regain the strength to resist.

Cassidy started to rub the fabric of his jacket with his thumb. He glanced at Beck, then at the bed. Any minute now, Fitz thought, he'd ask if he could go and lie down. Beck would make some crude joke about him sleeping in the same room as two men. The atmosphere would go, and all his work would be wasted.

Fitz got up and went and sat on the edge of the coffee table near Cassidy. Beck was watching him with the sneering expression Fitz had grown so used to during the night.

Fitz ignored him. Sooner or later, he'd find the way to take Beck down permanently. He was sick of the man enough to want to do that. But now wasn't the time. Now it was Cassidy's turn.

'Confess,' Fitz said. He kept his tone reasonable, but without any trace of forced gentleness that Cassidy might interpret as condescension. Cassidy was a teacher. He'd recognise that tone when he heard it. 'Plead guilty. It'll be over in a flash.' Cassidy looked at Fitz. A muscle at his jawline jumped. 'Deny it and there'll be a trial. Week upon week, detail on detail. Your mother squirming and cringing – '

'You've done this.' Cassidy twisted round in his seat. The look he shot Fitz was pure venom. 'My flat, my job, my mother, Lesley. All because you decided I was gay.' He was furious now. Two bright spots of colour appeared high up on his pallid cheeks. 'What gives you the right?' he shouted. 'What makes you so bloody arrogant you can decide that after five lousy minutes?'

Good, Fitz thought. If he's angry I'm getting to him. He could manipulate Cassidy's emotions – fear to anger to remorse – easily enough. That awful blank-eyed staring had been the dangerous thing, the thing that would have locked him out. But it was over now. Cassidy didn't know it yet, but he had already lost.

Abruptly, Cassidy got up and started across the room.

'Because I'm right,' Fitz said to his back.

Cassidy turned round by Beck's chair. 'You're wrong.' He stared at Fitz for a second.

I've hurt him, Fitz thought. He'll want to hurt me back. He wondered what it would be – his weight, his drinking, his smoking?

'When was the last time you gave your wife a good seeing-to?' Cassidy demanded. Bastard, Fitz thought at him. 'When was the last time?' Cassidy persisted.

Beck was watching him. A sly smile played around his lips. Up yours, too, Fitz thought at him. Cassidy was standing behind Beck's chair now, so that for a second it seemed that the two of them were ganging up against Fitz.

'That's my business,' he said to Cassidy.

'Well, you've poked your nose into mine for long enough.' Cassidy's voice had that phony-patient quality beloved of teachers and counsellors everywhere. Without wanting to, Fitz found himself thinking of Graham. Graham in bed with Judith, giving her what Cassidy would term a good seeing-to.

'I haven't killed somebody. You have.' He was almost shouting. That wasn't very professional. Too bad. He'd give Bilborough a discount off his bill.

'I haven't,' Cassidy yelled. He leaned across and picked up the phone. He thrust it at Fitz. 'Bring her down here. She's probably gasping for it.' He glanced at Beck, who was grinning broadly now. 'I'll slip her one.' He sneered. 'You can ask her what she thinks.' He slammed the phone down so hard it was a wonder it didn't break, then came slowly back to the sofa.

Judith in the duty room, making him listen while she told him she'd had sex with Graham. Not slept with him. Screwed him, then came home and tried to pretend nothing had happened.

You're dead, he thought at Cassidy. Whatever happens, before you leave this room I will nail you – nail you to the cross, crucify you, leave you for dead like you left Tim.

What would get him? His sexuality. But not just calling him gay. He was used to that by now. What was the one thing that he would have been clinging to, all through this long day?

Cassidy sat down. Fitz leaned close to him. He didn't shout. He didn't need to. 'All those times you've made love to Lesley? She faked it every single time.' Bullseye. Cassidy looked away. For a moment Fitz thought he might cry. 'Why else would she believe you're gay?' He was taking away the only thing Cassidy had to hold on to, but he didn't care. He was probably setting back the interrogation several hours, letting himself rage at the suspect just when he should have been worming his way into his confidence. He didn't care about that, either. 'She felt the need to fake it, Nigel. She knew you needed reassurance.' He'd lost Cassidy now. The blank look had come back into his eyes. 'She knew, deep down, that something was wrong.'

Cassidy sank back into the sofa. His voice was dull. 'I marked books. I jogged – '

226

'And then you marked more books,' Fitz finished for him. He smiled a little, as if to say, 'OK, we've both scored points, so now we can stop arguing.' He leaned back into his own chair, mirroring Cassidy's body language. It was a cheap trick, a counsellor's trick, to put him at his ease. He sighed deeply. He wanted Cassidy to think he was fed up with the situation, desperate to get it over with. It wasn't so very far from the truth. 'Did you ever tell Tim off?' he asked.

'Of course I told Tim off.'

Beck was watching them both. Let me show you how it's done, Fitz thought. 'More than the other children?' he asked.

'No.' He was wary.

Never let a predator see you're afraid, Fitz thought. He went in for the kill. 'He was special. You'd have to hide that – you'd tell him off more than the others.'

'No.' He blinked.

Liar, Fitz thought. He stood up. He took a pace forward. His shadow fell across Cassidy's face, but the man didn't look up. Fitz began to create a fantasy, a lie that would reveal the emotional truth of the situation. When he was done, Cassidy would have nowhere to hide, nothing to look into that did not reflect his soul. 'You're standing. He's sitting down, head bowed – ' just as Cassidy was sitting. Fitz put steel in his voice. ' "Look at me when I'm talking to you boy. Look at me." ' Cassidy kept looking at his hands. 'Look at me,' Fitz said. For a moment he thought it wasn't going to work. He was suddenly very aware of Beck's gaze on him, assessing him. Then Cassidy looked up. 'And he looks up.' His voice drifted along, weaving a spell, a spell that couldn't fail to enchant Cassidy. 'Blue eyes, those long blond lashes, more a girl than a boy. And his eyes were saying, "Please stop this. Please stop this. Please stop this" . . .' he let his voice trail off, then added, 'How did that make you feel, Nigel?'

Cassidy stared into space for a long, long moment. 'Grey,' he said at last.

'What?' Fitz said, taken off guard.

Cassidy twisted round and looked straight up into Fitz's eyes. 'They were more grey than blue.'

Gotcha! Fitz thought. You're mine now, you bastard. But he had to stick with it, keep the dialogue going till Cassidy was so far into it that he wouldn't be able to stop. ' "See me Tim. See me Tim." ' Fitz realised he didn't know what happened in a modern classroom. If he got it wrong, Cassidy might break free of the spell. He'd have to risk asking him, even though that might let Cassidy realise he wasn't totally in control of the dream he was weaving. 'And then what? He'd go to your desk?'

'I'd go to his.' His voice, too, was soft. Good. He was collaborating now. But then he went on, 'Not just his, every pupil's – '

Fitz cut him off. He didn't want Cassidy to talk. If he did, he might talk himself back to the real world, where there were plenty of places he could hide from the difficult truths of Fitz's fantasy.

'Ah,' Fitz said. 'And you'd squat.' He sat down. 'He'd be really close. Touching. Going through his work. You'd exchange glances. Be inches away, inches away from those eyes . . .' Cassidy looked at him, his face full of wonderment. Fitz knew that expression: 'How did you know?' and 'You do understand, don't you?' and 'You will protect me, won't you?' No, he thought at Cassidy, I won't protect you. He let his voice pick up speed, so Cassidy would be pushed to reply. 'And that was it – the moment you'd been waiting for, the moment that would get you through the rest of the day. He really was that special to you, wasn't he, Nigel?'

Cassidy let his head fall back over the back of the sofa. His Adam's apple moved in his bared throat. Say it, Fitz willed him. You've given in, you've exposed your throat to my blade. Now say it. Say you killed him. Say it.

'He disgusted me,' Cassidy said.

'And what were they saying, those eyes, the last time you

228

saw them?' Fitz asked. He tried to keep his voice mild, but he couldn't do it. ' "Please stop this, please stop this, please stop this." ' He heard the anger and contempt in his own voice: anger at Cassidy for murdering Tim, anger at society for forcing Cassidy to repress his sexuality to the point where its expression was unnatural, violent.

'You want to atone,' he said gently. For the first time that night, he spoke with genuine sympathy.

Cassidy considered this. 'Yes.'

'That's why you tried to kill yourself. A life for a life.'

He sounded more certain now. 'Yes.'

It was time, finally, for Fitz to spring the trap. 'I don't want that much, Nigel. Just confess.' Cassidy didn't speak, simply stared at him as if trying to remember how to turn a thought into a word, a sentence. 'I know you want to confess. You've killed a child, Nigel.' Fitz gave Cassidy a moment to think about that, to remember whatever there was to remember. 'That's a terrible, terrible burden. You want to share it.' He paused again. 'I'm here, Nigel. I'm willing to share it.'

Hatred. That was the expression Cassidy was struggling to articulate. It was written into the lines on his face. 'You're willing to share my burden?' The words were mild. The tone was contemptuous.

'Yes.'

'I won't let you forget you said that.'

The words hung on the air. 'I won't forget it,' Fitz murmured.

There was silence then. It stretched out, became unbearable. Beck took a long drag on his cigarette, then breathed the smoke out. He looked as if he might be about to speak. Don't say anything, Fitz thought at him. Don't. He didn't.

Cassidy stared at Fitz, with eyes full of hatred and despair, contempt and pleading. 'I killed Timothy Lang,' he said.

TWENTY-FIVE

Bilborough dabbed at Catriona's forehead with a damp sponge. She was slick with sweat, and her eyes were pools of shadow. Her hand grabbed at his. She managed to dart him a quick smile before she screamed.

'Come on,' Bilborough said. 'You're the most beautiful woman that ever lived. Come on. Come on – '

Her back arched. He heard a sheet tear as her feet scrabbled for purchase. Her lips skinned back from her mouth. She moaned.

Bilborough wiped his face with the back of his hand. It came away wet.

Then, suddenly, it was over. The midwife was holding something small and wrinkled out to Catriona, but Bilborough was crying too hard to pay much attention. He touched the tiny face with the edge of his thumb, and it was only later he registered what the nurse had said: 'It's a boy.'

He had a son. By God, he had a son.

TWENTY-SIX

The interview room was deadly quiet. Cassidy sat on one side of the table, with Begum near him on the short end. Bilborough clicked the button on the tape machine. Its twin recording decks whirred into life.

'Interview commences eleven thirty-five a.m. Present are Nigel Cassidy, Shazia Begum acting for the accused, DCI David Bilborough, and police psychologist Doctor Edward Fitzgerald.'

Penhaligon and Beck had wanted to be in there when Cassidy finally, officially, coughed; but Bilborough had been afraid that Begum might claim there had been intimidation if too many people were present, so he'd banished them to watch on the monitors.

'Please repeat for the record what you said at the Hotel Royale this morning,' Bilborough said.

'You do *not* have to do this, Nigel,' Begum said. 'A confession made under duress, without witnesses and without the proper procedures being followed is not admissible in a court of law.'

Bloody woman, Bilborough thought. But he'd managed to grab a few hours' sleep when he finally left the hospital, and he was in far too good a mood to let Begum worry him. Let her try and turn Cassidy. All it meant was that she'd have less of a case if the defence tried to pull the intimidation routine in court: and God knew, Bilborough wanted Cassidy, but he wanted him nailed down tight. No comebacks. No 'innocent man wrongfully imprisoned' crap six months after he was sent down.

'It's all right,' Cassidy said. 'I want to do this.' He cleared his throat. For a second, the only sound was the steady hum of the tape deck. 'I killed Timothy Lang,' he said.

Bilborough could almost hear the cheering from the duty room even with the doors shut.

Bilborough was surrounded by people the second he came out of the interview room. There was a lot of backslapping, a lot of cheering and whistling. Penhaligon hung back, unable to relax till she'd had a private word with him.

He pulled out a couple of notes. 'Here,' he said to Beck. 'Go and get some booze in.'

'Cheers, boss.'

A bit after that, Bilborough went into his office. Penhaligon waited a moment, then followed him.

'Can I have a word, boss?' she asked.

'Anything you like,' Bilborough said. The unhealthy pallor had vanished from his face. 'Anything you bloody like.'

'I was wondering – could I take some leave?'

'Well, yeah – book it out through Admin and I'll sign – '

'No. I meant, like now. I've got a couple of weeks due, and no disrespect, but I've about had enough. I need to get away.'

Bilborough stared at her. His good humour seemed to have vanished. For a moment she was sure he would refuse. Then he made an odd little snorting noise. 'I haven't been easy to work with these last couple of days, have I?'

'No, sir,' Penhaligon said. What the hell. He could only say no.

He grinned wryly. 'Honest to the last – that's what I like about you, Penhaligon.' He fiddled with something on his desk. 'Go ahead – make sure you've handed everything on to Jimmy, your paperwork and caseload, the lot, first though. I'll square it with Admin.'

Penhaligon smiled.

• • •

232

Judith had always found gardening therapeutic. Planting, for instance, reminded her that however bad things got, there was always hope for the future. Collecting seedheads for dried flower arrangements showed her that even the most useless facets of her life might yield dividends. She'd collected a lot of seedheads during her marriage to Fitz.

Today, however, Judith was weeding. Throwing out everything that was bad, so that the good might have a better chance to grow. It wasn't just the symbolism involved that pleased her.

Behind her, the rhythmic blat, blat, blat as Mark and Katie played swingball told her all was right with them. A proper little family she thought. For all she and Fitz still had a lot to work out, she was happy to be home. If only he would be happy to have her . . . she shoved the trowel into the earth and scooped out a dockweed. Another. The next was stuck. The tough stem bit into her fingers even through her gardening glove.

A shadow fell across her. She turned. Fitz was standing there. He stared at her for a second – a stranger, she thought, he looks at me as he would look at a stranger – then came round and squatted beside her.

For a moment he didn't speak. Blat, went the swingball. Blat. It took Judith a moment to comprehend the look on his face: embarrassment. It wasn't an expression she was used to seeing there.

'I'm thinking of going away for a while.'

For a moment she thought he meant he wanted to take the family on holiday, but that didn't square with his expression. Someone else? Ridiculous. Who would have him? And yet . . . 'On your own?' she said with a touch of asperity, to let him know that she thought the idea that he might be going off with someone was too stupid for words.

If he were going off with someone else, she didn't want to know.

'Yeah,' he muttered. He wasn't looking at her.

He wouldn't lie to her. He wouldn't.

'You look terrible,' she said. It was true. His scratches and scabs were livid against the pallor of his skin. His eyes were red-rimmed.

'Well, I haven't slept.'

'So sleep,' she said. She sounded impatient even to herself. With Fitz there was always some complicating factor. She went back to her weeding, wondering if he knew that even her impatience was a sign of her love.

'How often have you wished me dead?' he asked.

The question took her by surprise. Ridiculous, she thought. 'Lost count,' she said, and laughed.

Fitz didn't join in. 'So you could sleep with other men.' She looked at him. He was joking. He had to be joking. 'With a clear conscience.' He meant it. There was no keeping the hurt off her face. 'I've put it to dozens of couples,' he said quickly.

As if that mattered. As if it made everything all right. It made her feel like a bacterium under a microscope: no, you couldn't dissect a bacterium. A rat then, pinned out alive for some scientist to slice open, all in the cause of science.

Judith dug the trowel hard into the earth. 'I couldn't give a damn how many people you've put it to. You're wrong.' She looked at him again. He couldn't see it, couldn't see how much he'd hurt her or what he was doing to their marriage. 'Look, I've had opportunities, Fitz.' She was going to hurt him. Something in her wanted to stop, but it was too late for that, too late for niceness. 'Men see me, see you sitting next to me – overweight, pissed, arguing with someone on the next table, totally ignoring me until you've smashed him into an intellectual pulp – ' Fitz snorted. If he could recognise himself, and laugh at what they saw, maybe there was still hope. Stupid, Judith, she said to herself. How many disappointed hopes had there been since she'd first left him? Too many. ' – they assume I'm available.'

'Yeah. I know.'

234

She had hurt him. She hadn't finished. 'I enjoy it – '

'Yes, I've seen it – '

She wondered suddenly if he'd seen it when it had started – early in their marriage – or only lately, when she'd been so unhappy she'd begun to play on it.

When did hurting each other become natural to us? she wondered. And though she didn't want to, she had to acknowledge that though Fitz's behaviour had been unbearable to live with, he'd never used it to hurt her intentionally. Whereas she had used her leaving and her adultery to punish him . . .

It was time to let him off the hook. 'All that effort to impress, and it's wasted because they haven't got a tenth of that – ' she pointed at his head, and then at his heart. 'Or a twentieth of that – ' She meant his heart, the compassionate core of him that he tried so hard to hide; but she also meant the sheer physical bulk that no other man could match. She looked at him steadily. For a moment he met her gaze, but by the time she stopped speaking, he had looked away. 'I've loved you for twenty-five years, and I have never wanted anyone else.'

Look at me, she wanted to say. Look at me. But he didn't look at her, and she knew then that he was going away with someone else.

Penhaligon held the party dress up to herself in the mirror. It was dark green, shot through with silver thread, and it suited her hair beautifully. She glanced at the suitcase that lay open on the bed. It was already nearly full. What the hell, she thought as she folded the dress carefully and put it in. She could take another case if she had to. She added a pair of flat sandals, and a pair with heels.

A key turned in the front door. Damn, she thought. She'd meant to leave before Peter got home. She hadn't wanted to face another row. Not one in which she would have been lying.

235

She heard his footsteps in the hallway, and knew that she should go to him and explain, before he found out the hard way. Instead, she picked up her one-piece swimsuit and folded it. She'd already put a bikini in. Another costume wouldn't hurt. There was room if she wedged it down the side and –

'What are you doing?' Peter said.

Penhaligon looked up from the suitcase. 'Going away,' she said.

'I don't understand.' Peter's eyes flickered from her to the wardrobe.

Penhaligon suddenly realised he thought she meant permanently. 'I'm taking a couple of weeks' leave.' She saw the relief in his eyes, rapidly followed by understanding and then hurt. 'There's food in the freezer. You'll be OK,' she said, and immediately felt guilty. It was a stupid, brutal thing to say. Besides, he cooked more often than she did. But she'd wanted to be certain he understood he wasn't coming with her, and she didn't want to get into long conversations about it.

'I thought we were going together – '

'Changed my mind. I tried to tell you when I came into the store yesterday – '

'I was busy – ' She was hurting him. It wasn't that she didn't care, she realised, but that she cared about what they had lost, not what he was feeling now.

'You were busy. I'm busy. We never have time for each other any more.'

'I know. I said – ' He was right. She knew it. He'd been saying the same thing over and over for weeks, but only so he could suggest she change her shift pattern. He didn't seem to realise it wasn't really up to her. 'That's why I thought we should go away together.'

'Sorry,' Penhaligon said.

Peter stared at her for a moment. She wouldn't look away. Eventually he did. His gaze shifted to the bed, where the tickets were lying half out of her handbag.

236

Two tickets. The top one was hers, but the other one – Fitz's – was poking out from under it. From where she was standing, the words *Dr E Fit* were clearly visible, though the rest of Fitz's name was hidden. Penhaligon wondered if Peter could see the writing from where he was, and if he could, whether he'd make the connection. She'd talked about Fitz often enough after all.

'Who are you going with?' he asked.

'A couple of the girls from Admin,' Penhaligon said. It was a ridiculous lie, a lie he was sure to catch her out in. Who on earth could she say it was, if he asked? Penny? She was broke, and had been complaining bitterly about it the last time she came round to dinner. Gillian? Her husband kept her on a pretty short leash.

She reached over and swept the tickets into the bag, then closed it firmly and put it over her shoulder. 'Got to hurry. Promised the lads I'd go back to the station for the bastard-coughed party,' she said, and flapped the case shut.

He was watching her intently. She could feel it. Say something, she thought at him. Ask me who I'm really going with. Say you don't want me to go. But he didn't speak. She picked the case up and went past Peter to the door. He followed her out.

She stopped in the corridor outside the flat. 'I am sorry,' she said.

'So am I.'

'I'll send you a postcard,' she said, and reached up to kiss him good-bye. He moved his head away.

'Have you got your keys, Jane?' he asked.

'Yes, of course – '

'Just in case I'm not in when you get back.'

Penhaligon nodded. So that's that, she thought as she walked away. She didn't look back.

Fitz settled down in a corner of the duty room. He found a pad of paper and started jotting down notes on Cassidy, stuff he'd need when they called him as an expert witness when the trial finally came to court.

Repression, he wrote. Guilt complex arising from conflict driven by suppression of sexuality and – Minutes later, he realised that he had written nothing more, but had covered the page in triangles. Triangles and eyes. Very interesting, he thought. All that sixties stuff about the eye in the pyramid: global conspiracy theory and the Illuminati who were supposed to rule the world. What was his subconscious trying to tell him here?

Nothing complex came to mind.

Sometimes, Professor, he told himself, a banana is just a banana. He was drawing triangles because he was stuck in one: him, Judith, Panhandle; and eyes because they were archetypal symbols of womanhood and love.

'Don't go getting too comfortable,' Beck said. Fitz looked up at him. 'Your pretty-boy pal wants to talk to you – '

'What?' Fitz said. He stared at the page in front of him. Crudely drawn eyes stared up at him. Illuminati. Conspiracy theory. Fit-ups and shake-downs. Cassidy staring numbly up at him from the hotel sofa. He couldn't want to withdraw his confession. He'd had his chance that morning, surely?

'Cassidy,' Beck said, all feigned patience. 'Wants to see you.'

'Yeah,' Fitz said. 'Tell him I'll be with him in a minute.'

'You tell him. I've got things to do.' Beck started to go, then he turned back. 'Could be your luck's changing, eh, Fitz?'

Moron, Fitz thought at him, but he didn't bother to say it. He stared at the paper again. This is ridiculous, he thought. I promised I'd help him get through this, share his guilt, whatever it takes. He's realised how deep in he is, and now he's calling me on my promise. He said he would. This is just a little earlier than I expected.

But the eyes and the pyramids stared up at him. He heard himself lecturing, telling a class of freshers that the subconscious mind was a powerful tool that knew far more than mere consciousness ever could.

Load of crap, he thought firmly at himself. Sort of thing you tell first years to scare the bejesus out of them.

Feel the truth with your hearts and your guts. That was another thing he'd told them. He'd felt Cassidy was guilty; so had Bilborough and Penhaligon; even Beck had felt it. The man himself had admitted it twice. He couldn't be innocent.

There was one way to find out. Fitz started to stand up. His heart was pounding, and his mouth was dry.

Evidently his subconscious had its own ideas about Cassidy. Well, he wasn't going to see him in this state. The man would just have to wait until later.

TWENTY-SEVEN

In the duty room, the whole of Anson Road Police Station got ready to party. They'd managed to get a result on a major murder enquiry in three days flat, and avert a riot at the same time. That had to be worth a celebration. A bottle of champagne stood in a plastic bucket of luke-warm water, and someone had produced a few packets of crisps from somewhere.

Penhaligon stood leafing through the holiday brochure. In a couple of hours, she'd be on her way to Kos, with Fitz beside her. She could almost feel the sun on her face, taste the retsina, feel his hands rubbing oil into her back. She grinned – couldn't help it. Maybe by the time she came back she wouldn't feel so fed up with the lot of them.

She glanced round. There were good friends here, even if they did drive her mad sometimes.

One of the constables rushed in, carrying a couple of six-packs. 'He's coming,' he said urgently.

'Say nothing,' Fitz said in an undertone.

Everyone found something business-like to do – reading, or filling out reports.

Beck came in. He was carrying two bottles of champagne, but everyone ignored him carefully. There was a pinkish place under his nose where his moustache used to be.

'Yeah,' he said, brandishing the bottles. Still nobody paid him any attention. Bilborough came out of his office and leaned against the doorframe. Beck was standing with his back to him. 'I got a bit sick of the jokes, right? I was going to keep it – just to prove that I've got nothing to prove.' He thought about this while he found a couple of plastic cups.

240

'But I haven't got to prove I've got nothing to prove, so I got rid of it.' He looked around, as if expecting applause for this triumph of logic. 'Right?'

Someone began to laugh. Beck glared at the man, unaware that Bilborough had taken a couple of steps forward. He produced a fake moustache and held it to his face with one finger. 'Could you give us that again, please?'

The room exploded into laughter and jeers. A couple of people clapped. Beck turned round. 'Ahh bollocks,' he said, but he was laughing.

'Calm down. Calm down. Calm down.' Bilborough had Beck off to perfection.

Beck popped the champagne cork, and suddenly everyone was laughing and joking. Fitz applauded. Penhaligon whooped. Someone else let out a piercing wolf-whistle. Cans of lager were opened. Someone saw to another bottle of champagne. Penhaligon put the brochure in the wastepaper bin. Somebody offered her a cup of champagne, but she turned it down. Time to go, time to go.

Fitz was holding out a cup to be filled with champagne. She smiled at him fondly. He looked up, and for one long moment there was no-one in the room but the two of them, sharing the secret of what they were about to do.

Penhaligon broke the exchange first. She looked around nervously, but no-one seemed to have noticed. She began to thread her way between the tables to the door.

'I'm off,' she said to no-one in particular, loud enough so it could be heard over the noise.

Somebody shouted, 'Have a good time – '

'Have one for me – '

' – sand, sex and sun – '

' – all she has to worry about – '

'You've got to have just the one,' Beck said as she passed him. He pushed a cup into her hand. She took it and sipped from it as she walked. Warm champagne. Best thing she'd tasted in weeks.

'Hey,' Bilborough said. Penhaligon turned. 'Tell Peter you want a tan – he's got to let you out of the bedroom now and again.' Penhaligon made a mock curtsy. It was good to see him so relaxed. He pointed at her. 'And don't speak with your mouth full.'

Penhaligon pulled a face. She looked away, only to find that she'd caught Fitz's eye. Hurriedly, she turned and left.

It was time for Fitz to make good on his promise to Cassidy. Time to forget the celebration and do what he could to help the man come to terms with what he'd done, though in truth Fitz wasn't sure that living with his guilt shouldn't be a large part of Cassidy's punishment.

He walked along the passage to the holding cells, clutching two cups of coffee along with his lit cigarette. It was godawful stuff, the worst kind of machine instant money could buy. The smell of it mingled with the odour of stale urine and disinfectant.

The passage was chilly. It's the tiling, he thought; that and the fact that it's in the basement. But it was more than that. It was the thought of what Cassidy was facing. Years and years in gaol, every move controlled by someone else. And Beck had been right, of course. His fellow prisoners were going to give him a rough time.Whatever he thought now, Fitz reckoned Cassidy couldn't imagine what they would put him through. Give him a week and he'd be screaming for Section 43.

The duty officer opened the door. He went in. Cassidy was sitting curled up on the end of his bunk, back to the wall. He seemed remarkably calm, Fitz thought. Then again, he'd probably managed to get some sleep; in which case, he was the only one who had.

'Coffee?' Fitz asked.

Cassidy took it. 'What do you want?' he asked. He leaned forward, so that his arms and legs moved away from his body. He rested one arm on his knee, so his hand dangled loosely. Fitz automatically assessed his body language – open, not friendly but confident: neither challenging nor overly defensive.

Whatever tricks Cassidy's subconscious was playing on him now – however it was making him out to be the hero of his own story, and thus producing this body language – it couldn't last. Sooner or later, the guilt would overtake him, and the understanding of what the law would do to him. Fitz might not be around then. He had to help Cassidy now, because otherwise he'd have no help at all, or worse, some prison counsellor or chaplain.

'I've come to help you,' he said. He took a long drag on his cigarette.

Cassidy grinned, but only with his mouth, not his eyes. 'I've lost my job. My flat's been destroyed. Lesley's walked out. And my mother's being persecuted. Apart from decapitation, what else can you do for me?'

Humour. It was a good defence, as Fitz well knew. He couldn't let Cassidy get away with it. 'You were living a lie,' he said. He couldn't be sure whether Cassidy had yet admitted it to himself or not. Making him do so was the first step to helping him.

'You're a happily married man,' Cassidy said. 'Are you? Hmm?' He put his head on one side, like an adult uncomfortable at having to talk to a toddler. Fitz felt his jaw clench. His hand went tight on the coffee cup. He took another hit from the cigarette. It didn't help. 'Never thought of adultery?' Cassidy was good, Fitz had to give him that; it was that or believe that everything he'd ever thought about Panhandle was obvious to everyone who knew the two of them. 'Or just walking away?' This is what it feels like, Fitz thought, all those times I've taken people apart and never understood: this is what it feels like. Cassidy was still speaking. 'But you don't. You go on living your lie.'

You murdering little shit, Fitz thought. 'There are worse things, Nigel.'

243

Cassidy crossed his arms on his knees, so his face was partly hidden. Whatever he's going to say next, Fitz thought, he's afraid of how I'll react. 'To hell with the consequences. To hell with who gets hurt – just as long as you can expose lies. Not your own, of course.' He paused. It isn't like that, Fitz thought. It isn't like that. So why this sudden uprush of anger, why the desire to shove Cassidy's head through the wall? Well, he'd think about it later. He didn't have to dance to Cassidy's tune. Cassidy continued, 'Other people's. That's got nothing to do with truth.' He spat the final words out as if they were blows hammering nails home. 'That's just utter selfishness, you *bloody* hypocrite.'

Enough, Fitz thought. 'You're the murderer. Get out of the pulpit.'

Cassidy reached down and put his coffee on the floor. 'You said you were willing to share my burden. You remember that?' It was a challenge, as if he were putting Fitz on his honour to acknowledge what had been said.

'Yes,' Fitz said, emphasising the word with a nod. How could he forget? Though in truth, after what Cassidy had just said, he regretted the promise. He stared at the floor between his feet.

'I didn't kill Tim.'

The words were like a body blow. They couldn't be true.

Fitz studied Cassidy. He had settled himself back against the wall, still with his legs drawn up and his arms across them, but this time in such a way that Fitz could see his face. There was no hint of tension in it.

If he'd been looking at the man when he spoke, Fitz might have been able to be certain. As it was he could only go on his gut reaction. 'Don't believe you,' he said, making the words as positive as he could.

'I'm not gay. I fancied Tim because he was a girl.' His voice was matter of fact.

This was ridiculous, Fitz thought. A ridiculous piece of

trumpery that he'd dreamed up to get himself off the hook. They'd better hope to God he didn't have some weeks-old bruise somewhere on him, or he'd be yelling police brutality. 'Nigel, I don't mind you telling me lies, but come on – '

'He knew.' His voice had gone just slightly dreamy. 'He'd talk to me at school. In the staffroom, they'd laugh.' He put on a camp voice. ' "Takes one to know one," they'd say. I'd laugh too.'

He paused. My God, Fitz thought. It was no wonder that Lesley had believed he was gay. At the time she'd have thought he was just being a good sport, but if the other teachers had constantly made Cassidy the butt of their jokes . . . Something terrible occurred to Fitz. If Cassidy were lying now, why was he saying this? It would be so much easier to make people believe his confession was false if he kept denying any hint of homosexuality. But the man was speaking again. Fitz made himself concentrate. 'But then he came round to my flat. He needed to talk. It frightened me, brought things out in me – ' He had to be telling the truth. He could easily have accounted for Tim's behaviour simply by saying the boy had been unlucky enough to fall for someone who was resolutely heterosexual. 'I chased him away. He died that night.'

For a moment, a glorious moment, Fitz thought Cassidy meant he'd killed Tim, but accidentally. But he had to be sure. 'Are you saying you didn't kill him?'

Cassidy rubbed his hand up and down his upper arm. His hand rasped against the cloth until he spoke again. 'I as good as killed him.' Damn you. Damn you to hell. Give me a straight answer, Fitz thought. 'All you saw was guilt. The same kind of guilt that Andy must have felt, that his parents must have felt, or anyone who ever knew him.' It was possible. It was so, so possible. 'That's all,' Cassidy said. 'No more.'

Fitz could hardly breathe. He felt something snap inside him. He leaned forward. 'Tell me you didn't do it.'

245

'I did not kill Timothy Lang.' The words were slow, paced so Fitz couldn't possibly misunderstand. There was no way he could avoid believing them. 'What's wrong, Fitz?' The words were a taunt. 'An innocent man's confessed? The killer's still out there? No. You were wrong – that's what's bothering you.' Fitz couldn't find the words to reply. 'Isn't it?' Cassidy demanded. 'You arrogant bastard.'

Fitz looked away. His throat felt closed off. His gut had turned to water. An image of his fist impacting with Cassidy's face flitted through his mind. Breathe, he told himself. In through the nose. Pause. Out through the mouth. Breathe. Cassidy had felt guilt, rightly or wrongly. He couldn't deal with it through any healthy mechanism – good old British male response, repressing every emotion till it deformed under the pressure into something unholy – so he'd done this – 'Look, if you want to punish yourself, that's fine. I'll fix something up for you, you selfish, twisted little prick. But there's a killer out there, and he's going to strike again.' Cassidy just gazed at him. 'Retract your confession.'

'I want him to kill again.'

He couldn't mean it. No-one could mean it. 'Retract your confession right now,' Fitz yelled. He leaned towards Cassidy using every trick of intimidation he'd learned in forty-four years of being the biggest, cleverest person around.

'I want him to kill again,' Cassidy repeated, this time spacing his words out. There was a long, long silence. Nothing Fitz had ever come across had prepared him for this. 'You said you'd share my burden,' Cassidy said, almost plaintively. 'That's my burden. I'm responsible for the death of a child. If he kills again, you'll be able to share it.' He was using that logical, plain-as-daylight tone beloved of teachers.

Fitz saw it now, saw the trap Cassidy had laid for him. He even knew why, now. It was nothing to do with the standard reasons people make false confessions – the desire for notoriety, to validate one's own existence by taking part in something that had become public property. After all, Cassidy was already involved in the case.

No, this was something darker and more devious, infinitely harder to understand. All his life, Cassidy would have been the one to take the responsibility for things, and the blame when they went wrong. He was probably an eldest child, probably from a religious background – maybe one like Catholicism, with its emphasis on personal guilt and the damnation of unrepentant souls – which he might consciously have rejected. Christ knows, Fitz thought, enough of us do. But subconsciously? Oh, the subconscious is a wonderful thing. It never forgets. So all this time, all these long, repressed, lonely years, Cassidy had been searching for someone to share the blame. Not to take the blame for him. That would be wrong. You have to own up to what you've done, otherwise you'll burn in hell, or maybe the bogey man will creep out from under your bed and gobble you up. But to share the blame. Oh yes, a twisted little bastard like Cassidy would want that all right.

Fitz could hardly breathe. He couldn't look at Cassidy.

'You did promise? Am I right? You did promise?'

'Oh my God,' Fitz whispered. He got up and banged on the door, and he didn't stop till the officer came and opened it.

TWENTY-EIGHT

Andy hadn't wanted to go to the press conference, but it seemed to mean a lot to his mum, so in the end he agreed.

By the time he'd stood around in the reception area of the police station for twenty minutes, he was beginning to regret it. There was him, and his mum and dad, and Mr Lindsay, and a few other local people. Apart from that, the place was packed with journalists, all with their notebooks out, and their fancy tape recorders over their shoulders. It was as bad as being in church. Everyone stood round talking in whispers, and no-one would admit it was useless.

Bloody police. What was the point in wasting time listening to them, when in the end Cassidy would get off with a slap on the wrist?

Nice, middle-class Mr Cassidy. He'd get some fat-cat lawyer, who'd talk a lot of guff about his client's previous good character, and how Tim had provoked him. Andy could hear it all, already. They'd be lucky if he was inside for more than a year or two.

'Andy!' He heard Melanie's voice, coming from outside. A policewoman was barring her way.

Andy pushed his way through the crowd. 'Let her in,' he said to the copper. 'Please.'

For a second he didn't think she'd do it, but then she smiled at him and stepped aside.

Pity they weren't all like that, even if she wouldn't let Mike in too, Andy thought as he led Melanie back to his mum and dad. They were standing close to each other, not quite holding hands.

A woman journalist came over to them. His mother glared at her, and she backed off. He heard her mutter something to one of the other hacks. She sounded angry, but he couldn't hear what she was saying.

A copper came down the stairs. He stopped a few steps from the bottom. 'All right, everyone,' he shouted. 'You can go in now.'

The crowd started to move forward. Andy slipped his hand into Melanie's. He glanced back. She smiled encouragingly at him. Behind her, he saw, rather than heard, his father say something to his mother. She turned to look at him. He smiled. It was only there for an instant, and then it was gone; but Andy was quite sure he'd seen it. It had been a long time since he'd seen his father smile.

It was amazing how relaxed he felt about press conferences these days, Bilborough thought, as he went down the corridor from his office to the conference room, holding his statement in one hand. Not a year ago he'd fumbled his way through his first, with the producer or director or whatever she was wincing at his every word.

That was then. This was now. He could be home in three-quarters of an hour with Catriona and the baby. He couldn't stop himself from smiling. Not yet a day old and it already looked like him.

'Oy,' Fitz called from behind him. 'Oy.'

Bilborough turned just as Fitz caught him by the arm. He was out of breath. 'He didn't do it,' the psychologist said.

Oh for Christ's sake, Bilborough thought. But there had been other times Fitz had only been right on the second go. 'How do you know?'

'I've just spoken to him. He told me.'

Bilborough's brain kicked in. He thought about the forensic evidence, the circumstantial stuff. It could be wrong. It just could be wrong. 'And you believed him?' he said.

'Yes,' Fitz said impatiently.

Oh God, Bilborough thought. Oh please God, not this. Not now. He still had to square things with Allen over the scenes with the mob earlier. He'd managed to forget that for a while, but now he couldn't think of anything else. If he had to tell him Cassidy wasn't their man, there'd be hell to pay. 'Is he going to retract his statement?'

'No.'

'Then what's the problem?' Bilborough managed to make it sound as if he'd never thought for a moment that he had anything to worry about. He turned away and walked towards the conference room, hoping to terminate the conversation.

Fitz followed him. 'He didn't do it,' he shouted.

They got as far as the duty room. Beck was standing near the door. 'Boss? They're ready for you – ' he gestured at the door that led to the stairs down to the conference room.

Bilborough paused. 'We got a result. The rest is up to the CPS,' he said. He didn't add, *and I'm going to make sure they have enough to nail that bastard, retracted confession or not*, but he thought it. There was too much riding on this for him not to make certain of it.

'Oy, Sarge,' someone yelled to Beck. 'Sarge.'

All three of them looked over. A couple of constables were lounging around at a desk, like they didn't have anything better to do. One of them was wearing the fake moustache, wrinkling his upper lip to keep it in place. He blew on it, and it flew off and bounced in the air, suspended on a piece of elastic.

Like bloody kids, Bilborough thought. They never knew when to stop. 'Will you behave yourselves, the pair of you? Just grow up.'

'Look,' Fitz said. He sounded as if he were having trouble keeping his temper. 'I don't give a shit about a result. He didn't do it – it's the truth that counts.'

He was begging, Bilborough thought. It was a startling thought, but it was just tough. 'I've got a press conference.'

He brushed past Fitz towards the conference room.

'I got the statement off that man. That means I'm the one responsible, and I have to live with – '

Enough, Bilborough thought. 'DS Beck got the statement,' he said over Fitz's voice.

'What!'

Beck had followed them. Bilborough gestured at him. 'DS Beck got the statement. "After shrewd and persistent questioning by DS Beck the witness made his statement," ' he spoke too fast for Fitz to interrupt.

'That man couldn't get Edward the Confessor to cough,' Fitz said, sneering. 'I got the – '

'Piss off,' Beck shouted.

' – statement.'

'Why don't you just piss off – ' Beck forced himself between Bilborough and Fitz.

'Jimmy – ' Bilborough said.

' – and give us a rest?'

'Jimmy?'

'Look, I've had to put up with you all bloody night and the novelty's wearing a bit thin.' Beck jabbed his finger hard at Fitz. 'Do you know what I mean?'

'Why don't you just button your baldy lip?'

Bilborough had never heard Fitz shout so loud. Beck backed away.

Time to put an end to this. 'Tell them I'm coming,' he said to Beck, to get him out of the way.

If looks could have killed, Fitz would have been the next murder they investigated. But at least Beck did go to the conference room without saying anything else. Now Bilborough only had Fitz to deal with.

Fitz cleared his throat. 'If you don't stop this now, we're finished.' Blackmail, Bilborough thought. It just proved even the great Doctor Fitzgerald could read someone completely wrong occasionally. 'Understand? I'm out of here.'

'Have you finished?'

251

'It's the truth that matters. Not "the result",' he mimicked Bilborough's accent, badly. 'The truth!'

Condescending bastard, Bilborough thought. 'Here endeth the lesson, yeah?'

'Yeah.'

OK, Bilborough thought. OK. He thought, maybe if he gives me one scrap of a lead on another suspect, anything I can go with, maybe I can wait a day. Just a day and we'll check it out. Christ knew he didn't want to go with this if it was going to blow up in his face later. But he knew in his heart – and he was honest enough to admit it – that no matter what Fitz said he would go ahead with the conference. 'If I let him go, what have we got left? Nothing. What do you want me to do?'

But he knew what Fitz wanted him to do.

'He didn't do it,' Fitz said. He sounded almost desperate. There was something else working on him, Bilborough thought, but he didn't give a damn.

'You told me he did,' he said. 'I've pursued one line of enquiry, one sole line of enquiry, and now you want me to tell the boss it was wrong? I'd be back pounding the bloody beat.' He glanced towards the conference room. In a couple of minutes he was going to have to face the people in there, and not so long ago most of them had been part of a raging mob. 'You want me to tell that lot out there I was wrong? They'd lynch me.' He realised he was shouting and lowered his voice. 'You want me to tell Tim's mother I was wrong?' Fitz just glared at him. 'I'm charging him.'

Bilborough walked away. Fitz's shouting voice pursued him. 'He's innocent.' Bilborough looked back. 'Can you live with that?' Fitz shouted. 'Because I can't.'

Bilborough went through the door and slammed it behind him as hard as he could.

Fitz stood in the middle of the duty room, staring at the door Bilborough had just gone through. He was a bloody fool, and the only pity was that he wouldn't have to pay for his own stupidity.

If I had any sense at all, I'd call his bluff – walk out and not come back, Fitz thought. The only trouble was, that would leave how many more members of the public at the mercy of Mr Plod?

Maybe I'll do it anyway, Fitz thought. He stalked – in so far as someone with his bulk could stalk– out of the duty room, down the stairs and into Anson Road.

It was only when he was safely sitting in a taxi that he realised that he had finally worked out what had been getting to Bilborough. He'd said, 'I'd be back on the beat in no time.' That was the key. Bilborough had been promoted young – too young, some people thought; he worried about it constantly, even when he was at his most relaxed. Then there was Catriona's pregnancy. Bilborough seemed to have blamed himself for the miscarriage she'd had last summer. So, here he was, faced with the murder of a child, and an investigation that had blown up in his face – and with witnesses who had left Timothy Lang to hang in the woods rather than risk themselves by coming forward.

Bilborough, Fitz concluded, had transferred their failure to act as adults – to care for Timothy – to himself. It was partly that old voodoo magic: he was scared that if he involved himself with them, their behaviour would some-how rub off on him, until he, too, was unfit to be a parent. And partly he almost certainly felt they epitomised every-thing that was wrong with society, every reason someone might think they shouldn't bring a child into the world. If he hadn't made them cough, Bilborough would have failed in his first duty as a father.

It was all perfectly clear to Fitz now. He leaned back, well satisfied. Pity he'd worked it out when it was too late to be of any use.

It would be all right, Julie Lang thought. They would hear

253

what the police had to say, and she would know for certain that the man who killed Tim was going to pay for what he had done.

Then she might be able to accept that her son's death hadn't been her fault. What had Fitz said? 'Guilt soon goes. Grief remains. But grief is your friend. It allows you to mourn.'

All right then. They would tell her that they were going to punish the man who had killed Tim, and then she would mourn. She and her family.

Andy was next to her. He was much calmer now, thank God. Melanie was next to him. They were holding hands. She was good for him, that girl. Julie hoped they had sorted things out. Andy shouldn't be alone too much. Not now.

And Stephen. Stephen was behind her. Maybe when this was over she would ask him to move back in with her. She knew he wanted to.

She stared around the room. Of the other people there, a few were neighbours. Some had been strangers before this had begun, but they had been involved with the search, and then the picket. Perhaps some of them would become friends. And then there were the journalists. Voyeurs the lot of them. She wanted nothing to do with them.

The young policeman, Bilborough, came in and sat down. Julie took a second to identify the dark-haired man next to him as DS Beck: he'd shaved his moustache off. There was a woman on Bilborough's other side, but it wasn't Jane, the nice sergeant.

Flashbulbs popped. A tape deck whirred. 'OK? Everyone ready?' A microphone dangled in front of Bilborough's face, then rose slightly. He looked straight at her. There was something wrong, she was sure of it. Get on with it, she thought. Get on with it. He looked down. Cleared his throat. 'A man was arrested this morning in connection with the murder of Timothy Lang.' His voice was lifeless. Julie had thought he would be elated. He'd got a result, after all:

wasn't that what they called it? 'That man has since been charged and will appear in court this morning.' He was looking at her again. But if they'd charged a man, it must be all right. He'd probably been up all night. That was it. He was just over-tired, like they all were. 'That's all.'

The journalists all started shouting.

'What evidence do you have for arresting this man?'

'Who is it?'

'Is it the teacher?'

But Bilborough went out the door without answering any of them.

It's all right, Julie told herself. There's nothing wrong now. I can cry now. I can cry.

TWENTY-NINE

Fitz threw a shirt into the suitcase. He pressed the clothes down hard, then realised what he was doing and grinned wryly at his own foolishness. He was still pissed off with Bilborough, so he was taking it out on the clothes.

Pretty damned stupid when you came to think about it. Especially when he had to admit he wasn't half as angry at Bilborough as he was at himself. He'd made a mistake, the kind of half-arsed mistake a counsellor like Graham would make. He'd failed to find out about Cassidy's background, and that meant he'd read the man all wrong. And he was wrong about another thing, too. He wasn't the one that was going to have to live with it. Cassidy was.

Well, he'd made one mistake today. He wasn't going to make another. You got one chance. One shot at happiness, and he was going to take his.

He zipped the case up. He was late for meeting Panhandle, but that was OK. He could call a cab and be at the airport in twenty minutes, plenty of time before they had to check in.

In the garden, Judith was arguing with Mark.

'You get a job by Christmas or – '

'But I'm at college now – '

'Then why don't you ever go to classes?'

'Because it's crap, that's why.'

That's my Mark he thought. Illogical to the bitter end.

God, two weeks on Kos, with no family to annoy him, no Judith nagging him to give up gambling, give up drinking, give up being himself.

Sun. Sand. Panhandle. He thought about her in a bikini, turning golden brown. Her skin would feel like silk he thought. Oiled silk. Let her out of the bedroom? Not bloody likely. Not if he had his way.

'I'm serious,' Judith said. 'It's either get a job or go back to college.'

His Judith. What had she said in the garden? 'I've loved you for twenty-five years, and I have never wanted anyone else.'

He wished he could say the same. He wished he could turn the clock back, so that he'd never met Panhandle.

I love you, Judith, he thought. If he did this it would never be the same again. Even if she didn't catch on, it would never be the same again.

The phone rang.

Fitz went into the front room. He knew that it would be Panhandle, wanting to know that he was on his way. Judith and Mark were still arguing. He was just about to pick the receiver up, when he heard Katie giggle. She'd just told Mark her favourite dinosaur joke-of-the-moment. He guessed that, because she'd told it to him twice already, and she always cracked up before she got to the punchline. He could see her now, through the window, batting the swingball around, while Mark lounged on a sunbed and Judith sat sipping iced water in a big shady hat that hid her face from him.

His family. For better. For worse.

He punched the on/off switch on the answering machine. It ran through the out-going message, then beeped imperiously. Panhandle's voice said, 'Message for Fitz from DS Penhaligon.' She paused. He could hear airport noises in the background. 'I think you've forgotten our appointment, Fitz.' She didn't sound particularly upset, but Fitz knew her too well to be fooled.

I'm sorry, he thought at her. He knew, in that moment, that he had never really intended to go with her.

The phone started to make strange beeping noises at him. He ignored it.

Maybe if he hadn't screwed things up with Cassidy. Maybe then he'd have gone with her. But he'd failed there, and failed to fix it once he'd realised his error.

The parallel with his marriage was stark.

If he went with Penhaligon, he might fail there, too, fail to entertain her, to keep her interest once she saw all those bronzed young musclemen, fail to satisfy her.

He couldn't face that. But if he stayed with Judith, there was a chance he might be able to get it right at last.

He went out into the garden. Judith smiled at him. He eased himself into one of the garden chairs. It was a little too small for him, like most things –

But not my marriage, he thought fiercely at himself. My marriage is not too small for me. Something in the tone of that reminded him of Mrs Lang, saying desperately, 'My son did not commit suicide.' She had been right, but it hadn't helped her. If I'm right, Fitz thought, will that help me? Maybe even if I am right, I'll have to make myself too large for the marriage.

He wouldn't think of that. Didn't dare. It explained too many things. He tried to listen to Mark instead, to think of some way of persuading him that Judith was right and he ought to go back to college; but all the arguments seemed spurious.

He picked up the drink Judith had poured for him. Mineral water. He sipped it, more to show willing than because he wanted it, though his mouth felt full of ashes.

Judith was staring at him. Her eyes were large and full of pain.

He ought to say something, he knew. Tell her he'd changed his mind and wouldn't be going away after all. But that made him think of Panhandle, sitting at the airport surrounded by her luggage. He wondered how long she would wait before she decided he really wasn't going to

258

show. She'd go anyway, he was fairly sure of that. She'd probably pick up some musclebound waiter and have a wild time, a regular Shirley Valentine of a time.

But thinking all of that didn't answer the unspoken questions in Judith's eyes, and once he'd thought of that, and of Panhandle's accusing eyes, he couldn't help thinking of triangles, and then pyramids: and then, of course, Cassidy, trapped in his cell by his false confession, just as much as Fitz was trapped in his marriage.

But it *wasn't* the same. Fitz's love for Judith was true, the truest thing in a life dedicated to truth.

Truth like you told Panhandle? he asked himself severely, imagining her fastening the seatbelt round herself. Truth like you let Bilborough tell the Langs?

There can be too much truth, he thought, and sometimes it doesn't stay the same from day to day. He put the mineral water down. Judith smiled at him. He smiled back, and turned to watch Katie as she whacked inaccurately at the swingball.

Today I'm with my wife and my family, he thought. And that's the truth. For today.

Mar. 23/17
JC- 38
Lost Dec 16

D 12
J 5